THE PIED PIPER

For Zoo

And the Piper advanced and the children follow'd,
And when all were in to the very last,
The door in the mountain-side shut fast.

—Robert Browning, *The Pied Piper of Hamelin*

1

■ It was 8:24 A.M., July the twenty-third, 1972. A young man, as alone as any human being can be, sat quietly on the curb in front of the house at 3030 Aston, West Haven, Connecticut. He was slight, about five-seven, and weighed about 135 pounds. He was dressed in faded jeans, dirty T-shirt, and sneakers with no socks. He sat with his head hunched down, his arms wrapped around his knees. From between the nicotine-stained fingers of his right hand a cigarette sent a steady wisp of smoke up into the humid air. His body trembled slightly. He was sobbing, softly, steadily.

A police siren sounded in the distance, coming closer and

closer, finally reaching Aston and then dropping an octave as the patrol car halted suddenly in front of the boy.

Sergeant William Rathers, fifty-two, West Haven Police Department, left the car and approached the curb.

"Been some problem here, son?"

The boy looked up, squinting through his reddened eyes in the morning sunlight. "Yessir."

"You the one who called the police?"

"Yessir."

"Well, you going to tell me about it?"

The boy dropped his cigarette just as it started to burn his fingers. "It's Earl. I left him in there." He nodded toward the house behind him.

Sergeant Rathers looked back. On the porch steps, sitting close to each other, were another young man and a young girl. This second young man looked directly at Rathers; the girl looked into the distance as though dazed.

"Earl who?"

"Earl Harmen. That's his house. He's inside."

"What's the matter with him?"

"Earl's dead. I killed him."

"You killed him?"

"Yessir. He told me to."

Sergeant Rathers unsnapped his holster flap and walked up the sidewalk to the porch. The boy and girl on the steps moved slightly to let him pass. Carefully, he looked inside through the aluminum screen door, then walked in. The three young people waited silently in the muggy New England morning. After less than sixty seconds, Sergeant Rathers reappeared, moved purposefully to his car, and got on the radio. He spoke a few terse sentences, clicked off, and returned to the curb.

"We're all gonna go to headquarters in a minute and see if we can't straighten this thing out, hear? So everybody just relax till the other car comes."

All three nodded.

Rathers pointed to the couple on the porch. "All right now,

you two. Why don't you come down here so we can all be close together."

The couple complied wordlessly.

Rathers took out a pad and ball-point pen. "Now, suppose you tell me your names. You, miss?"

The girl looked off into the distance. "I'm Veronica Metcale."

"You?"

"Don Simonds."

The boy on the curb fumbled in his pockets for another cigarette.

"And what's your name, son?"

"Me? Criley. Lee Criley."

Walter Lee Criley, seventeen, had been born and lived all his life in West Haven, a suburb of New Haven. While not a homely youth, he was not handsome either. Since the age of fourteen, he had suffered from an acne condition that caused him continual annoyance. His eyes were a light, almost milky blue, nervous eyes that avoided prolonged contact. His teeth were stained from heavy cigarette smoking, and his thin light-brown hair fell across his face in limp, dirty strands.

Lee was the second of two sons born to Emma and Philip Criley. His parents had been married for eleven years before the father's drinking bouts caused the final breakup and eventual divorce. Even Philip Criley's friends thought him a "mean drunk," and although Lee continued to see his father from time to time, he had never lost his fear of him.

Emma Criley never remarried, but brought her mother, Mrs. Gladys Stevenson, to live with her and the children. With what Mrs. Criley could scrape together as a part-time waitress, saleswoman, or laundry worker, with occasional checks from Mr. Criley, and with Mrs. Stevenson's small monthly pension, the family of four was able to make ends meet. Within the lower-income area in which they lived, the Crileys were only a little worse off than average.

With four people in the small one-floor, three-bedroom house, Lee had to share a room with his nineteen-year-old brother Michael. Michael was more sports-minded than Lee and was especially good at baseball. The relationship between the two brothers was not particularly close and the two saw little of each other except at home.

Of all the members of the household, Lee was closest to his grandmother. She spoiled her younger grandson, who could do no wrong in her eyes. Although he took advantage of this to a certain extent, Lee did feel a warmth for his grandmother. He would tease her about her regular churchgoing, then suddenly smile and tell her he was only fooling, and she would tell her fine grandchild not to make fun of the Lord like that, even in jest. Lee would say he never would, and the two would be fast friends again.

A sickly, asthmatic child in his early years, Lee was forced to repeat the first grade at Washington Grammar School because of numerous absences. He always achieved passing marks in school, and in sixth grade was scored an acceptably high 113 on a full-scale IQ test. At that time, his teacher described him as "a sensitive, withdrawn boy—shy in class—does adequate work but never up to his full capacity."

Lee made few friends at school, was not interested in extra-curricular activities, and was unsure of himself around girls. His attendance dropped lower and lower, until at age sixteen, in the ninth grade, Lee dropped out of school permanently. Few of his classmates noticed he had left. Prior to dropping out, his one confidant was sixteen-year-old Otis Hesler—Otis John Hesler—who was in the same class and lived just a few blocks from Lee.

Throughout the latter years of his school career, Lee was smoking marijuana heavily, on a daily basis. From the age of fourteen, he had also been experimenting with mescaline and LSD as well as amphetamines and barbiturates. He tried heroin twice, snorting it through his nostrils, but did not particularly enjoy the feeling. In addition, he was drinking heavily. By the time Lee Criley was sixteen and left school, there were few moments in his waking life when he was not under the influence either of drugs or alcohol. He had become a totally drug-dependent personality who did not consider himself able to function without chemical help.

Emma Criley was at first distraught about Lee's leaving school, believing that the only way her children could better themselves was by continuing their education as far as they could. But when he explained to her that he thought it was time he started contributing to the family welfare and get himself a job, she finally agreed. With his mother's help, Lee found work as a busboy in a nearby diner. He worked without missing a day for a little under five weeks. Then he missed one day, and then two days, and was fired. He worked for a week as a truck loader but found the labor too strenuous. At his mother's insistence, Lee scanned the papers for job openings, but when she didn't press him, he did not make the effort on his own. In a short time he settled into a pattern of sleeping into the afternoon, playing records, plunking at his guitar, and spending a lot of time away from home.

During this period, Lee spoke occasionally of joining a band and playing his guitar professionally. In fact, he knew only a few chords, and he was able to sit through only three lessons before he decided he could learn better on his own. Some afternoons he would spend hours gyrating in front of a mirror, rhythmically striking two or three chords as his stereo blasted behind him.

The one good sign, as far as Mrs. Criley could see, was that at last Lee seemed to have some close friends. Always a loner, now Lee was often in the company of two companions. Otis Hesler often called for Lee. Although Otis and Mrs. Criley did not get along, Mrs. Criley would have welcomed anyone who got Lee out of the house. Otis told Mrs. Criley that she should allow her son more freedom, and Mrs. Criley didn't approve of Otis' unkempt appearance and arrogant attitude toward her.

The other friend was much more warmly received in the Criley home, not only as a suitable companion but almost as a member of the family. He was older than Lee, and that was good, because Lee so badly needed a stronger, stable influence in these confused years of growth and unsureness. And he was polite, always respectful to Mrs. Criley, never taking her hospitality for granted. He was invited for meals at the Criley home; he sometimes spent holidays there; he was the older brother whom Lee could turn to, the father who was the source of wisdom and strength, the good friend who could always be counted on to understand and lend support. This other friend was a bachelor in his thirties, a telephone repairman named Earl Howard Harmen.

"Now, as clearly as you can remember it, son, I want you to tell me everything that happened last night when you say you shot Harmen."

Lee Criley sat at a table in a small cubicle in the West Haven police station. It was a cool, air-conditioned room, windowless, lit by fluorescent tubing. The table was gray formica, the two chairs were green leatherette waiting-room chairs. Lee Criley looked steadily into the ashtray Sergeant Shaunessey had placed in front of him, tapping his freshly lit cigarette on the edge of the ashtray. He was silent.

"I know you want to tell me about it now, don't you, son?"

Sergeant Raymond Shaunessey, a large, beefy Irishman who retained the litheness of his former days as an athlete, had been on the force for eighteen years. He had a quiet, almost mystical sense of his obligation to be gentle with his fellow man. He was a good cop; he knew it and was proud of it. It had fallen to him to conduct the initial interrogation of Lee Criley.

A tired, respectful voice finally answered "Yessir, I do." It was a voice that Sergeant Shaunessey had heard many times in the past eighteen years, the voice of someone who wants to confess, to unburden his soul.

"That's fine. Now you just take it easy, son. Nobody wants to pressure you, you understand that. Suppose you start where you think it makes the most sense."

"You mean last night?"

"All right, last night. What did you do last night?"

"I went over to Earl's house."

"Earl Harmen? The man you shot?"

"That's right. And he said it felt like a good idea to have a party."

"A party?"

"Yeah, you know. Smoke a little grass, sniff some paint or something, I don't know."

"Did you ever have parties like that before at Harmen's house?"

Criley was silent for a moment before he nodded. Shaunessey sensed the reluctance, sensed the break in the thoughts of the youth, and quickly brought him back to the events of the night before.

"All right, so you were going to have a party. Then what?"

"Well, like usual, Earl said for me to find somebody, and that's what I did."

"And who did you find?"

"Well, at first I couldn't find anybody and I was getting a little worried about what I was going to tell Earl. Then I ran into Don Simonds."

"Where did you run into him?"

"Over on Fairfax."

"About what time was that?"

"I don't know what time it was. It was late, that's all. I don't know what time it was. I don't have a watch."

"All right. You ran into Simonds. What was he doing?"

"He was sitting in his car, fooling around with his chick."

"Veronica Metcale?"

"Yeah."

"And then what happened?"

"Well, I was getting a little uptight about not finding anybody, see, like I told Earl I would, so I figured why not ask Simonds if he was interested in a good time that night."

"And was he?"

"Him and Veronica was going to run off somewhere just that night. I don't know what they were planning to do, get married or something. I don't know. But they said okay."

"And the three of you came back to Harmen's house? How did you get there?"

"Simonds has this old Chevy, I think it is. I wasn't too hot on bringing Veronica along. I mean, I think I knew all along she'd be trouble."

"Why?"

Lee Criley shuffled in his chair. He glanced up quickly at the kindly, curious, reassuring face of Sergeant Shaunessey, then back into the ashtray.

"Well, I mean, usually we didn't have chicks at these parties. It was kind of . . . well, we just never had chicks, that's all."

"But you brought Miss Metcale anyway?"

"Yeah. I don't know. I figured that her and Simonds were planning on running off, and Earl and I were planning on going to New York for a while. . . . I guess that doesn't make too much sense, but I just didn't think a girl would make any difference this one time."

"Did it make a difference?"

"Well, not at first, anyway. I knew Earl was surprised about me bringing this chick to the place, but he didn't say anything about it. Usually I can tell when Earl gets mad about something. But not this time."

"So you went ahead and had your party."

"Yessir."

Sergeant Shaunessey was a good interrogator. He knew his business. He knew that the confused boy sitting at the table across from him wanted desperately to say what he had to say, to vomit up the whole story of the events that led up to the shooting of Earl Harmen. And he understood that it wouldn't be easy for Criley, that many resistances and fears would have to be overcome by the natural human need to unburden his conscience. Shaunessey had seen it a hundred times, and he knew that the process could not be hurried, that everything would have to happen on its own, that the inner struggles this youngster now experienced would have to be resolved in their own time. He mustn't move too quickly, mustn't press the boy, but instead must soothe him, let him feel secure, let him know that at last it was all right.

"You're doing fine, son. There's no hurry. You just take your time and get everything straight in your mind. How about some coffee?"

Lee Criley nodded, and Sergeant Shaunessey stepped into the

large open area of the detective division. Slowly, patiently, he began putting instant coffee and instant cream into two small styrofoam cups. A shorter man in shirt sleeves, the ever-present .38 on the belt, approached.

"How's it going, Ray? Got anything for us yet?"

"No, not yet. I think he'll come around in a little while, though."

"You know, they found some crazy-looking stuff in that house."

"What kind of stuff?"

"Well, they had a lot of handcuffs. And they had, if you can imagine this, boards—with holes in them. Jesus, what could they be doing with something like that?"

Shaunessey breathed out heavily. "I guess we'll know pretty soon."

Closing the door carefully behind him, Shaunessey handed Lee Criley a cup of coffee and again sat down opposite. He watched the boy as he sipped the hot liquid in quick gulps, watched his eyes staring beyond the table into empty air, watched his fingers tremble as the cigarette burned its way down. He even felt as if he were watching the tiny wheels turning in the boy's mind, trying to fit it all together in some orderly sequence, trying to work up just the right degree of momentum to let it all out. And then, as Lee Criley's eyes shifted back into focus and he firmly extinguished the butt of his cigarette, Shaunessey knew that now prodding would no longer be needed. The boy would talk now.

"I'd been tripping on some pretty good mesc that day," he said, "so I was a little high anyway. But right after we got there Earl turned us all on to pot. Real strong stuff. Pot and mescaline, they're a good mix, each makes the other better, so I guess I was pretty zonked out right away. What I mean is, at first I wasn't paying much attention to what everybody was doing. I think I spent about three hours watching a couple of goldfish Earl had in there.

"I think Earl was talking some kind of shit to Simonds, the

way he usually does, giggling and laughing and everything. And I remember Veronica was playing the radio, dancing around, doing this real horny stuff, like a stripper or a go-go girl, dancing like that. She was trying to interest Simonds, but for a while there she was getting to me too. She's not so pretty, Veronica, but she got me going all right. Earl was watching her and I could tell he wanted to pull her head off."

"Was Earl smoking marijuana, to your knowledge?"

"Earl? No, I don't think he ever smoked. Maybe once or twice, a long time ago. Usually, though, he never did. He said he could turn on with a beer and get just as high as he wanted. Earl didn't go in for drugs too much. He always had plenty around—grass, pills, shit like that. But only for parties. And nobody ever did any scag in Earl's house. He was real uptight about that."

"All right, so Veronica was dancing around. What then?"

"Well, she kept making these moves for Simonds, grabbing his pants, and Earl was getting madder than hell. Then, I guess more to keep Veronica away from Simonds than anything else, he said we should get really wasted and sniff up some paint. I knew he was mad, and that he blamed me for it, because when he got up to get the paint, he put his hand on my shoulder, buddy-buddy like, but he grabbed that little muscle, the one between the shoulder and the neck, and pinched the goddam thing. I was so out of my mind I don't think I screamed, but it hurt like hell, I can tell you. And it still hurts." Criley rubbed his shoulder cautiously, wincing a little.

"Earl kept smiling while he was pinching that muscle. It really gave me the creeps to see him smile like that, especially at me. Then he said something like 'You had to bring a chick, didn't you?' He wasn't too happy about Veronica being there.

"So he went to his closet, where he always kept the stash, and he brought out some tubes of acrylic paint and some bags. By that time, what with the pot and some pills Earl gave us, we were pretty far along already. Earl made damn sure that Veronica was the first one to start sniffing the paint. He practically pulled her off Simonds. He pretended he was just joking around, but I could tell he wanted Veronica out of the picture. Maybe none of it would have happened if Veronica hadn't been there. How was I supposed to know?

"When Veronica started nodding off, Earl set Simonds up, telling him how far out he would get, shit like that. Then it was my turn, and man, did I get blown away! A couple of sniffs of that stuff and the lights went out. Maybe it was the mix of the mesc and the pot and everything, but man, I crashed but good."

"You were unconscious?"

"Man, was I!"

"For how long?"

"I don't know. It's hard to tell. Maybe just a few minutes, or it could have been a couple of hours. I don't know. You get so wasted on that paint you lose track of time completely.

"But when I woke up, I was cuffed to the board. He'd taken all my clothes off and I was cuffed to the board. Simonds and Veronica were cuffed up too, but only Simonds was stripped down. Veronica still had her clothes on. And there was Earl, sitting in his big easy chair, smiling crazy the way he does. Simonds and Veronica were still pretty doped up, and they weren't too sure what was going on. I was pretty groggy too, but I knew what was happening, and I was scared clean out of my mind, I can tell you that."

"What about that board? What kind of a board?"

"Well, Earl had these boards. They had holes drilled in them, so that when you laid down on it, he could handcuff you, hands and feet, and you couldn't go noplace. And he had us all three cuffed up that way. I don't know how long he had those boards. He had them when I first knew him."

"And you were frightened. What did you think was going to happen?"

"You didn't know Earl. I didn't *think* anything was going to happen. I knew what was going to happen. Earl was going to kill us."

"How could you be sure?"

"Sergeant Shaunessey, you just didn't know Earl like I did. He was going to kill us all right, sure as hell. Sure as hell . . ."

Shaunessey saw Criley begin to drift off back into his own world. He didn't want to be too abrupt with the boy and possibly frighten him out of telling the rest of the events of that night, but he couldn't let him fall back into his own thoughts.

"Do you need any more cigarettes, son? You look like you're about running out."

Criley looked up. "Yeah. Thanks. Thanks, Sergeant."

Shaunessey got up and called to someone outside to bring in a pack of the brand Criley was smoking.

"I'd like to pay you, but they took all my change."

"That's all right, son. It's on the house."

"I guess you have to be pretty smart to do this kind of work, don't you?"

Shaunessey studied the boy to see if there was an edge of sarcasm to his remark. He could find none.

"Not so smart, son. Just ready to listen."

"Yeah, but you don't come on too strong or climb all over me with questions. You're good at it."

"Are you ready to tell the rest?"

"Yeah. Okay. I was telling you how I know Earl was going to kill us. He was.

"I've never been so scared in my whole damn life, and I knew that unless I could talk him out of it fast I was going to get wasted.

"Earl was really out of it. He kept jumping around, giggling, waving this pistol and a hunting knife around. He kept saying how he was going to have some real good fun, he was really going to get his kicks, and then he was going to kill all of us. I don't think Veronica could believe it. She thought it was some kind of a joke. But I knew it wasn't no joke.

"So I started sweet-talking Earl. It didn't do any good to beg your way out with Earl, because that only turned him on more. I couldn't let him know I was scared. I forget just what I said, but I think I told him how it would be better to let me out, because then the two of us could have some fun together with Veronica and Simonds. I think I told him I wanted to try out some new trick. I don't know what the hell I said, but I was talking about a mile a minute. And I prayed to God that if I ever got out of there alive, it would all be over."

"And Earl finally let you out?"

"Don't ask me why, but he did. He let me out."

"And then what?"

"He gave me the knife. And then he told me to cut off the chick's clothes, just slice 'em off. And that's what I did. Veronica was getting a little panicky, so Earl put some tape over her mouth. Simonds was just waking up and Earl taped his mouth, too. Then we both went into the kitchen. Earl was going to get some kind of goo or something. I went because my throat was dry as dust. I think I drank about a gallon of water."

"What was the goo for?"

Criley paused. "Earl, well, Earl was . . . he was going to . . . he was going to fuck Simonds."

"Did he tell you that?"

"No. He didn't have to."

"All right. Then what happened?"

"Simonds was still pretty groggy, like he didn't know what was going on. Earl unlocked his cuffs and pulled him off the board he was on and dragged him over to Veronica's board. Veronica just watched him, her eyes getting wider and wider, breathing hard through her nose because of the tape over her mouth.

"Earl gave me the gun to hold . . . no, I guess I already had it in my hand. I'm not sure. Anyway, he pulled Simonds up to Veronica's board and cuffed him up just like she was, only face-to-face. Belly-to-belly, too, because they both didn't have any clothes on. Then Earl just got crazy, giggling all over the place. I never saw him lose control so bad. He started taking off his clothes, too, dancing around, slapping Simonds on the ass. He was slapping him hard. Earl always hit as hard as he could, which was pretty damn hard. By the time Earl got all his clothes off, throwing them all over the place, Simonds' ass was red as a beet. And Simonds was beginning to wake up.

"I'm pretty sure Earl even forgot I was there, because when I asked him what he was going to do, he looked surprised, kind of.

And he said something like 'Just you watch, just you watch.' He grabbed Simonds by the hair, getting up real close behind him, his hands going all over the place. It was like the three of them, Veronica, Simonds, and Earl, were all rolled up in one big ball. Simonds started moaning, because he had that tape over his mouth, and Veronica kept breathing hard and kind of panicky.

"Then Earl said, 'Go ahead, honey, stick it in her. She wants it, honey. Go ahead.' And all the time Earl was climbing onto Simonds' back. That's when I told him to stop."

"What was going through your mind then? What were you thinking?"

"I don't know. I just knew it was time to stop. Like I had made that little prayer before about getting out of there, but I don't think that's what it was. I just knew that it all had to stop right there, and that was it. It wasn't like I gave a damn about Veronica or Simonds, because I didn't. It wouldn't have made much difference to me whether Earl would have killed them or not. That wasn't it. It was just that I knew for sure that now it all finally had to stop. I guess that doesn't make too much sense."

"Yes it does, it makes a lot of sense. Did he stop right away?"

"Yeah, he stopped, and he looked at me real mad, and said something like 'You better put that down.'

"To tell the truth, I didn't realize until just then that I had the gun in my hand. I told him to get away from them, to leave them alone, that I was going to let them go. And Earl looked right into my eyes, like he saw me for the first time, and he said something, I don't know what. He began to come at me, looking real mean at first. And then it was worse, because all of a sudden he started that crazy laughing of his. It could really scare somebody to hear Earl laugh like that. And then he stopped laughing and a funny look came over his face and he said something about it being all right for me to kill him."

"And then you pulled the trigger?"

"Then I pulled the trigger."

"How many times did you shoot him?"

"I don't know. I just kept firing till there was no more shots left."

"Did you check if he was dead?"

"No. I knew he was dead."

"And then?"

"Then I uncuffed Simonds and Veronica and called you guys. And here I am."

"That's all?"

"Yes."

Shaunessey watched the young man carefully. Something was a little off here, he thought to himself. The whole story wasn't sitting quite right. The sense of relief at having finally told the story wasn't apparent. Lee Criley had confessed to murdering his friend, but somehow Shaunessey had a feeling he was holding something back.

"When you shot Harmen, did you fear for your own life?"

"Yeah, he was going to kill me all right. I just killed him first."

"Did he have a weapon in his hands then?"

"I guess he must have. I don't know. Maybe he had the knife. I don't exactly remember that."

"So you think you shot him in self-defense?"

"I guess you'd have to say that."

Shaunessey got up wearily. "All right, boy, I'm going to have a stenographer come in here, and I want you to run the whole story, just like you told me. Do you mind doing that?"

"Yeah. All right."

"And then I want you to sign your name to that story, all right?"

"Sure."

In two other small rooms in the West Haven police station, two other similar statements were being made, taken down, and signed by the principals. Donald Simonds and Veronica Metcale told police officers essentially the same stories though not as detailed as that of Lee Criley, simply because they had not been conscious for the same length of time as Criley. All three statements meshed, and it appeared that a somewhat bizarre but finally quite plausible case of justifiable homicide was developing.

No charges were filed against Simonds or Veronica Metcale, who was a minor. Both were referred to the West Haven Hospital, where they were treated for sexual assault and shock. Later that day they would be released to their parents, with the understanding that their statements might eventually have to be repeated in open court.

    As Sergeant Raymond Shaunessey headed toward the door of the tiny cubicle he had shared with Lee Criley for several draining hours, he thought that his job was now accomplished. The facts had been drawn out of the boy, a clear and consistent sequence of events had emerged, and another day's work was done.
    "Sergeant, aren't you going to ask me any more questions?"
    "Is there more you want to tell me, son?"
    "I think I'd better tell you the rest."
    "The rest? What rest?"
    Lee Criley ground out another cigarette.
    "About those kids. Those kids we killed."

2

■ It was autumn in the sleepy New England town of Hanover, Connecticut. There had been just the right combination of sunshine and rain that year to create a spectacular display of fall foliage. And in Hanover, where apple trees and pumpkins grew, the children were looking forward with fearful and delightful anticipation to Halloween, when monsters and witches and ghosts and vampires would wander in the darkness of night.

In October, in the year 1937, a baby boy was born in the sleepy New England town of Hanover. A pretty baby, with dark laughing eyes. He was healthy, the doctor assured the mother, and normal in every way. He was named Earl Howard Harmen.

■ The small bedroom reeked of sex. The bedclothes shifted and jerked and from them issued the grunts and moans and heavy breathing of love. The bed creaked, squeaking, rocking back and forth, back and forth, rock-a-bye baby.

Little Earl, two years old, rocked himself back and forth in his blue crib, back and forth, smiling, rocking with the creaking of the bed. Pretty baby. Such lively, dancing brown eyes.

The movement on the bed stopped. For a moment all was silent.

"Gimme a cigarette over on the table." Marion Harmen smoothed the sheet over her body, covering her full breasts, and waited for the man at her side to do as he was asked. He put the cigarette in his own lips, lit it, took a deep drag, and passed it to her. Without being beautiful, she was more than merely attractive. Her figure was not perfect but full, plump, curvy. Her reddish hair, contrasting with her pale skin, haloed the soft, regular features of her face. The memorable feature was her mouth, a mouth that sought contact, a hungry mouth. Marion Harmen, twenty-four, wife and mother of a handsome little boy, was a woman men looked at twice. This was pleasing to her. The man to whom she had just made love was not her husband. It had been her decision, one fine day several months ago, that there was no reason why he had to be. It had been a fast decision, surprisingly easy to make, and one that relieved more tensions than it created. She would have her lover, maybe even a number of lovers, and her husband could like it or lump it. Why should she be faithful to someone she didn't love? Besides, she was faithful to the one person in all the world she cared about—her little boy. She didn't need anybody else. Earl was the real love of her life.

She smoked in silence, letting the last waves of her lovemaking course through her body. The man started putting on his clothes, obviously in a hurry. "Listen, why don't you make some arrangements to get away for a whole night or something? These quickies are making me nervous. What if he comes back?"

The woman looked up from her catlike relaxation and gazed at the man's hard muscular body with appreciation.

"He won't be back. Don't worry about it."

With the beginning of a conversation taking place, the pretty baby boy in the crib turned his head. He listened to the sounds, waiting for the reassuring cadences of his mother's voice, then redirected his attention to his yellow giraffe.

"Still, it's making me nervous. Honest, Marion, let's try to get off someplace. Just you and me. No worrying about the clock or your damn husband's footsteps on the porch. Let me make some reservations someplace."

"You know I can't do that, Jack. Why do you ask me?"

The man was almost fully dressed. "We can do it. Jesus Christ, there's no reason why you can't say you have to visit a sick girlfriend for a night or two."

"Don't swear at me like that. Not in front of the baby. I don't like it."

"All right, all right. I'm sorry. But you know how much I want to be with you all the time."

"I know. Come over here." The woman patted the bed beside her.

"Ah, there's no time. He'll be here soon."

"Just for a second. Come on over here." The man sat down, and as he did, the woman let the sheet fall away from her breasts. She put an arm around his neck and guided his face downward. With her free hand, she reached for the buckle of his belt. But suddenly the man jerked away.

"Goddammit, Marion. What are you doing to me? Are you nuts?"

The woman laughed softly and snuggled back under her covers. "Be back tomorrow?"

"Yes, I'll be back tomorrow."

"Good."

"Marion, what's the real reason you won't go off with me? It's because of the kid, isn't it?"

"Well, I couldn't hardly take Earl to a hotel with us, could I?"

"Why not, for God's sake? He sees enough right here in this room."

The woman looked at him coldly. "Look, Jack, any time this all gets to be more than you can handle, you just let me know. That's all you have to do."

The man was beaten. She would have her way. He scowled in self-disgust.

"Oh, come on, now," she said. "Don't pull such a long face. This is a pretty nice deal, isn't it? I'm here for you any time you want me, right? That's not so bad, is it? Come over, now. One more kiss before you go."

"I'm late. I gotta go."

"Tomorrow?"

"Yeah. Tomorrow."

Marion Harmen let the warmth of the afternoon sunlight pour through the window and over her body. She was a woman who liked the feel of things, a sensual woman. She glanced at the baby.

"And how's Mama's little darlin', hmm? What's Mama's little darlin' doin' over there all by himself?"

The baby looked up from his stuffed giraffe and cooed with pleasure, recognizing the loving tone of his mother's voice. A handsome boy, with such wide, dancing eyes. Marion Harmen went to the crib, standing naked over the baby. He stood up, reaching out his arms to her, and she bent down, lifting him gently to her, holding him close to her breasts, the nipples still hard from lovemaking.

"Mama's little boy. You were such a good boy when that bad man was here, weren't you? Such a good little baby. Such a sweet pretty little baby."

The baby held tight to her, gurgling with happiness.

"Sweet little baby. Mama's best boyfriend."

She carried him to the bed, and lay back again in the sunlight. She closed her eyes as he climbed happily over her soft familiar body.

When Howard Harmen came home, he found the baby sitting alone in the living room, playing with his yellow giraffe. He also had with him, clenched tightly in his little fist, a very long and very sharp kitchen knife. The baby glanced up, showing no sign of recognition, taking in the man with his wide, inquisitive eyes.

"Oh, for God's sake! Earl, give me that knife. That's a good boy, now. Give it to Daddy." He knelt down and gently, carefully, unwrapped the baby's fingers from the knife. "That's a good boy, now. Let Daddy have the knife." The little boy refused to give up the knife, screaming in rage and frustration, and the father was taken aback by his son's strange behavior.

"No, Earl. The knife is dangerous. You might get cut. Where's Mommy?"

The father eased the knife away.

"Marion? Where are you?"

The house was quiet except for the crying of the baby. Then he heard the sound of water running and saw the bathroom door was closed. He opened it, and clouds of steam poured out. She was there, all right, luxuriating in what appeared to be an all-day bath.

"You know the kid's out here all alone playing with a knife?"

"Hello, Howard. You're home early, aren't you?"

"No, I'm late, dammit. And the kid had a knife in his hand. He could have hurt himself."

"He didn't, did he?"

"No. I took it away from him. How about getting out of there?"

"Why? You have anything in mind?" She raised her shapely leg out of the water seductively. The man looked away.

"The kid's crying, the house is a mess, and there's no dinner. That's why."

"Tell you what you do. You give me a little while longer in here, and you go have a beer. Then maybe you'll change that tone in your voice and we can talk like human beings. All right?"

Howard Harmen left without replying and went to the refrigerator. He took out a bottle of beer and sat down at the kitchen table. He was a young man who worked too hard, looking older than his years. His eyes were tired, his hands were dirty, and he needed the beer. He finished it in four swallows and opened a second bottle.

The baby toddled in, cooing to himself and ignoring the man. "Hello, Earl. You wanna come and sit on Daddy's lap?"

Holding his toy giraffe tightly, the baby continued to ignore his father.

"Come on, son. Didn't you miss your Daddy today?"

"Mama?"

"Ah, she's in there. She's in the bathroom making herself beautiful." Howard Harmen finished his second beer, hesitated a moment, and went for his third.

Marion Harmen entered the kitchen, a look of disgust on her face. "What are you gonna do, get drunk again?" She wore a filmy-thin bathrobe, open provocatively in front. She sat down carelessly, exposing most of her full white breasts, and started working on her nails. Marion Harmen could look provocative in almost any situation. She didn't have to dress up or down for it. She was aware of the excitement she was causing in her husband.

"Just a couple of beers."

"Yeah, yeah. Sure."

"Well, don't worry about it, will ya?"

"Who's worrying about it? I'd be in trouble if I sat around doing nothing but worrying about it. Buster, you can bet I don't worry about it."

"And what the hell is that supposed to mean?" The third beer was almost gone.

"I'll tell you what, lover boy." She didn't bother to look up from her nails. "You don't worry about it, and I won't worry about it."

The man was almost begging now. "Marion, what do you do this to us for?"

"I don't know what you're talking about."

"Why can't we get something good going again? Why do we always drive each other crazy?"

"I don't know. Why?"

"Let's try again, Marion. I know we can make it work out. I love you, Marion."

"Good, Howard. That's good."

Howard Harmen walked to his wife and put his hands inside her robe, tentatively, clumsily. She put down her nail file and looked up at him for the first time. "Is it going to be this time?"

"I love you, Marion."

The woman stood up and pressed her body full against her husband's. She kissed him long and passionately, pressing her thighs and hips against him, grinding back and forth. Then, just as suddenly, she pulled away. He dropped his arms from around her and looked down, defeated.

"Ah, you're really something, Howard. You know that? You take the cake."

Howard went to the refrigerator. Only one more beer left. He took it.

"Yeah, have another beer. That'll make you feel better."

The man said nothing.

The woman went back to filing her nails. Then, almost incidentally, she said, "Howard, I think I'll take Earl on the bus this weekend to Boston. I've been meaning to visit an old girlfriend of mine, and she called today."

"I didn't know you had a girlfriend in Boston."

"She said she was sick and could use a little help. I told her I'd come down."

"What girlfriend?"

"You don't know her, I don't think. From before we were married. An old girlfriend from high school."

"What's her name?"

"Her name? Travers. Alice Travers."

The man's face reddened with growing anger.

"Are you lying to me, Marion?"

"Look, Buster. I couldn't care less if you believe me or not. I'm going to visit a sick friend, and that's that."

"You're lying to me. I can tell you're lying to me. Go ahead, you can tell me. There's somebody else, isn't there?"

"Oh, Howard, leave me alone, for God's sake."

"Tell me. Tell me the truth."

"Why don't we just leave things the way they are, Howard? Don't keep asking me questions that you don't want to hear me answer."

The man grabbed the woman by the shoulder, looking down into her eyes with rage and hurt. He was almost crying, yet his teeth were clenched tightly, and he spat the words rather than spoke them. "Tell me, you goddam whore, or I'll kill you."

The woman slapped his hands off her shoulders. "Okay, tough guy, you really want to know? You really want to know? I'll tell you. Yes, there's somebody else. There's been somebody else for five months now. And he makes me wet inside just to think about him. And he was here today. We fucked all afternoon. That's why the house is a mess and dinner isn't ready. It's not that I haven't been busy. I've been busy all right. I've been busy fucking a man, a *real* man, in your bed all day. And that's why I want to get out of here for a weekend. So I can stay in a hotel room and do nothing but fuck and fuck and fuck till I scream. And I'll tell you something else. You want to know everything? I'll tell you everything. I like the way it feels when he comes inside me, so I don't let him wear anything. And I think I'm pregnant right now. It's his baby. He made that baby because I like to feel him come inside me. Any other questions you want me to answer? Or do you think you know the score now?"

The man stood frozen as her torrent of words came gushing toward him. His fists were clenched at his sides and the tears started, slowly at first, then in great gulping sobs. He swayed, almost falling, and then lurched toward the woman, pouncing upon her. He threw her from the chair, falling on top of her, flailing wildly with his fists.

"You dirty goddam whore! You dirty goddam no-good whore bitch!"

The woman screamed, but a hand around her throat took her breath away, and abruptly the scream changed to spasmodic gurgles. With his other hand, the man punched again and again at her face. The first punch smashed her nose. He punched again, shattering a cheekbone. He punched again and blood dribbled out of the swollen mouth. The woman only moaned now, as the man's knees drove into her side, her ribs, her breasts.

The man continued to cry, chanting through his tears, "You dirty bitch! You dirty whore!"

The woman lost consciousness, but it was a few minutes before the man realized this, his punches and kicks raining down steadily on her motionless body. Then, suddenly, he stopped, sitting quite still as if in prayer.

The bathrobe had fallen open, leaving the woman totally exposed as she lay on the kitchen floor. Even the moaning had stopped now, and only soft gurgling could be heard as her breath came slowly and shallowly. Blood bubbled from her nose and mouth, the bright red liquid forming a tiny pool in which her head rested. Bruises had already become distinguishable on her white body.

Softly now, tenderly, the man lay down on the floor beside the woman, nuzzling against her broken face, trying to kiss away the blood from her misshapen mouth and cheeks. His tears were gone, replaced by a calm, faraway look.

"I love you, baby. You know I love you. It's going to be all right, just you wait and see. It's going to be like it used to be with you and me." He kissed her neck, and then her breasts. Quickly, still lying next to her, still kissing her, the man unfastened his pants and slipped them off. He rolled on top of her still body, whispering words of love into her ears, kissing her gently.

"You see how it's going to be all right. You wait and see. Oh, how I love you, baby. I love you."

The woman moaned softly as he moved on top of her, but she did not waken. It was over quickly.

The man stood up. He walked to the sink and held his head under the cold water. He shook himself dry. Without looking back at the woman, he walked slowly to the bedroom and fell on the bed. He was asleep immediately.

His eyes wide with interest, the baby had been standing off by himself in a corner of the kitchen. He stood holding his stuffed yellow giraffe close to him, watching. When the man left, the baby approached the unconscious woman, watching curiously as the red bubbles formed and then popped from the holes in her face. He sat down next to her and pressed his small body against hers.

The marriage of Howard and Marion Harmen lasted a total of five years. Family and friends marveled at how the couple stayed together for so long, considering the frequency and intensity of the outbursts that took place in the home. As sometimes happens in the most violent of marriages, each partner had grown into his role in the family drama and found within it a peculiar kind of peace and stability. Howard Harmen expected his wife to be unfaithful and to flaunt her infidelity. He expected her to challenge his manhood. In turn, Marion Harmen expected her husband to beat her unmercifully, occasionally into unconsciousness. As long as they both lived up to each other's expectations, the marriage lasted. When the undisguised infidelity and fierce rages ceased to interest either partner, the marriage disintegrated. In the end, it was boredom that brought about the divorce.

They parted amicably. Earl was told that his father had to move away and that he would soon have a new father. On the day Howard Harmen left, just before what would have been his and Marion's fifth anniversary, Howard hugged his son while instructing him to always be good to his mother, and went off to take up a new life in Philadelphia.

Marion Harmen remarried within the month. She married Alvin Marris, the owner of a service station and garage in Hanover. Fortyish, he took pride in his musclebound physique (the result of much weight-lifting in a local gym), and thought of himself as a "*real* man."

Earl Harmen would soon be five.

■ The summer sun was turning a bright orange. Cooling east-
erly winds blew in from Long Island Sound as the waves lapped
gently at the sandy beach. A few swimmers lolled about in the
clear salt water, and farther out a single water-skier skimmed
gracefully across the blue-green water, the whir of the outboard
motor barely audible in the wind. Still farther out, a tiny white
sail moved slowly on the horizon.

Four blue-and-white patrol cars pulled up in a semicircle
around the weatherbeaten white frame house. The pavement had
ended, and the cars halted in the weeds and sand that surrounded
the house. A dozen men got out, eight uniformed police officers

and three men and a boy in civilian clothes. Of the latter four, the men were dressed in business suits and the boy was clad in dungarees and T-shirt. His hands were cuffed in front of him, to allow him to smoke in relative freedom. Lee Criley looked small and insignificant surrounded by the larger, serious-faced men. But Criley alone appeared relaxed, confident of himself. There was a spring to his step, a certain lightness about him, the sense of exhilaration that comes from finally unburdening oneself of a terrible weight. He smiled inappropriately, continually, always puffing away at his cigarette, talking to anyone who would listen to him.

"Yeah, this is the place. That's Mrs. Kozler's house there. Real nice lady. She'll probably have a fit when she finds out what's going on." He spoke to no one in particular, and no one answered.

Detective Walt Harel was in charge of the group. He was a thin, humorless man who, like Criley, chain-smoked. He scanned the area quickly, noting in particular the dozen or so wooden boat sheds scattered just above the beach line.

"Which one of those sheds is it, Criley?"

The young man perked up, obviously eager to be of help. "It's the fourth one from the end, sir. You see it there? The green one? It's probably locked, though. You'll probably have to shoot the door down."

Harel nodded. It was clear he did not intend to get into any long conversation with this young man.

"All right, now everybody just wait here while I go talk to the lady of the house. Looks like we can't get to it right off, anyway."

Harel plodded his way through the sand, feeling it seep into his shoes. He passed a small, hand-lettered sign on the porch that read MRS. HELEN KOZLER—BEACH FRONT BOAT SHEDS —WEEKLY AND SEASONAL RATES. He could find no bell, and rapped sharply on the screen door. He rapped again, then a third time; finally, a tiny grandmotherly woman minced out to the door.

"All right, son. I'm comin' as fast as I can."

"My name's Harel, Mrs. Kozler. West Haven Police. I hope

we're not disturbing you, ma'am, but we'd like to have a look at one of your sheds. If it's not too much trouble, we'll be needing the key."

"Police? Oh, my. We don't have any trouble around here. No, sir. Everything's real quiet and respectable."

"I'm interested in a shed you rented to an Earl Harmen. Do you remember that name?"

The woman's face brightened in recognition. "Oh yes, of course. Mr. Harmen. I know right off—he has number eleven, down to the end of the beach. Such a fine young man. He isn't in any trouble, is he?"

"I don't think it's anything you need worry about, Mrs. Kozler. But if I could, I'm going to have to look inside that shed of his, and I'd appreciate it if you could let me have the key."

"Well, seeing as how you're a police officer, I guess it's all right. Such a fine man. Never any trouble. He always has a smile and something nice to say. Not like some of these sour-faced youngsters. A real fine man. I hope there's nothing wrong. Just a minute, now, and I'll get his key for you."

Harel waited until the woman returned. He thanked her again, assuring her that he and his men would be finished in a short time. Then he walked back to the waiting men.

"Lashlee, call in and see where the hell those prisoners are."

A uniformed policeman went to one of the car radios.

Lee Criley observed this exchange curiously.

"Prisoners, sir? What prisoners? What are you going to do with prisoners?"

Harel looked at the thin teenager with undisguised distaste. "You said we might have to do some digging, didn't you? That was in your story, wasn't it?"

"Oh, yeah, and you want to use the prisoners to do the digging. Yeah, I see. I guess that saves you guys some work, doesn't it?"

The uniformed officer returned to Harel. "They're on the way, sir. They had a little trouble getting clearance. Shouldn't be more than twenty minutes or so."

Harel spat into the sand. "Clearance, huh? You wait over

here for 'em, then. Criley, now suppose you take us on down to this shed of yours."

Criley smiled buoyantly. "Yes, sir. Right this way."

The young man, still handcuffed, bounded out in front of the men in the direction of the beach.

"Now just take it easy, there. Not so fast."

"What? Oh, yeah. Ha, ha. You didn't think I was going to escape, did you? Don't worry. You got me. I'm not going anywhere." And he continued to smile as the officer took hold of his upper arm.

As the men walked closer and closer to the shed, each experienced a growing sense of unease. This small shed, twelve feet by thirty-two, its faded green paint blistering and chipping in the hot salt air, this shed with the number eleven painted over its wide swinging garage-style doors, was somehow different. Of course, they knew the feeling stemmed from the ghoulish thing they had been told about the shed, but still there seemed to be a gloom, a darkness, a kind of evil that emanated from it. Each man felt it, each of these police officers accustomed to dealing with man's inhumanity to man on a daily basis, each knew that once he walked through those doors he would come face to face with the unspeakable.

Harel unlocked the door, and for one eerie moment nobody moved an inch. It was as if they could still turn back, still forget the whole thing, go back to their wives and their kids and return to the normal, comfortable rhythm of life. But once they passed through those doors, their choice would be irrevocable. To a man, they all knew this. Even Criley, happy, exuberant, unburdened of his secret at last, even Lee Criley understood the meaning of that pause and remained silent, respectful.

Harel threw the door open, flooding the inside with the late-afternoon light. Looking inside, these men could almost sense the movement of certain things, things of the darkness, things that vanished with the coming of light.

Harel tried to be especially matter-of-fact. "All right, men, now let's see what we got here."

With that, they were inside; the irrevocable step had been taken.

For some reason, they all kept close to the walls.

The air in the shed was a few degrees warmer than that outside, protected as it was from the cooling ocean breezes. And because there was less circulation of air, the shed had a musty, oppressive smell, not fresh and invigorating like the salt air but heavy and deadly. There was an automobile in the shed, taking up about a fourth of the available space. It was a 1965 Chevrolet, and the fine layer of sand on the body and windows indicated that it had been unmoved for some time. There were three sawhorses piled on top of each other in one corner. Hanging on the walls from nails and hooks, and wedged in between rafters, was an assortment of objects such as might be found in any boat shed—oars, ropes, an old lobster trap, fishnets, an anchor, life jackets, gasoline cans, paint cans, brushes, and two deep-sea fishing poles.

Against a wall, just barely visible, Harel noticed two other things: a garden spade and a nearly empty bag of quicklime.

There was no flooring in the shed. The floor consisted only of sand and was covered with footprints. The sand in the center looked darker, of a more rocky texture, than the sand around the edges of the walls. There was an area of about six by ten feet that looked as if it had been dug up and filled in again.

Harel motioned to Criley and pointed to the sandy area in the center. "Is that where we should start digging?"

Criley nodded. "Yessir. Right there. There's quite a few of them right there."

"You mean there's other places too?"

"Yessir. I told Sergeant Shaunessey all that. He knows about it."

"You told him all about it, did you? I know what you told him, but you come over here, son. I want you to listen to me real good. I'm not sure just what it is you're doing. But if it turns out that you've been doing nothing but handing everybody a load of crap, and this is all your idea of a joke, then you're gonna be one sorry boy, you hear me? You hear me, son?"

"Yessir, I hear you. But, honest, it's no joke. I wasn't trying to fool nobody. You'll see. Honest."

Harel just looked into Criley's pale blue eyes. He believed him. That was the worst part of it.

"All right, let's all move on out of here till the prisoners get here. Let's go."

Outside the shed, the men stood around in small groups, finding what shade they could. Criley spoke only to ask for a match now and then. They waited five minutes, ten minutes, and then the prisoners arrived. Six men—four white, two black—dressed in prison denims, all carrying shovels. Though they were trustees, two guards with short-barreled shotguns at the ready watched their every move. The older of the guards sought out Harel.

"Sorry we're late, sir."

"What the hell was the problem?"

"I don't know, sir. Seems like the warden didn't want anybody goin' on any work mission till he found out just what kind of good time these boys'll be gettin'. It messes up our body count to keep prisoners out during the night, and then we never know for sure how much to cut their sentence. I guess that's why, sir."

"All right, so long as they're finally here. Get 'em on inside there and have 'em start digging."

"Yes, sir. And just whereabouts should they start?"

"Criley, show them where to start."

"Right, sir." Criley was quick to respond, eager to resume center stage. He led the prisoners inside, and the police officers followed after, keeping always toward the walls. Criley drew a large circle in the sand with his foot. "Right there. That's where. Just keep digging right there, and you'll find 'em, just like I told you."

The prisoners looked to the guard for instructions. He nodded, and they moved into the circle, poking the sand tentatively with their shovels. Criley moved toward the wall, standing near Harel.

"Just like going after buried treasure, isn't it? I mean, in a way."

Harel looked at Criley in disbelief and said nothing. The shovels bit easily into the loose, soft sand.

The digging had gone on for some time before Harel became aware that the activity within the boat shed had attracted a number of curious onlookers. A small group of children and one or two adults were gathered near the open door of the shed. "Lashlee, take care of those people, and close the doors."

The uniformed policeman gently explained to the group that this was a routine matter and they should all go back to their swimming. Reluctantly the people drew back a few yards and the officer closed the doors. It became dark enough then to require the use of the one hanging light bulb. The light contributed to the rapidly rising temperature in the shed. With so many men inside and no air circulation, the heat quickly became unbearable.

"All right, Lashlee. You'll have to open the doors a bit. Post two men outside. I don't want any more beach parties wandering in here."

The digging continued.

At a depth of three feet, one of the men struck something.

The top layer of sand was cleared off with the tips of the shovels, then the rest was brushed away. It was a plastic bag, heavy green plastic of the type used in gardening and landscaping. A knot was tied at the open end, making it almost airtight. Even so, there was no mistaking the odor that filled the shed: the odor of decomposing human flesh, the odor of death.

"See? I told you I was telling the truth. I told you."

"Lift it out of the hole and set it down here. And be careful with it, for God's sake."

Two prisoners picked up the bag gingerly, holding their faces away from the smell.

"All right, one of you men cut it open. Cut it open, I said! What are you waiting for?"

One of the officers opened a jackknife and cut an even line the length of the bag. He peeled open the sides, exposing what lay inside. The stench was overpowering, and every man immediately started breathing through his mouth to decrease the effect of the odor of death and decay.

Death was inside the green plastic bag. Death was there in the form of a still-recognizable fourteen-year-old boy, naked, his flesh bloated, discolored, and rotten, his arms and legs twisted in a fetal position. The skull was misshapen, crusted brown. The body had been mutilated.

"Oh, Jesus God. Oh, God." Most of the police officers simply looked away. The prisoners, whose experiences had not brought them into contact with this aspect of death, gagged and dropped their shovels, heading for the cleaner air outside. Detective Harel looked from the body to Criley.

"You recognize that boy?"

"Yessir. That's Billy. Billy Breskin. His folks live over on South Main. Yeah, that's Billy Breskin, all right."

Harel spoke to his men. "All right, let's clear out of here. One of you call the morgue. Have 'em send a truck and a body bag over here. I guess you better call for a few body bags. It looks like we're going to be here a while. And don't let anybody come poking around that hole. Criley, come with me. I want to talk to you."

"Sure, Detective. Anything you say."

Criley followed Harel outside, both glad to breathe good air again. They walked about twenty yards from the shed, when Harel turned and spoke again to Criley.

"You say that's Billy Breskin in there?"

"Yessir. Just like I told you."

"How long has he been there?"

"Billy? Well, let's see. Not too long. Maybe three weeks, the most. I'd say between two and three weeks. I guess I'm not exactly sure."

"Were you there when he was buried?"

"Yeah, me and Earl were there. Otis wasn't in on that one."

"Otis?"

"Yeah. Otis Hesler. I told Sergeant Shaunessey all about him. Isn't Sergeant Shaunessey going to be here? I felt real good being able to talk to him."

"No, he won't be here today. And where was Billy killed?"

"Earl's house."

"Now, just who was it that killed him?"

"Earl killed him. I didn't kill Billy."

"How did he kill him?"

"I'm not too sure I remember. I think he hit him a couple of times in the head with a baseball bat. Yeah, that's how he did it. He didn't shoot him or anything."

"Look at me, son. Don't you have any feeling about all this? Doesn't it make you feel bad at all?"

"Oh, yessir. It does. I feel real bad about it, you bet I do. I guess I never felt so sorry for anything in my whole life as I do now. I feel bad, all right."

It was Detective Harel's impression at the time that Criley might just as well have been apologizing for breaking his mother's best plate.

Moments after the digging resumed, this time with the prisoners wearing handkerchiefs across their faces, a second bag was found. This bag was partially decomposed by a heavy layer of quicklime that had been spread over it.

The prisoners carried it out of the hole, and again the bag was cut open. Inside was the body of another boy. The face was unrecognizable.

"Who's that?"

"Well, if that's the one before Billy, and I'm not sure it is, then it's some kid we picked up hitchhiking. That was a month or two ago. It's pretty hard to tell right now, though."

Harel walked away. "Yeah, you're right. It is pretty hard to tell right now."

One of the prisoners, a muscular man named Sam, put down his shovel and approached a shotgun-wielding guard. It seemed to the guard that there might have been tears in Sam's eyes, but it could have been from the fumes of the quicklime.

"Hey, this ain't no job for me. I can't keep diggin' up them little boys. It makes me sick."

"If you don't want to work, Sam, I'll get somebody else. You volunteered to work, and that's what you'll do."

"Honest, I can't keep lookin' at these little boys. I don't like this."

"Goddammit, who the hell do you think *does* like it? Just shut the hell up."

The man walked back to the deepening hole and resumed his work.

A third body was found at about four feet. This one was not in a plastic bag, and so there was little but bone left. By the size, the body appeared to be approximately the same age as the other two.

Criley watched, still interested, but without any discernible emotion.

A little deeper. Another body. The fourth.

Criley tapped Harel on the arm. Involuntarily, Harel cringed from the contact.

"What is it?"

"Do you think it would be all right if I called my mom? I mean, she doesn't know where I am or anything, and I think I'd like to talk to her."

"You mean to tell me you didn't get a chance to call anyone since you were arrested?" Harel was incredulous.

"Well, no, sir. Because, first of all, I didn't really feel like talking to anybody. But I think I'd like to talk to somebody now. I think I'd like to call my mother. She worries quite a lot when I don't get home."

Criley dialed his home number from a phone in a bedroom of the Kozler home. Detective Harel stood near the door, having made it clear that there would have to be someone present when Criley made the call. Outside, two more uniformed police stood guard. Just in case.

The phone rang twice. Three times. In the middle of the fourth ring, Lee Criley's brother Michael answered.

"Hello?"

"Mike, it's me, Lee. Is Mom around?"

"Where you been, Lee? Mom's been going nuts. Where you been?"

"Just get her for me."

"Where are you?"

"Will you please get her for me?"

"Hold on. I think she's watching television."

Criley spoke to Harel. "She's coming. Have you got a match?"

He lit Criley's cigarette, tossing the match in a bedside ashtray.

"Thanks."

Harel nodded.

There was activity at the other end of the phone.

"Lee, is that you?" The woman's voice was strained, hysterical. She was near tears from relief at finally hearing her son's voice.

"Yes, Mom. Everything's all right."

"Where are you? Why didn't you call?"

"Mom, don't get too excited, but I'm down at the boat shed. Earl's dead. I shot him."

There was a pause. "What? What are you saying?"

"I told you, Mom. I shot Earl. I'm down here with the police."

The woman was starting to lose control. "How could you shoot him? You don't have a gun. What are you saying, Lee? Are you all right? Did you get hurt?"

Criley looked at Harel, shaking his head, as if to indicate that as two mature men they would have to be patient with a hysterical woman.

"Ma, I told you, I'm all right. There was a fight with me and Earl, and I shot him. And now I'm with the police. They're taking good care of me and I'm all right."

"And they arrested you?"

"Yes, Mom."

"And you can't come home?"

Criley smiled at Harel. "No, Mom, I can't come home. Not for a while."

"Can I come and see you? Lee, are they going to take you to jail?"

Criley spoke to Harel, and Harel answered curtly.

"Mom, they say you can see me at court tomorrow at the arraignment. There's some more things I have to talk to them about tonight."

"What things? Oh, my God."

"Just some things. Honest, Mom, there's nothing to worry about. I just wanted to talk to you for a while and let you know everything was all right."

"Was that Otis Hesler involved in any of this?"

"Well, yes, sort of."

"I knew it. I knew it. I warned you about that Otis. I told you he was a terrible boy."

"Aw, come on, Mom. That doesn't do any good."

"Doesn't do any good? And what does do any good? You tell me Earl's dead and you're in jail? What should I do?"

"Nothing. Don't do nothing. I told you everything was all right."

"Lee, are you sure? Are they treating you all right?"

"Please, Mom. You have to understand. I feel good. I mean I really feel good. The cops are watching me, but I feel free, Mom. So you don't have to worry about me. Can you understand that, Mom?"

"You feel free?"

"Mom, it's like I'm really alive for the first time. Earl's dead, but I'm alive now. I've been talking to the policemen here, one of them especially. I got a whole lot of stuff off my chest, Ma, and it's going to be all right."

"Lee, I'm so scared for you."

"Look, Mom, I think I got to go now. There's somebody else has to use the phone." Criley winked at Harel, who did not respond.

"I'll come and see you tomorrow."

"Good, Mom. Goodbye."

"I'll be praying for you, Lee. And Michael and your grandma will be praying for you."

"Okay, Ma. Thanks."

"And we all love you, Lee. We'll all be praying for you."

"Goodbye, Mom."

"You be a good boy, Lee. Goodbye."

He hung up, breathing a deep sigh of relief.

"Boy, mothers, you know what I mean? They really get up-tight."

Harel couldn't suppress his thoughts, although he knew it was pointless to voice them to Criley. "I wonder how the mothers of some of those boys out in the shed feel."

"Yeah, me too. I feel real sorry for them. I guess they'll all know for sure now." He said it almost with a smile.

The digging went on. A second shift of prisoners took over the work. At about four and a half feet, the remains of a fifth body were discovered. A skull and most of the skeleton were slowly brought out of the hole. The left foot was not found. The bones were placed carefully in a canvas tote bag, tagged, and put aside.

Criley continued to watch, showing only signs of fatigue. He had been awake for almost forty hours. He had not eaten, except for coffee and a hard roll at lunchtime. The effects of the previous night's drinking and drug-taking had long since worn off, and he was left with a slow, throbbing ache in his left temple. At first, during the day, he had been sustained by the telling of his story. Then the excitement of the events, the attention of the police, the digging, more questions, all kept him alert and interested. This excitement too had passed, and now Lee Criley was hovering near exhaustion, with only an endless chain of cigarettes to sustain him.

Harel spoke to Criley, bringing him temporarily back to alertness.

"How long did you know Earl Harmen?"

"Sir?"

"I said, how long did you know Harmen?"

"Two, maybe three years."

"And this . . . this kind of thing was going on all that time?"

"Well, yeah. Most of it. Yes."

"Let me just ask you once, that's all, and you don't have to an-swer me if you don't want to. But how in God's name could anybody do this kind of thing? Can you tell me that? How could this happen?"

Criley stuck another cigarette in his mouth. Harel didn't light it this time.

"Well, sir, it all just kind of happened, you know. I don't think anybody planned it. But you would have to know how Earl was. I can't explain it, but you didn't know Earl."

"He made you take part in all this?"

"No, I'm not saying that. What I did, I did. It's just that Earl was a very strange guy, and you'd find yourself doing things with him that you wouldn't ordinarily do. Something like that. I can't explain it."

The prisoners raised another plastic sack out of the hole. It had been buried deeper than the last body found, but the contents were not in such an advanced state of decomposition, perhaps because an effort had been made to make the bag airtight. In the bag were two bodies, young boys, naked. Most of the flesh had fallen away, but somehow there was an uncanny impression that the two bodies had very recently been alive, walking around, riding bicycles, playing baseball. Having been thrown into the single bag together, the limbs of the two bodies had intertwined, as if they were holding each other, as if they were shielding each other.

"I remember them."

"You remember them? Who were they?"

"Oh, a couple of brothers we picked up fishing or something. Cute guys, really. They're from around here."

"Did you kill them?"

"Only one of them. Earl killed the other one. Strangled him."

The digging went on. At Criley's direction, the hole was made wider instead of deeper. "None of them is more than six or seven feet down. We'd have been digging all year otherwise."

An eighth body was recovered. Criley had fallen asleep, leaning against the wall. He was awakened to see if he was able to recognize this body. He did not remember it.

Criley requested that he be taken back to headquarters as soon as possible to sleep. Harel agreed and Criley was led, still in handcuffs, to a patrol car that took him off into the night, away from the boat shed.

It was two in the morning. The digging continued. Before the digging was to stop, at this site and at others, it would come to light that Earl Harmen, with his two young accomplices, had committed the most heinous series of crimes in the history of the United States. And aside from those accomplices, not one single living person had known him as anything other than "a nice quiet man."

The door to the jail cell slid shut on well-oiled rollers and closed with a solid, final thud. Lee Criley had been locked up before for brief periods, for minor scrapes with the law. Always he had gotten out within hours. This time, when the door to the cell closed, he was suddenly aware that this was very different.

He had been awake well over forty-six hours now, and his body was churning with nervous energy. He was tired beyond exhaustion, beyond the ability to sleep or even to begin to relax. He paced the tiny cell in his bare feet, his thumbs hooked in the loops of his beltless blue jeans. His thoughts, jumbled, magnified, exploded in his mind like so many bullets, careening against the inside of his throbbing head, crashing into one another.

The thoughts seemed to reverberate against the gray, graffiti-covered walls, mingling with the echoes of despair and anger and confusion and lust of the hundreds of men who had occupied this tiny cell before him. Hundreds had heard the same terrifying closing of the door and felt the same absolute aloneness. With that closing of the door, the universe had demonstrated its rejection of these men and, now, of Lee Criley. It had no further use for them; it did not want them walking free, breathing free, sharing existence with the rest of human society. We don't want to see you any more, Lee Criley, we don't want to look at you any more. Stay here, away from our gaze.

And he though that first thought of all who are jailed or chained or locked away. He thought of the possibility of fire, of how he would be utterly unable to defend himself, to run away, should great sheets of red flame suddenly fill the halls outside, trapping him in this tiny cell. It wasn't fair, it wasn't right, that anyone should be that defenseless. No one should feel that all chance of escape and self-preservation had been denied him.

He thought of the two boys. The two brothers. Somehow more than any of the others, they were the ones who stuck in his mind, coming back to him at the least-expected hours of day or night. He had tried to tell Shaunessey about them, but he couldn't. The two brothers came back to him now, as if now, in jail, this untold part of the story had more room in which to twist and coil about in his thoughts. Shaunessey had been good for him, made him feel strangely free; but there was still so much more he had to tell. Those two brothers. Those two brothers kept coming back to him.

He used the john, the only furniture in the cell except for the steel cot that hung from the wall at a height of about two feet from the floor. He stepped on the flush handle, and an explosion of sound filled the cell. It took a long time for the bowl to fill again and for silence to return.

Then the silence itself terrified Lee Criley. The small cell grew smaller, and the thought of a fire suddenly overwhelmed him. He panicked. If only to hear the sound of his own voice, of any voice, he called out.

"Hey! Hey, out there! Is anybody out there? Can anybody hear me?"

"Shut the fuck up in there."

The closeness of the voice had an instant effect on him. He wasn't alone. There was someone else right next to him, locked up just as he was.

He called out again, though now the panic had subsided.

"Hey, let me out of here. Hey, out there."

"Ah, for Chrissake, shut your fuckin' mouth, will ya?"

A key turned in a lock, a heavy door swung open, and sharp footsteps sounded in the corridor.

"What's the problem in here?"

It was a cop Lee Criley had not seen before. He looked official and crisp in his blue uniform.

"I was gettin' a little nervous in here."

"You better try an' pipe down. You're not the only one here."

"I know that."

"All right, then. Get some sleep. You're going to need it."

And before Lee Criley could say a word, the footsteps clicked down the corridor again and were gone. The cell lapsed back into dead silence.

He lay down on the cot, which was impossibly short. He adjusted the one woolen blanket under his head and tried to lay on his side, but the hardness of the cot forced him to turn over on his back. Lee Criley stared up at the dark gray ceiling and for a moment he saw Earl Harmen's face looking back down at him with a smile as distorted as any nightmare image.

He squeezed his eyes shut as hard as he could, looked up again . . . and the face was gone. He knew he wasn't crazy; he was just exhausted and feverish. The leering face above him was a product of his own mental and physical state. He had certainly been under the influence of hallucinogens often enough to have learned how to maintain a kind of equilibrium, emotional and physical, by not completely trusting his own perceptions. Lee Criley knew that he wasn't crazy; yet he shivered all the same in cold fear.

They had been fishing. He was almost sure of that. He thought he remembered putting the fishing poles in the back seat of the car when they got in. Two brothers, off on a fishing trip. He remembered what a beautiful day it had been and how he had wished that he had gone fishing, maybe even with those two brothers. He had never fished much, never had time, never had anyone to show him how. He remembered that he envied the two boys, their closeness, their happiness.

Lee Criley shifted his weight restlessly on the steel cot. His body already ached from the hard surface. He could feel tightness in his joints, a slowing down of circulation, and he kneaded his shoulders and legs in an effort to release the tension of his body. And he thought of the boys, how they had remained fast to the boards with no chance of escape, all movement cut off, for hours and sometimes days, until the end came.

He realized that he was staring into the light bulb in the ceiling; it was shielded by wire mesh, shielded from the prisoner who might consider doing violence to himself or to others. His eyes were normally oversensitive to light, to sunlight especially, and Lee Criley quickly averted his gaze as first orange and then green afterimages floated behind his eyelids.

He couldn't remember the address, but he could see the room with absolute clarity, the room where he had handcuffed the older of the two brothers. A nice kid, really, not a wise guy like so many young punks were. He was cuffed to the board, like they did with most of them, and he was mumbling. Lee could hear him mumbling again, and he thought he was calling for his brother, the little guy. And Lee remembered that he had been shocked that this kid, this kid who was being tied up and beaten, was still worried about his little brother. Quite a kid, he thought.

There was a low moan and then a sound of retching. It took Lee Criley many seconds before he placed the sound as coming from the cell next to his. The sound filled him with disgust, yet he was gladdened in a way for the sense of reality it brought back to him. The reality was that he was confined, that he probably would be confined for a long, long time, and that now even this reality was to be desired over other darker, more insistent realities.

The moaning grew louder. Though he could not see him, Lee Criley sensed that the man from whom the moans came was rolling about on the cold cement floor, probably holding his stomach in sick spasms.

"Oh, Christ, help me, will ya? Give me some water, will ya?"

The moaning and shuffling sounds continued. Lee Criley listened intently. There was no response from beyond the corridor.

The boy was moaning from behind the white adhesive tape, and his eyes were red and swollen. The small body was bruised and broken in many places. The boy's head raised up as Lee entered, and his eyes widened just perceptibly. Lee didn't know whether it was through the sudden shock of seeing another human being or whether the boy expected that it was now all over, that help had appeared, and that he would soon be freed and sent home. They all expected that, deep down. They all thought that they would be freed and sent home.

There had been a phone call, Lee remembered. Earl's idea. For no reason, really. They would never have let him go.

"Mom, it's me," he had heard him saying. "It's Buddy."

"Hey, bud. Ya got a smoke?"

Lee Criley's mind strained at the intrusion.

"Hey, buddy. How about a smoke? Ya got a smoke?"

He couldn't quite understand where the voice came from, and his disorientation increased.

"What's the matter in there, bud? Ain't ya got a smoke? What about it?"

The wounded boy receded back into nothingness. It was the prisoner in the next cell.

"No, man. They took everything away from me."

A long phlegmy cough rattled from the cell. "The son of a bitches. What're you in for?"

At that moment, Lee Criley realized that he didn't know what he was in for. All he knew was that now, at long last, it was all over.

"I don't know. What difference does it make?"

The disembodied voice in the next cell apparently accepted this as an appropriate answer, and went on.

"Me, they say I got drunk and drove into a couple of cars. I ain't drunk, for Christ sake. I don't get drunk on a couple of beers, goddammit."

Lee Criley could actually feel the chill coming over his body. He shivered on the steel cot and drew the blanket up close around his chest. He felt as if he were in a refrigerator, and yet he knew that August nights in southern Connecticut, particularly in an airless jail cell, were not cool.

Shaunessey had seemed to care. He listened kindly, never rushing him, and he seemed almost to offer a hope of forgiveness. Maybe things hadn't been so bad. It was easy to see how anyone might get involved with someone like Earl and how one thing could lead to another. Shaunessey seemed to realize that Lee wasn't so different from anybody else, and how a lot of guys get into trouble in some way or another. He was a cop; he had seen lots of stuff like this before and, okay, you get into a little trouble, you get busted, pull some time maybe, but that's it. Nothing special. No big deal. He was only human, wasn't he? He was just another seventeen-year-old kid who messed around with some things he shouldn't have. Anybody could understand that. Sergeant Shaunessey, big-boned, gray-haired, compassionate, had seemed to the troubled boy a kind of holy man, a priest, who offered the promise of peace and salvation.

Criley had tried to tell him everything, as best he could, and the old cop had listened gravely, quietly, nodding from time to time, encouraging him to go on, to cleanse himself. And for a while, for so brief a time, Lee Criley had allowed himself to think that somehow things could be made right again. But the joy and relief lasted only until he began to speak of the incident with the two boys, when he suddenly felt the distance stretching between himself and the old man, and he had realized with a sickening certainty that no, Sergeant Shaunessey did not understand and that yes, he, Lee Criley, had removed himself irrevocably from things human.

He barely heard the insistent pleading from the next cell as he sank deeper into his memory of Earl Harmen, a memory that grew stronger and clearer as the cold penetrated the very depths of his body, and beyond.

The two boys. The two brothers. It had all changed for Lee Criley on that day. Up to that day, he had gone along with things, hardly realizing what he was doing, fooling himself into believing that all those earlier beatings, all the killings, had been nothing more than a frightening game. It had been a joy ride, a cruel, terrifying joy ride that Earl Harmen had taken him on, that he had let himself be taken on—but it was just that, a joy ride, something exciting, dangerous, something against the law, but really not serious at all. Until that day, when the two boys had been brought to the house, Lee Criley was unaware of what he and Earl and Otis were doing. And if he had actually considered it, he would have thought, deep down, that after all the games were over, all the boys would get up out of their sandy graves and everything would be the same again. It was a game. It wasn't real. Nobody was really getting hurt.

But with the two brothers, with their fishing poles, with the older one so protective and concerned about his little brother, it had all changed. That day Lee Criley first began to realize the truth. He began to understand that these two boys, and all the others, would in fact not get up to go home again. And he began to understand—not completely, of course, but a little—that it was no longer a game that was being played. It was instead something that could only result in his damnation.

"Don't kill me, Lee. Please don't kill me. I won't tell anybody, ever. Please, Lee, don't kill me."

The understanding had first dawned on him then, as the boy was pleading for his life. It had jarred him and paralyzed him for an instant, and then he was able to push it back, to forget, and to go on.

"Please, Lee. Don't kill me. Please."

He killed the boy anyway.

But this boy, unlike the others, would not stay dead. This boy, unlike the others, made Lee Criley see the truth that he would have to live with forever.

"Please, Lee. Please. Don't kill me, Lee."

He had killed him, but the boy would not stay dead.

The face of the boy who would not die floated before Lee Criley.

"Please, Lee. Don't kill me. Please."

There was an explosion, and a small red hole appeared in the boy's forehead.

"Please, Lee."

Another explosion, and another.

The guard was shaking him, slapping him. "Hey, what's the matter with you? Are you all right? What the hell's the matter with you?"

Lee Criley looked up into the angry, puzzled face of the guard, then beyond him to the gray walls of the cell, the bars on the door. Jail. He was in jail.

"I'm all right. I'm all right now."

"Keep it quiet here, boy, or I'll have to take you into isolation."

"No, it's all right. I'll be quiet. I won't make any more noise."

"You make sure of that."

The guard left him alone, and this time Lee Criley fell into a deep, dreamless sleep.

4

■ "Get the hell down here, goddammit! Get down here when I call you."

The voice, enraged, furious, terrifying, boomed through the house, shattering the quiet.

"Get down here, you! Don't make me come up and get you."

Earl Harmen, now twelve, sitting on the floor of his room, froze in terror. He knew he would have to go down, that there was no escape from what awaited him downstairs. But he was unable to move. He was physically unable to command his body to respond to the voice downstairs, so great was his fear.

"Can't you hear me, goddam you? Get down here!"

It sounded as if his stepfather were drunk again. His voice had that full, gurgling sound that meant his rage would know no bounds. Carefully, Earl put down the pieces of the model plane he was working on, but because his hands were shaking, he spoiled the whole plane. He stood up, opened the door of his room, and went to the head of the stairs. His voice, as contrasted with the one downstairs, was faint, abject.

"Yessir?"

"Don't you yessir me, you goddam little bastard. Get down here when I call you. Get down or you'll be one sorry little bastard."

Earl walked down the stairs slowly because he dreaded going to his stepfather, and yet he could not go so slowly as to appear disrespectful.

He held onto the banister tightly, his knuckles showing white under the skin, the palms already slimy with sweat. His mind racing, Earl wondered what he might have done to enrage his stepfather. He had left no mess downstairs, he had made sure of that. His bicycle was put away; he had done his chores. What could it have been, what could he have forgotten? What had made his stepfather so mad again?

"Are you down here yet?"

"I'm coming. I'm coming down."

He was sitting in the living room, and from the redness of his face, the watery, glazed look in his eyes, and from the smell, Earl knew that his stepfather was drunk. Maybe so drunk he would fall asleep soon. Earl prayed that this would happen.

"Where's your mother?"

"I don't know."

"You don't know. Is that all you can say? What the hell's the matter with you, anyway?"

Earl said nothing. He hung his head, looking at his shoes. He was dizzy with fear.

"Answer me when I talk to you, damn you to hell."

In the years since his mother had married Al Marris, Earl could not remember that he had ever called him by name. Instead, there had been beatings. The beatings weren't so bad when his mother was there, and she would step in and pull the boy away when they threatened to get out of control. And other times, when his mother wasn't there, the beatings would be worse. Marris would use his belt, his thick black leather belt, to beat respect into the boy, to teach him to listen to his elders. Earl had dreamed about the big black belt crashing down on him and had wakened in terror, screaming for his mother, unable to tell of his fear of the man she had married.

"I thought I told you to mow the goddam lawn."

The lawn. That was it. The lawn. But he had cut it only a few days ago, and he was going to cut it again on the weekend. Right now, it really didn't need cutting. Surely, it was a mistake about the lawn. He couldn't be in trouble because of that.

"But I already cut the . . ."

The man sprang out of his chair with a speed one would have thought impossible for such a bulky body. He grabbed Earl by the shoulder, breathing his foul breath into the boy's face. His own face was red with alcohol and rage.

"Don't you back-talk me, boy. Don't you ever back-talk me."

He slapped the boy with such force that the blow would have knocked him over if he hadn't still held him by the shoulder. Earl could not help but sob softly. He had learned it was best to make no noise at all, and he tried his utmost to hold back the tears of pain and humiliation.

"I think it's high time I teach you a lesson. Get upstairs. Get upstairs right now. And when I get up there, I want you laying on the bed with your pants off. Do you hear me?"

Earl opened his mouth, but no sound came out.

"Did you hear me, boy? Did you hear me when I tell you something?"

He could only whisper a soft "Yessir," and then he did as he was told.

Inside his room, Earl unbuckled his belt, unzipped his pants and let them fall around his ankles. He let his underpants fall over them and then, taking a few clumsy steps, he lay across his bed and waited.

The minutes dragged on like hours. He knew his stepfather

would keep him waiting like this for a long time, and he knew that as much as he tried to convince himself that he might have forgotten, he never did. Sooner or later, his stepfather would come up to him, his great black belt slapping menacingly in his open palm.

Earl cried softly, steadily, into his blankets.

The bedroom door crashed open, and the big man strode into the room.

"Next time maybe you'll remember not to back-talk me and to do like I tell you."

The belt cut through the air and exploded on the boy's bare buttocks. He bit into the blankets, stifling his scream.

The belt rose and fell again and again, and this time the boy could not keep from crying out.

"A crybaby, huh? A real little goddam sissy, huh? Is that what we got here? A little sissy boy?"

The belt struck again, and Earl screamed in pain.

And then there was nothing. The next blow did not come as expected. Earl heard the belt drop to the floor. At first he dared not move, and then, tentatively, fighting the fear, he turned slightly to look at the man.

There was a strange expression on Al Marris' face, a look Earl had never seen before. It was a hungry, twisted look that frightened him more than the look of rage.

Marris was unbuttoning his pants.

"Turn around, goddam you. Who the hell said you could look at me, you goddam little sissy. Turn around."

Earl did as he was told. He buried his face in the blankets.

"You are a little sissy boy, aren't you?"

Earl didn't know whether he should respond or not.

"Aren't you? Aren't you?"

"Yes, yes, I am," he said through the blankets.

And then, suddenly, Earl felt the huge body of his stepfather on top of him.

When it was over, the man stood up, buttoned his pants, and slid the great black belt back through the loops. Then he walked around to the other side of the bed, to where the boy's head hung limply over the edge.

He reached down and grabbed the boy by the neck, his huge hand fitting easily all around it, and he pressed his thumb into the boy's windpipe.

"If you ever tell your mother about this, I'll kill you. Do you believe me? Do you believe I'll kill you?" He pressed his thumb in deeper, cutting off the boy's air. Earl's face turned red and then went dark. His eyes started to turn up into his head.

The man loosened his grip.

"Do you believe I'll kill you?" he asked again.

"Yes," Earl choked out.

Almost two years after that day, Alvin Marris was driving home after a night of drinking with some friends. An investigation concluded that he must have fallen asleep at the wheel, driven into the bridge abutment, and died instantly.

Throughout his mother's second marriage, Earl had been terrified of telling her anything. And even afterward, when he and his mother went to live with his grandmother in Brookline, Massachusetts, Earl was still unable to tell his mother.

The A&P on Home Street in Brookline stayed open until nine o'clock on Friday to accommodate the payday shoppers. By nine-thirty, the floors were swept, merchandise was replaced on the shelves, the meat was put back into the cold storage area, lights were switched off, time cards were punched out, and the doors were locked. Earl Harmen, aged fifteen, tagged along with three older boys, a quiet, withdrawn figure in the loud, laughing group. Earl usually went straight home after work. That night he didn't.

The boys walked along in the summer night, only a bit behind the girls, four cashiers who had clocked out just before them. Tonight there was going to be a party. Jeannie Megan's parents had left for the weekend, and she had invited the boys to come over and listen to some records. Earl was invited, too. He was the youngest of the group, he had never spoken to any of the girls except when he had to, and he had no idea how to relax or joke with them. Yet, somehow, he was invited. He had been to a few birthday parties, but never to a party when there were no adults at home. He wanted to go, yet he was frightened and completely unsure of himself. Maybe they had asked him to join them, he thought, just to have someone to laugh at, to poke fun at, if the party got dull. But nothing would have stopped him from going. His grandmother would just have to wait.

There was a girl there in whom Earl had a special interest—Patsy Loughman, a small, shy girl of sixteen, with hair in a ponytail and silky down on her arms. Earl's eyes had locked onto Patsy the very first time he walked in the store, and since then he had avoided all contact with her. Patsy would be at this party. Could it have been her idea that Earl be invited?

The boys hung back from the girls, keeping about half a block behind them for the duration of the five-block walk. While they were older than Earl, none of the three other boys had had much experience with parties at girls' homes. To ease their nervousness, they kept up a chorus of wisecracks and jokes. To this repartee, such as it was, Earl could contribute nothing. The girls looked around occasionally, pretending indifference. Only Jeannie called to them now and again, telling them to hurry up and not get lost.

The Megan home was literally on the other side of the tracks—the wrong side, a fact that Earl did not fail to note. The house was just beyond the railroad crossing, and though trains rarely ran on the old tracks, it was apparent that any train would shake the house to the rafters. Jeannie Megan led the three girls through a back doorway and into the house. By the time the boys arrived, there were records on the phonograph and Jeannie had come out to greet them.

"Hey, whatsa matter, you guys comin' in or not?" Jeannie shouted.

"Sure. What do you think?"

Jeannie was a coarse, lumpy girl. At sixteen she had already developed heavy breasts. She was heavy all over, with rolls of bulky flesh visible beneath her tight-fitting jersey. She wore thick make-up to cover her bad skin. While not considered an outright tramp, the word among the boys was that she was fast, that if the circumstances were right you could get some action. Earl Harmen considered her disgusting.

The boys followed Jeannie inside, with Earl the last. The house was incredibly shabby, with great gaping holes in the upholstery, big enough, Earl thought, for a rat to crawl into. Everything Earl touched felt greasy and dirty, and he wanted to leave as soon as he got there.

Patsy and another girl were dancing together in the living room, the third girl was nowhere in sight, and Jeannie was sprawled on a chair, sipping from a can of beer. Earl had never seen a girl drink beer before. He himself had never tasted beer in his life.

"You guys can have a beer if you want, but don't drink it all or my old man will kill me."

"Hey, let me at some of them suds. We won't drink much of it, Jeannie. Just what we can get our hands on."

"I ain't foolin'. My old man will beat the crap out of me if he finds out about this. So don't go nuts, will ya?"

The three boys sipped their beers awkwardly, feigning drunkenness after the first two or three swallows. Their joking grew louder, more daring, but still there was no real interaction with the girls, all of whom were now dancing together. Earl watched, sitting on the cleanest chair he could find. He hadn't said a word since he came in.

Tim Wallin, the one boy with whom Earl had any kind of a friendly relationship, looked over at the lonely younger boy.

"Hey, Earl, ain't you gonna have a beer? It's on the house."

"No, I don't think so."

"Aw, go on, it won't hurt you. Join the party, fer cryin' out loud."

"I don't like beer."

"Jeezus, this is a party, ain't it? Have one."

"Maybe I'll have a Coke."

The three boys roared in derision. Tim Wallin shrugged and

didn't bother Earl any more. More beers were passed around, the records got louder, and finally Ed Carne, the oldest of the boys, worked up enough courage to ask one of the girls to dance. Earl watched in misery as Patsy Loughman accepted Ed's semi-intoxicated invitation. The dance ended quickly enough, with Ed returning to his friends and more beer, winking and leering while the girls danced again with each other.

Earl watched it all, alone in his misery. Even the girls must now be aware of his status as the outcast. He burned in quiet shame, hating himself even more than the others. But he couldn't leave. He was glued to the chair, unable to make a move that would free him from his humiliation. The noises, the laughter, the dancing went on around him, ignoring him as if he weren't there. No one even looked at him.

He watched as Ed Carne led Patsy Loughman through a door that closed behind them.

Jeannie came out of the kitchen with a can of beer and turned out the lights in the living room. The only source of illumination now was from the kitchen, making it shadowy and dark in the living room. Two dancing couples giggled and moved closer together. Earl grew accustomed to the dark, relieved that he could almost disappear now. He watched as hands groped and caressed in the semidarkness. He listened to the sounds of "Don't" and "Stop" and "Aw, please." that rose just slightly over the sound of the music.

A door opened and Patsy Loughman walked out, followed by Ed Carne. Patsy appeared quite prim and proper, but Ed was straightening his clothes, tucking his shirt into his pants. They sat together on the couch, nuzzling, whispering.

"Well, look who's here. Back to join the party. You better be good, you kids. An' if you can't be good, be careful. An' if you can't be careful, name it after me." Jeannie broke off into her loud laughter. Still whispering together in the darkness, neither Patsy nor Ed responded. The record ended.

"Hey, Jeannie, how about some more sound, huh? What kind of a honky-tonk are you runnin' here, anyway?"

"Ah, shove it you-know-where." She dropped a stack of long-playing records on the phonograph, and then turned off even the kitchen light. The room was in complete darkness.

Earl was startled, completely unprepared for the warm pressure he felt on his right side. Someone was pushing into the chair, crowding in next to him.

"Who is that?"

"Me. Who do you think?" Earl felt himself being enveloped in Jeannie's breath. Smelling the beer rushing into his nostrils, he almost gagged.

"What are you doing?"

"Just saying hello. How come you're so quiet over here by yourself?"

"I don't know." Her arm reached around Earl's shoulders, playing with the hair at the back of his neck. Her breasts were pushing into him, hot beneath the sweat-soaked jersey.

"What are you doing?"

"You like me, don't you?"

"Sure. I mean, you're a nice girl."

"You have pretty eyes, you know that?" She brought her lips close to Earl's face, but he pulled away before she could kiss him.

"You're cute. I like you." She put both arms around Earl, smothering him in her tight clasp.

"You like me, don't you? Don't you?"

Earl struggled to get free. "I don't think we should do that."

Jeannie grabbed Earl's hand and brought it to her breast. In the darkness she had unbuttoned her jersey, and she brought his hand in under the brassière, rubbing it back and forth against her warm breast. "You like that, don't you?" She was whispering heavily, excitedly.

"What are you doing? Don't do that." Earl was paralyzed in terror and disgust.

"Go ahead, you can touch me. Touch me all over, touch me down here." She took his hand and forced it between her legs, rubbing it against her body. In her frenzy, she was unaware of the response she was causing.

She brought her face close to his, this time finding his lips. She kissed him hard and long. At last, as the nausea was rising up in him, Earl snapped out of his frozen fear, punching as hard as he could in the short distance between them, feeling his fist strike the soft flesh of her breast. He was crying in rage and disgust.

"Goddam you, goddam you. Leave me alone, for God's sake. Goddam you."

Jeannie jumped away from the chair, and immediately the light came on. The other couples stared at the two in surprise. Jeannie had lost her breath, so intense was the pain. She held both her hands over her right breast, her eyes wide in disbelief.

"What the hell's going on?" Tim Wallin asked.

Jeannie continued to stare at Earl. "He punched me. The dirty fucking little faggot punched me in the tit."

Ed Carne moved toward Earl. "Give me a hand here, Tim." The two older boys grabbed Earl by the arms and pulled him to the door.

"I think it'd be a good idea if you just get the hell out of here. You understand?"

Earl nodded. They threw him down the three or four stairs into the darkness. He landed, unhurt, in some grass.

When he finally got home it was almost midnight. He unlocked the door as quietly as he could, but a light was still visible in his grandmother's room.

"That you, Earl?"

"Yes, Grandma."

"You're home late, aren't you, Earl? Is everything all right?"

"Yes, Grandma. Everything is all right. Good night."

"Good night, Earl."

Earl took a bath that night in the hottest water he could stand. He scrubbed himself until his skin was red and raw. He brushed his teeth until his gums started bleeding. He lay in bed, looking at the ceiling. When his grandmother called him several hours later to do his Saturday chores, he was wide awake.

It was late March, seasonably warm in Boston, warmer than spring and yet still cooler than summer. It may have been the single most pleasant day of the year.

Earl was going home from school two periods early. His grandmother's physical condition had deteriorated and, because his mother worked, he had received special permission to take his classes one after another at the beginning of the day, like the athletes, and then be excused for the latter part of the day, hours that ordinarily would have been spent in long, boring study halls. While most of the students given this privilege spent the extra time playing football, basketball, or baseball, Earl Harmen used these hours to help his grandmother, to bathe her and shift her from her wheelchair to her bed, to clean and cook as much as possible, and then go on to his part-time job at the supermarket. At first, he had found it difficult to go back to the A&P after his experience with his co-workers at the Megan house, but when he found that everyone simply ignored him he decided to stay on.

He walked past the ballfield, feeling the warm sun on his arms and back. He watched for a moment or two as an outfielder ran after a long fly ball, caught it, and threw it with all his might back to home plate. Earl was fascinated by the physical beauty of the action, the smooth coordination of the outfielder. He wished he could play like that.

Leaving school earlier in the day meant that he always walked home alone. Earl had made few friends, so it didn't make that much difference to him. In fact, he preferred it this way. He would be alone, anyway, and he didn't need the presence of groups of laughing, whispering boys and girls to remind him of his aloneness. The walk home was usually the best part of his day. It was a bridge between the tensions of the classroom and the tedium of helping his grandmother and working in the store. It was a quiet time, when there was no one he had to respond to. He savored this walk; he drew it out.

He enjoyed the walk even when it was raining, or when it was snowing and he lost his footing on the icy sidewalks. Today, in the warm, fresh air, under the yellow sun, the blue sky, with buds just popping out on the trees, today was sheer pleasure. It would have been even better if there had been someone with whom to share the magic of the day, but that was all right. Earl Harmen was as happy as he had ever been.

He had passed the ballfields now and was on Maple Street. He would cross over to Church Street, then cut through a woody area in back of an old mansion.

As he walked, Earl was singing, softly his favorite song from *The Wizard of Oz*, "Over the Rainbow." He didn't know all the words, and he whistled where he wasn't sure. Earl Harmen did not usually sing, even when he was alone, but it was that kind of day.

He wasn't sure just when he became aware of the dog. He caught it out of the corner of his eye, to his right. All he knew was that there was a dog across the street. It flickered in and out of his consciousness. And then the car appeared, tires squealing around the corner, speeding, much too fast for the residential area. The car was behind him when he heard the awful sound. It was the sickening soft impact of a body against metal. There was a high-pitched yelp hanging in the air as Earl turned around. The car sped out of sight without slowing down.

The dog was lying in the gutter, whimpering. Its two hind legs were smashed. It was part spaniel, a mutt, black and white. And red from the blood.

Earl rushed over to the dog and stroked its head gently, murmuring over and over, "That's a good boy. There, there, that's a good boy." The dog tried to lift its head, but the effort put too much strain on its spine and it fell back quickly.

"That's a good boy. Don't you worry, now."

He looked down the street, seeing no one. With infinite care, Earl slowly lifted the dog into his arms, cradling it like a baby, exerting almost no pressure on the broken hind legs. The dog felt the pain—even the slightest movement caused him to whimper softly—but he put up no resistance, looking up into Earl's eyes, seeking and finding reassurance.

"That's a good fella. You just be quiet now. Nobody's gonna hurt you."

Earl's shirt was splotched with blood and dirt as he walked slowly away with the dog in his arms. It was a silent, almost holy, scene, as the rays of healing sunlight streamed down on the boy and the broken dog.

Gently, gently, he placed the dog down on sun-dried moss,

nestling him among the great roots of an ancient maple tree. Gently, he arranged the shattered hind legs so the dog could now move his head without straining his whole body. And with gentleness he stroked the dog's head, rhythmically, softly.

"Poor old dog. That's a good dog, now. Just you be quiet now."

He cleaned the spittle away from the dog's mouth, gazing down with sadness and love, a kind of love Earl had never known before, a complete loss of self and of time in his concern and care for this wounded creature.

They sat for a long time together—the minutes could easily have stretched to hours, or even longer. Time was meaningless under that tree. In that bit of eternity, the boy and the dog reached a kind of intimacy in which there could be nothing hidden any more. The sense of intimacy grew and grew until, inevitably, it reached its climax.

The dog looked up at Earl mutely, with pleading eyes. Then it began to whimper.

Suddenly there was burning, uncontrollable anger and hatred in Earl's heart. He stood up, hating the dog, hating its fragile, broken, useless body, hating its dumb submissiveness, hating its groveling, its whimperings and its cries.

Time was picking up now. It was speeding, hurtling, screaming past the boy's ears. He kicked with all his might into the dog's belly, feeling the ribs bend and finally break under the fury of his kick. The trees were spinning around him as the dog howled piteously. And the louder the dog howled, the harder Earl kicked, now completely out of control. He found a rock in his hand, though he couldn't remember picking it up. He grasped the rock with all his strength and approached the moaning creature.

The first blow caught the dog in the eye, spattering blood back at Earl. Again and again he struck, the ferocious rage within him demanding that he continue until it was all over. At last, the mangled body of the dog was completely inert. The shrill scream within Earl subsided. It was all right now. Things were back to normal.

Methodically, using his hands, then a stick, and finally a flat rock, Earl Harmen dug a shallow hole. The ground was soft and digging was not difficult. He rolled the dog's body into it, then piled the dirt back on top. On this mound he piled twigs and leaves. He looked around, checking to see if the mound was noticeable in the grove of trees and was satisfied that it was not. He brushed himself off—his clothes and, especially, his hands—as best he could, and walked in the direction of home.

He walked easily, gracefully, his hands in his pockets. He was whistling "Over the Rainbow."

The sun had fallen low in the sky, and the chill of winter crept back into the air.

He hastened his pace. He hoped he wouldn't be late.

■ During the early morning hours of Monday, July 24, 1972, while the rest of the world slept on, the digging continued in the small boat shed that had been rented to Earl Harmen. By the time the late editions of the morning papers hit the streets, when the daily commuters had switched on their car radios for the eight o'clock news, and when New Haven housewives sat down in their kitchens for the first cup of coffee, the number of recovered corpses had risen to eleven. Three more bodies of young boys had been dug up during the night, while Lee Criley had lain in an exhausted, almost comatose sleep in the West Haven jail. Three more small skeletons had been brought up out of the damp, stinking sand. There was no doubt now that there would be more. Lee Criley's story had been only too horribly corroborated. The digging did not stop.

The story exploded in the newspapers and on television and radio. The city of New Haven, Connecticut, which is no stranger to violent and senseless acts, was stunned as never before by the news. When the first headlines of MASS MURDER and BODIES IN SANDY GRAVESITE appeared, New Haven was completely off guard, unable to respond, unable to come to terms in any way with what it confronted. It was a city at the mercy of the unfolding sequence of events, shocked and frightened by the abyss opening up before it. The headlines were fascinating, hypnotic. They demanded total attention, absolute surrender. To do otherwise, to conceive of doing otherwise, was impossible. The good people of New Haven, Connecticut, looked on in horror as details began to accumulate of how their sons had died.

In all New Haven no one hung onto the news with more terrible urgency than the parents of runaway boys, teenagers who had disappeared, leaving no trace, no word, never getting in touch with their families again.

A rather incredible fact began to emerge. In the city of New Haven alone, there were more than two hundred young boys a year listed in the police files as "Runaway." And because of this large number, it became apparent that once a name had found its way into this file it was effectively forgotten. There were simply too many young boys taking it upon themselves to head for the open road for any kind of thorough police investigation to be undertaken. Any young boy reported to the police as missing by his family was placed on the active lists for a few days. Unless there was significant evidence of foul play (and there usually wasn't), if he did not turn up in a few days, he would be relegated to the runaway file, where he would be quickly and officially forgotten.

Asked to comment on this state of affairs, in light of the mass murder that had just been uncovered, the embarrassed and somewhat irate police response was that, yes, there was indeed a runaway file and, yes, there were thousands of boys who disappeared without a trace, and, no, there was not any continuing investigation being done on these cases. This was all true. But every large city in the country has the same problem; more than a million juveniles are reported missing each year in the United States. No police department was equipped to deal with a chronic situation of this magnitude. This was also sadly true.

Immediate research into the problem of runaways, however, revealed that a disproportionate number of young boys had disappeared from West Haven within the last three years. Distraught families of missing boys, who had gone through the anguish of losing a child into thin air and the frustration of trying to convince the police that their little Johnny or Billy or Jimmy wasn't like all the rest, that he was a good boy, that he was happy, that he had no reason to run away from home, were plunged into new dimensions of despair. Mrs. Edward Salley remembered that she had often told her son Frankie, missing for fourteen months, that she didn't approve of his hanging around that older man, that she didn't want Frankie accepting anything more from him. Mr. Walter Kelvin recalled that his boy Wally, Jr., had often gone for rides with a bunch of other kids in a white van driven by Earl Harmen. Perhaps the cruelest memory of all was the one that came back to Mrs. John Cunniff, who was still running ads in underground newspapers, hoping that her son Bobby, after seventeen months, would finally answer her.

The Cunniffs' search for their missing son had been long and intense. Not only were ads put in papers, with offers of rewards, but posters were placed in store windows and pictures of Bobby distributed throughout the city, hundreds of hours were spent cruising around the city streets. Inquiries were made in all the large cities, to the police departments of New York, Los Angeles, Dallas, Chicago. And as the face of Lee Criley emerged from the front page of the New Haven *Register*, Mrs. Cunniff remembered something that made her dizzy with horror. She remembered how helpful Lee had been during the weeks immediately after Bobby had gone. She remembered that he offered to pass out posters and promised to keep an eye open for Bobby. She remembered how Lee would come by to see if there was any news at all, if she were all right, if there was anything he could do.

And Mrs. Cunniff remembered that one day Lee Criley had smiled at her reassuringly and said, "I'm sure he'll turn up for you, Mrs. Cunniff. You know, Bobby could be right here, right here in West Haven. He could be right under your nose and you'd never know it."

There was a large number of families in West Haven that became aware of one another for the first time, finding that their lost sons were a common bond. Some experienced a sense of relief, a feeling that now, at least, they would know for sure, once and for all.

As Monday wore on and the first shock of the news subsided, other, stranger questions hung in the air. Was it possible that murders as obscenely violent and cruel could have taken place in New Haven? In Connecticut? On the planet Earth? The only precedent for such undiluted horror was the holocaust that took place over a quarter of a century ago, on another continent. How could it be that such things could go on, and on and on, right in the middle of New Haven? How could it be that young boys could be plucked out of the air, like so many apples from a tree, one after another, month after month, year after year, without detection?

The fact was that this nightmarish reality had taken place in the heart of New Haven, and could easily have continued unexposed for years. The machinery of terror broke down of its own accord, not because it had been detected and destroyed.

And out of all this, suddenly rising like a dark specter over the young boys' unheard cries for help, was the now enigmatic figure of Earl Howard Harmen.

Many people in West Haven had thought they knew Earl Harmen. He had been such a nice, quiet man, a man who always had time for kids. A big brother, a good influence, a gentle man who was generous with all the boys, giving them treats and soda pop and letting them hang around his place.

And everyone who knew Earl knew that he was a bachelor in his mid-thirties, and that until his mother, a seamstress, had moved away—to Massachusetts, somebody thought—Earl had helped support her with his job as a shoe salesman.

Such a nice quiet young man, so reliable, a man who liked kids.

This was Earl Harmen, good neighbor, good friend, respectable citizen, rape-murderer of young boys, the Pied Piper.

As of noon, July 24, 1972, the known number of victims had grown to fifteen. Fifteen bodies, or what was left of them, had been dug out of the sand in the tiny boat shed. And still the digging continued.

Shortly after noon that day, a nervous, heavily perspiring young man walked into the West Haven police station, presented himself at the front desk, and stated that he was Otis John Hesler, age eighteen. The desk sergeant did not immediately recognize the name and asked what he wanted. The young man stated that he knew something about the murders. "You know, about those kids they're digging up."

During seven hours of questioning, Hesler's role in the crimes began to emerge.

Otis Hesler's story was that he had known Earl Harmen since he was six or seven. He used to play around the Harmens' place, and Harmen would give him bubble gum and sometimes money. When Hesler was about eleven, Harmen disappeared for a few years and the relationship ceased.

There were three children in Hesler's family, both parents were alcoholics, and they paid little heed to their offspring. Otis came and went as he pleased—a street kid. At fourteen, Otis met Harmen again, and a sexual relationship developed. Harmen gave the boy spending money in exchange for his sexual compliance, and young Otis, raised in near poverty, responded to the first security he had ever known. Now there was always money, and there was always someone he could turn to.

Otis Hesler became wise in the ways of the world at an early age. By thirteen he had come to an understanding of how to deal with certain older males, and he understood immediately how to satisfy Harmen, how to play an active role. Otis did not consider himself a homosexual. "I was never a fag, man. I just did what he wanted me to. I didn't get anything out of it."

From the beginning, Otis was making money from Earl Harmen. He was soon collecting five and ten dollars from Harmen for his favors. Shortly thereafter, Harmen asked Otis to move in with him. Harmen would continue to pay the rent, to buy food, and to keep Otis in spending money. Otis complied. In all, they shared three different apartments in the course of nineteen months. Earl Harmen liked to move around.

It was a few months after the beginning of their cohabitation that Otis Hesler first became aware of "funny stuff going on."

One afternoon, Otis came home early and saw a sight he did not immediately believe. He found Harmen naked, standing over two boys who were handcuffed to boards in the living room. Harmen was angry and told Otis to get the hell out of there, that he had no business walking in on him like that. Then he changed his tone, told Otis not to worry about what he had seen, that it shouldn't make any difference between them, and that if he would promise never to tell anyone about it, Earl would buy him a new car.

"Did he buy you the car?"

"Yeah, a real pig. A sixty-two Chevy that burned oil. It wasn't worth it."

Hesler told the police how he had introduced Criley to Harmen, and how gradually Criley came to replace him as Harmen's favorite. He explained that the killings had gone on over a two- or three-year period, but that when Lee came along they seemed to be more frequent, more vicious. Otis Hesler denied that he had killed anyone, insisting that, although he knew what was going on and was present at many killings, he was never anything more than a bystander.

"My conscience is pretty clear on that," he told the police. "I never killed nobody. It was Lee and Earl that did everything. At least I can say that."

Hesler stated that he had started getting fed up with all the viciousness and cruelty, and that he had wanted to break his ties with the past and start leading a new life. He was tired of Harmen, tired of everything he stood for. He moved out of Harmen's house and back with his parents but had been unable to break away completely. He still brought boys to Harmen; he still helped bury them. Only he never killed anyone himself. From his point of view, that made him innocent.

Two weeks earlier Otis Hesler had married Sharon Minton and moved in with her family. He would have to start working now, especially with a baby on the way. Yet he was unable to get away completely from the old life. Somehow, he always kept returning to Harmen.

Hesler told the police that he had often wondered how long it could go on, and how he could ever cut himself loose from it. He wondered if he would ever be able to lead a decent life, working, taking care of his wife and kid, and living like a normal person. In a way, he was glad it was all over now. He was sure it was for the best.

After seven hours of questioning, Hesler was exhausted. He told the police he would cooperate in every way possible, that he wanted to clear up everything. He was asked if he would sign a statement as to his involvement with Criley and Harmen, and he agreed. Hesler did not ask for a lawyer at that time, and none was offered to him. His father was called in, and he agreed with Otis that it would be best to cooperate with the police and sign the statement. It was a significant decision.

The statement was long and detailed, ungrammatical, and yet carefully worded, as if the young man was trying as best he could to tell the truth without involving himself any more than he had to. He also had the assistance of his father in the wording of the statement. But for all the care that went into it, it was a thoroughly chilling document, a document that gave the police the first clearly focused look into the monstrous events that had been going on "right under everybody's nose":

The first killing that I remember happened when Earl was living at the Soundview townhouse. There were two boys there and I left before they were killed. But Earl told me he killed them afterwards. I don't know where they was buried or what their names are.

The first killing I remember was a boy named Ronald Hankens. Earl and I were the only people involved in that one. But Earl did the killing. I was just there and didn't have nothing to do with it.

I also remember two boys who was killed at the Upland Apartments. They were brothers and their father worked next door where they was building some more apartments. I wasn't there when Earl killed them. But I think I was there when they was buried. I don't remember. The youngest of these two boys was the youngest that was killed, I think.

I remember one boy who was killed on Dwight Street at Earl's house. This was just before Lee Criley came into the picture. Earl kept this boy around the house for about four days before he killed him. I don't remember his name but we picked him up on a road outside town. I think I helped bury this boy also, but I don't remember where it was. This was about two years ago. It really upset Earl to have to kill this boy because he really liked him.

A boy by the name of Jenner was also killed at the Dwight house. I had taken him home one time, but he wouldn't stay there because he wanted to go back to Earl's. I took him back. And Earl ended up killing him.

It was during the time that we lived on Dwight Street that Lee Criley got involved. Lee took part in getting the boys at first, and then later he took part in the killings. Lee liked causing pain.

Most of the killings that occurred after Lee came into the picture involved all three of us. I never took no part in the killings but nearly always all three of us were there.

In all, I guess there was between twenty-five and thirty boys killed. And they was buried in three different places.

I was present and helped bury some, but not all of them. Most was buried at the boat shed. There was three or four buried at Lighthouse Point, I think. I'm sure two are up there. I helped bury the first one at the Point. Then the next one we took to the Point, and when we got there Earl and Lee found that the first one had come to the surface and either a foot or a hand was above the ground. When they buried this one the second time they put some type of sheet on top of him to keep him down.

The third place that they buried bodies was on the beach at Woodmont. This was right off the beach road. The bodies are on the right-hand side. I never actually buried one there, but I always drove the car. I know that one of the graves had a large rock on top of it. I think that there are five or more bodies buried at this location.

*I am willing to show officers where this location is and I will try to
locate as many of the graves as possible.*
I'm sorry that this happened and I'm sorry for the kids' families.

When the statement had been typed, it was given to Otis
Hesler for examination and signature.

"What's this here?" he asked.

"It's the statement you just made," the officer told him. "Read
it, and if everything's okay, sign it."

Otis Hesler shifted uneasily in his chair, fumbling with the
paper. His father, Alton Hesler, nervously cleared his throat.

"Otis, uh, he don't read so good. He wouldn't be able to read
that paper."

"Didn't you say he went to high school?"

The father tried to speak softly, so as to be unheard by his
son. However, this was impossible in the small room, and the effect of his conspiratorial whispering and gesturing was ludicrous.

"Well, yeah, they kind of just kept pushing him along. They
said he was kind of, you know, dumb." As he said this, Mr.
Hesler put his finger to his head. Otis Hesler saw the gesture,
and reddened.

"I can read okay," said Otis Hesler, his voice thick with
anger.

"All right," said the officer. "Read this over and tell me if you
want any changes."

Still indignant, Otis snatched the papers from the officer's
hands. Slowly, his lips moving silently, Otis read the confession.
The officer waited patiently till Otis had finished.

"You understand all that?"

"Yeah, I understand."

"Can you sign your name, Otis?" There was just a trace of
sarcasm in the officer's question.

"I can sign my name," said Otis belligerently. "I ain't no
dummy."

Clenching the pen in his fingers, Otis Hesler laboriously,
childishly, scrawled the letters of his name.

The officer watched without smiling.

The statement was completed at 7:45 P.M.

Because of the growing darkness, it was decided that he would not be taken to Lighthouse Point to search for the remaining gravesites until the next day.

The digging at the boat shed had stopped by then. The last of seventeen bodies had been recovered from that location.

At the same time, Lee Criley was at Woodmont, where he had been directing recovery operations through the afternoon.

Lee Criley stood on a bluff overlooking most of the beach at Woodmont. He was handcuffed to a police car. Standing next to him, tall and silent, was a deputy sheriff armed with a twenty-gauge shotgun. Lee Criley had asked him jokingly if he would use the gun if he tried to run. The deputy sheriff had only looked at Lee, not replying. The question was answered.

The beach had been skimmed by four bulldozers to a depth of about two feet for a distance of about two miles. Another stretch of about a half mile had been dug out deeper, at some places to five or six feet. It had been a long, hot day, and it was now growing too dark to see. The dozers had been shut down, the crew had left, and the white police ambulance had driven off quietly, no siren blaring. Inside the ambulance were four stretchers, containing the remains of the four bodies recovered.

Lee wasn't sure how many were buried out here. Maybe four was all. He thought it might have been more.

Three reporters had found their way to Lee Criley, and in the brief interval between ceasing operations on the beach and his transporation back to the West Haven jail, they were able to ask if he wanted to talk about what had happened. Lee was pleased with this attention. He would be glad to tell them anything he could.

"How many are there, Lee?"

"Here? I'm not sure. They found four today. I think there's some more."

"How about all together? How many boys altogether?"

"I guess around twenty or so. I don't know. Earl was doing this with Otis Hesler for a while before I knew about it. I'd say around twenty, though."

"All boys?"

"Yeah. You know how it is."

"No, we don't, Lee. How is it?"

The deputy sheriff made a move to fend off the reporters.

"All right, you guys. That's enough. You shouldn't be talking to this kid."

"He doesn't mind, do you, Lee?"

Lee smiled. "Not if I can get a cigarette off you. Besides, I got nothing better to do."

A reporter placed a cigarette in Lee's mouth and lit it for him. The sheriff shrugged and leaned against the car.

"How do you feel about all this, Lee? About all these boys that are dead?"

"How would anybody feel? I feel bad about it. I'm sorry it happened. Some of those kids were real nice kids."

The reporter shuddered.

"Who were those boys? How did you pick them?"

"Well, Earl told us he'd give us fifty bucks for every kid we got him. What a crock of crap! It was more like five bucks. Anyway, we'd just go get kids for him."

"What kids? Where did you find these kids?"

"Well, sometimes they'd be kids we'd know, kids from around the neighborhood. Mostly it would be kids hitchhiking that we picked up in Earl's car. We'd ask them if they wanted to go to a party. And that'd be it."

"Hitchhikers?"

"Yeah, a lot of 'em. Listen, you want me to give you some free advice? Don't hitchhike!" Lee guffawed.

Three uniformed police hurried to the patrol car, and the handcuffs were unlocked. Lee was placed in the back seat. They drove off without another word.

The digging around New Haven had ceased for the night. The count now stood at twenty-one bodies recovered. The search would begin again in the morning.

6

■ On April 10, 1964, Earl Harmen was inducted into the United States Army. He was twenty-six years old.

He had volunteered, figuring that he would be drafted anyway and that by volunteering he at least would be able to maintain some control over his fate. Someone had told him that by enlisting he might have some choice of assignment, either his duty station or his job title. In 1964, a lot of young men were worrying about being sent to Vietnam, and Earl Harmen was among them.

Although he was apprehensive about the idea of being at the mercy of a vast, arbitrary system, there was another element in

Earl Harmen's thinking. In a way he had not quite fully admitted to himself, he was longing to get into the Army. He was longing to be in uniform, just as thousands of others were, to enjoy the complete anonymity of being a name, rank, and serial number rather than a personality. Earl Harmen had failed at the personality game. He was a loner; he did not enjoy people and they did not enjoy him. In the Army, the personality aspect of things would be superfluous. Everything would be mechanical, regimented, and by the numbers.

And on a deeper level, there was the hope that perhaps in the military environment, where he would be forced to live with hundreds of others on a daily and intimate basis, a different Earl Harmen might blossom. He would find friends and buddies; he would share good times and bad, he would have hearty laughs, and for once he would be one of the boys. It was a very dim and well-concealed hope, for Earl Harmen had had his share of disappointments and shattered illusions. But it was a hope nevertheless, and for that reason he felt a little thrill of exaltation on the April afternoon when he and a hundred other young men raised their right hands and said "I do."

It took Earl Harmen about three days to find out that he had been completely wrong, that life in the Army wasn't different, it was simply more intense, with the acute extra disadvantage of affording no escape whatsoever. Earl was not welcomed as part of a group of men sharing the same life. He found himself among youths who showed nothing but contempt for the gangly, uncoordinated, nervous twenty-six-year-old. There was no circle of friends who would accept him, as he had hoped. Instead, there was only the constant nagging presence of orders and inspections and drills. Worst of all, he saw the same looks of contempt he had sensed all his life but had hoped to escape in the Army. No, it was not the same. It was worse.

He spent nine weeks as a recruit in basic training at Fort Dix New Jersey, getting through for the simple reason that he was terrified of incurring the attention of the brutal black platoon sergeants. He went home for two weeks and did nothing but watch television and sleep. He cried in his mother's arms the night before he was to report to his next assignment.

Earl Harmen reported to Fort Benning, Georgia, on July 1, 1964, and remained for twelve weeks, training in radio repair. He did well in his courses, and his disciplinary record was clean. He made no friends and he wrote to his mother each night. Very quietly, he also began putting the paperwork in for a hardship discharge. His mother needed him, he wrote, his mother was getting older, suffered from hypertension, and was unable to continue working. Earl Harmen was needed desperately at home.

He had also decided that, unless he got out of the Army quickly, he would commit suicide.

In March 1965, Earl Harmen, now with a rank of E2, was reassigned to a permanent duty station at Fort Dix, New Jersey. This meant that he would probably not go to Vietnam and that he would be able to go home and stay with his mother, at least on some weekends. For a while the despair lifted and he began to relax a bit. There was something else that made life a little easier at Fort Dix. It was there that he made his first and only friend while in the Army.

It was Sunday afternoon in Barracks B10, a hot, boring, lonely, GI Sunday afternoon. It was free time, your own time, but somehow it only made things worse, because you knew you were a dumb GI with nowhere to go, nothing to do, and nobody to give a damn about you. On Sunday afternoon, a GI's money is long gone, his books have been read, his letters written, and he can't force himself to sleep one more hour. Sunday afternoon is the worst time in the world for a GI who has no buddies.

Earl Harmen lay on his bunk, staring up at the ceiling. He was one of four men in the barracks. One was playing a guitar poorly; the other two were straddled over a footlocker playing payday-stakes poker. Harmen was thinking about getting dressed in fatigues and going to eat some lousy Sunday chow. Chow was always lousy on Sunday. Cold cuts, process American cheese, gherkins, and beans. It was a meal consistent with the tone of the day. He was thinking that he might spend his last few dollars on hamburgers at the PX instead of going through the chow line. It was about five-thirty, and he would have to make a decision soon.

His reverie was interrupted as a duffel bag hit the floor. Harmen looked around and saw a young soldier, dressed in summer khakis, smiling through the sweat dripping in his eyes. He was a short, cute-faced boy, probably no more than eighteen. He smiled at Earl Harmen apologetically. "Hiya. Is anybody using this bunk? The sergeant at the orderly room told me there'd be an empty one over here."

Harmen propped himself up on one elbow. "Yeah, its empty. You can have it."

The young soldier rolled out the mattress and slumped down on the bed, resting on the pile of bedding he had been issued.

"Whew. Sweet baby Jesus, that feels good. I've been sleeping in airports since yesterday morning. Sure is good to be home in the good old Army."

Harmen looked at him incredulously.

"My name's Bob Fitzpatrick. What's yours?"

"Earl Harmen."

The boy extended his hand. "Pleased to meetcha, Earl. How is this place, anyway?"

"Not bad. About average, I guess."

"How about inspections and shit like that? I mean, do they bother you with a lot of that chickenshit here?"

"Like I said, about average. Not too bad."

Fitzpatrick lit a cigarette. "I tell you, I put in for Vietnam. This stateside stuff ain't for me. I don't go in for inspections and saluting and all that shit. I put in for Vietnam. That's why they sent me to this place. Everything in the Army goes by the opposite. I know guys who'd give anything for stateside duty, but *they* go to Nam. Me, I want to go, but here I am. Ain't it a bitch?"

Harmen sat up on his bunk. This was the longest conversation he had had with anyone since he had been in the Army. The longest social conversation, anyway.

"Don't tell me you're one of those loonies that wants to go over and get killed."

"Get killed? Who said anything about getting killed? Nobody's fixin' on getting killed, man. I just want to get where the action is. Because it's there, you know what I mean? Hand me that butt can, will ya? Thanks."

"Well, it's your ass. If you want to get it shot off, that's your business."

"Nah, it ain't my ass. This ass is property of the U.S. Government. LBJ just lets me carry it around for him. It ain't my ass, so why should I care?"

"That's one way of looking at it, I guess. Where you from?"

"Macon, Georgia. The heart of Dixie, boy."

"Georgia! You're one hell of a long way from home, you know that?"

"No, Earl. I didn't know that. Thanks for reminding me, though. It's good to have that kind of information."

"Smart-ass Southerner."

"You got it, Yankee. How's chow around here?"

"Not so great. I was thinking of getting some hamburgers at the PX. How does that sound to you?"

"Fine, man. Let's go."

And so it happened that Earl Harmen and the boy from Macon, Georgia, became fast friends. For Harmen, it was the difference between misery and happiness, between loneliness and joy. It was to be the single closest relationship he would ever have, a relationship in which he allowed himself the luxury of speaking as freely as he could, as freely as he knew how. Earl Harmen learned to joke and smile for the first time. This eighteen-year-old soldier from Georgia was showing twenty-six-year-old Earl Harmen how to be one of the boys.

The two became close friends, spending all their time together, going to movies, playing miniature golf, and all the other small entertainments a GI can afford. When questioned as to how he could spend so much time with such a creep, Bobby answered: "What the hell do you guys care for, anyway? Afraid you're missing sump'n?" Harman could only watch in awe and admiration as his friend turned antagonism into just another joke. What a friend to have!

All the ribbing from the others only served, in the long run, to bring Harman and the boy from Georgia closer. The tall, nervous-looking man and the short, wiry, smiling redheaded boy walking along together became one of the familiar sights around the post. Just another couple of lonely GIs, hanging around together, huddling together for warmth.

It was the last week in May 1965, payday. The two soldiers, their wallets filled with $92.50 apiece, walked by the orderly room bulletin board to make absolutely sure there was no problem in getting downtown that night. They looked over the long list of names and duties, until Bobby Fitzpatrick jumped up in the air, shouting in triumph.

"It came through, it came through. Sweet baby Jesus, it came through!"

"What? What are you talking about?"

"Look at it, man. I'm getting reassigned. I'm going to the First Air Cavalry Division, Republic of South Vietnam. Oh, boy, oh Jesus, it came through."

"Oh, God! Did you really do that? I can't believe you could really be that stupid."

"Yep. This is it, Earl-boy. No more stateside chickenshit for the kid. Whoopee!"

"How could you do it? How could you do it?"

"Tell you what, Earl. Tonight we'll go downtown and have ourselves a farewell party. No sense in saving money now, I guess. Oo-wheee. How much is combat pay, I wonder?"

That night, for the first time in his twenty-seven years, Earl Harmen got drunk. The two soldiers hit every bar on the strip of the sad little soldier-town near the base and they got rip-roaring, vomiting, GI drunk. It was payday, and there were hundreds of other soldiers doing exactly the same thing. For Earl Harmen, however, this particular payday represented the end of something unique and beautiful. He felt that the only real friendship he ever had was slipping away through his fingers. This young soldier from Georgia had grown to be all-important, had come to be essential to his very existence. Earl Harmen could not conceive of returning to the empty life he had lived before he found this one friend. And now, after all the good times and laughs and ping-pong games and movies, now this friend was being taken away, needlessly, foolishly. Earl Harmen felt like a man in a nightmare, running through sand that pulled his feet down, chasing an ever-elusive something that he needed for his survival.

When the party was over, the two soldiers found themselves sitting on the back steps of barracks B10. It was three-thirty in the morning. They were tired, their money was gone, they stank of beer. And sitting in the heat of the New Jersey night, they were getting sober.

"You really want to go over there and kill gooks, huh, Bobby? You want to go over there and win the war?"

"Yeah. I want to be an all-American hero. I want the fuckin' Congressional Medal of Honor. The fuckin' generals will be saluting me."

Harmen put his arm clumsily around the younger boy's shoulder. "And what if those gooks kill you instead? What happens then?"

"Mom would be proud."

They both chuckled drunkenly, and the younger man lit a cigarette. "Live fast, die young, that's my scene."

They sat in silence. Above their heads, hundreds of bugs buzzed around the naked light bulb that hung from the eaves near the corner of the barracks.

"Hey. Don't go."

"Don't go? Are you kiddin'?"

"Tell them you changed your mind. Tell them you want to stay here. Here with me. Like it used to be."

"What?"

"Stay here, will ya? It's not right that you go now. It isn't fair."

And at that point Earl Harmen lost control of himself and drunken tears rolled down his cheeks.

"Aw, come on, Earl. Quit that, man."

"It's not right. It's not right." The younger boy put his arm around Earl Harmen's shoulder, and Harmen's immediate reaction was to throw his arms around the younger boy. He pushed him over backward, covering his face and neck with clumsy, slobbering kisses.

"Please, please, stay here. We can stay together."

The younger boy sprang away in disgust and shock. "Hey, what the fuck are you doing?"

Harmen could only choke on his sobs, moving again to the younger boy, his arms outstretched.

"Hey, Jesus Christ, keep the fuck away from me, will ya? What the fuck kind of shit is that? Hey, man, back off. I'm not joking about this."

"But I need you. Can't you understand?"

"Hey, man, you don't need me. Not this boy. You got it all wrong, man."

Again Harmen moved closer.

"Listen, faggot. Back off, hear? Back off or you're going to be one sorry mother-fucker. Just keep the fuck away from me."

Then, suddenly, Earl Harmen's tone changed. He became instantly sober, realizing what he had done. And he knew that he had to clear this up, somehow. He had to make up for the dreadful, terrible mistake he had made.

"Oh, hey, look, I was only fooling. Don't get sore like that, okay? It's just a joke."

The younger boy kept moving backward, slowly. "Yeah, sure. A big joke."

"Where are you going?"

"Nowhere, man. Just a little walk, you know what I mean?"

"Don't be silly. Come on back here. Come on."

"See you around, Earl."

And then the younger boy strode off, around the barracks and into the darkness. Earl Harmen waited on the steps for a while, then went back inside to his bunk. Bobby would be back. He had no doubt about that.

The next morning, Earl Harmen woke up with a hangover. He smiled and looked across to the young soldier's bunk, and his smile faded. The bunk was stripped down and the mattress rolled up. Bobby Fitzpatrick had gone during the night. Earl Harmen would never see his friend again. Nor would he ever be quite the same again.

Later that week, the men in Barracks B10 were assigned a new squad leader—Sergeant Rick Coffee, twenty-one, fresh back from a year in Vietnam. He had less than six months to go in the Army, and he was determined to stay as drunk as he could for as much of those six months as possible. He quickly became a figure of awe for the others in the barracks, men perhaps older but less experienced. For many, he was the only Vietnam veteran they had ever seen. Coffee could well have taken advantage of his situation as the one battle-scarred old soldier among a flock of admiring, untested trainees. Instead, however, he kept to himself, barely making formations and drinking heavily, usually alone.

No one was more fascinated by the enigmatic figure of Sergeant Coffee than was Earl Harmen. He was determined to find out what this soldier had seen in Vietnam, to find out what it had "really been like." But he knew that Sergeant Coffee was not responsive to questions of this nature.

It was Sergeant Coffee's habit to head immediately to the NCO Club after duty hours, thereby catching the happy hour when drinks were ten cents apiece and affording him a good start on the evening. By eight o'clock he was drunk, by ten o'clock he was incoherent, and by midnight someone would drop him off at his barracks. The pattern varied little, and Earl Harmen discovered the pattern quickly.

Earl sat down one evening next to Sergeant Coffee, who was

slowly sipping a drink and chain-smoking. It was about seven-thirty.

Earl did not want to drink, but he ordered a glass of beer. He looked over at Sergeant Coffee. "Uh, hello," he said self-consciously.

The sergeant looked up, squinted at Earl, and grunted.

"I'm in your squad. Harmen. From Barracks B10."

Sergeant Coffee nodded. "Oh, yeah. How ya doin'?" He didn't wait for an answer, but returned his attention to the bottom of his glass.

"Good. I hear you're getting out in a few months, right?"

"Right."

"What'll you do then? Got a job lined up?"

"No. Just go home and get drunk there for a while."

"Where you from?"

"Indianapolis. Hey, gimme another Scotch and water, will ya?"

"Indianapolis? No kidding. Lemme pay for that."

Sergeant Coffee shrugged and accepted. "Thanks."

Earl nursed one beer and then a second, and continued buying drinks for the sergeant. He didn't press him, realizing that it would be counterproductive to approach the sergeant too abruptly. Finally, after about an hour, Earl Harmen began asking what was really on his mind.

"You're wearing a First Cav patch, aren't you?"

"Yep, First Cav. Yep."

"They're the ones that see most of the action, right?"

"Yeah, you could say that."

"The reason why I'm asking is that a buddy of mine just got reassigned to the First Cav, you know? And I was wondering what kind of stuff he'd be likely to get into. You know what I mean?"

"How do I know? Depends on how lucky he is."

"Guys can really get killed there, huh?"

"If they're not killed, they sure give a good imitation of it."

"Did you ever see anybody get killed?"

"Sure. How about another drink over here?"

"Anybody you ever knew?"

"Sure. I knew this lieutenant who got it just before I rotated back to the States. Hah. Yeah, he got it all right. Good old Lieutenant Geeson."

"What happened?"

"He was a hero. He liked playing soldier, sneaking around the woods like he was playing capture-the-flag. Only he sneaked out too far."

"On a patrol?"

"Yeah. He just disappeared. We only found him in the morning when it got light."

"Dead?"

"Just about. He didn't last too much longer."

"He was wounded?"

"Nah. The VC worked him over during the night."

"Tortured him? What did they do?"

"Oh Christ, I don't know what they did. They wiped him out, that's all."

Earl Harmen pressed for more of an answer. "What did they really do?"

Sergeant Coffee swallowed the rest of his drink. "They tied him up to a tree and they proceeded to make things miserable for the poor bastard. I don't know what the hell they did to him. What are you so curious for? You got orders to go?"

"No. Not me. A friend of mine."

"Then what the hell are you worried about? Hey, Sarge, how about another drink over here."

7

■ Tuesday, July 25, 1975. The Reverend Woodruff Lovell found himself self-consciously addressing an audience of two: Mrs. Marion Harmen Marris and her ex-husband, Howard Harmen. It was a difficult task for the Reverend Lovell to have to speak to Earl's parents of God's forgiveness and mercy, when the Reverend himself could neither forgive nor feel mercy for Earl Harmen's damned soul.

Both parents' faces were grim, set. Neither understood nor wanted to understand what had happened; they only knew that their only child was dead and would be buried as a Christian. There were no tears.

For this brief, final ceremony quiet dignity had been attempted and achieved. The cemetery, date, and time of the funeral had successfully been kept secret; there were no curious onlookers, no thrill-seekers, no press.

All three—the reluctant minister, the unhappy parents—intoned the Lord's Prayer as the coffin was lowered. Marion Harmen Marris and Howard Harmen then tossed two handfuls of loose dirt into the grave. For Earl's parents, it was all over.

Before going their separate ways once again, the former husband and wife met that afternoon in the home of Howard Harmen. They spoke very little of Earl, only briefly mentioning how he had remained close to both in spite of their divorce. Most of the time was spent in small talk, pretending to discuss plans for meeting again and commenting on how too much time had passed since they had gotten together. But it soon became apparent that Earl Harmen's mother could not force herself to partake in the polite, strained conversation. She soon became silent, drinking coffee, her jaw set.

Finally she put down her cup, excused herself, and walked out to her former husband's back porch. She looked up at the clear sky, feeling the sun warm on her face. High grass swayed gently in the midafternoon breeze.

She sat down on the top step, leaning back against the wooden railing. Hadn't he always been a kind boy, a happy boy? Surely this madman, this monster who killed and tortured, surely this strange man people were talking about could have nothing to do with her son Earl. Earl was a good boy, a kind boy, a boy who loved Jesus. It was a mistake, that was all. It would soon be cleared up once and for all, and then everyone would see the kind of boy Earl really was, that it was foolish to think he could have done such horrible things.

She didn't know how long she had been sitting there, lost in her thoughts, when she became aware of Howard Harmen standing there, looking down at her.

"Are you all right out here, Marion?"

"Oh yes. I'm fine."

"Can I get you anything? A cup of coffee? A Coke?"

"No, no, Howard. I'm just fine."

Howard Harmen was silent for a moment. "You mind if I sit here with you for a while?"

"I think I'd like that very much."

Howard Harmen sat down. He took the woman's small hand in his gnarled, workman's hand and patted it. Earl Harmen's mother looked questioningly, pleadingly, into the eyes of her former husband.

"He wouldn't have done those things, would he, Howard?"

"No, of course he wouldn't."

"Why are they making up all those lies?"

"I don't know."

"He was a kind boy, wasn't he, Howard? He was such a kind boy, wasn't he?"

"Yes. He was a kind boy."

And, for Earl Harmen's mother, the tears came at last. As she wept, Howard Harmen held her in his arms, telling her everything would be all right.

Marion Harmen Marris had found God later in life than many. She came to Him after two husbands, many lovers, and a life of sin, but He came to her with forgiveness, salvation, and love everlasting. Jesus Christ was the personal savior of Marion Harmen Marris. She knew this with absolute certainty, from the very core of her being, from every cell in her body. Jesus Christ was crucified, Jesus Christ suffered in agony, and Jesus Christ rose from the tomb, all for her, that she might seek and find the Kingdom of God within. Two weeks before her forty-third birthday, the God of her parents had appeared to her, and Marion Harmen Marris knew ecstasy and peace, and she knew that Jesus had died for her.

He had come to her at night, perhaps in a dream, she was never quite sure. At first she was only conscious of a feeling of something warm, a great sense of bliss, and without knowing why, she found herself crying as she hadn't cried since she was a little girl. And then she saw Him, His lovely blue eyes, His soft, delicate features, the thorns tearing cruelly into the white skin of His forehead, the gentle arms opening to receive her soul. And from that night on, Marion Harmen Marris was saved.

It had been Marion Marris' intention to go back to Boston immediately after the funeral, but now, having come to West Haven, having felt the atmosphere of hatred, fear, and repulsion that had surrounded the death of her firstborn, she found that she could not leave. Not yet. There was something she had to do in West Haven, something that only a mother could do.

Mrs. Marion Harmen Marris remembered that there had been another mother, two thousand years ago, who had seen her firstborn taken in the prime of His manhood, had seen Him become an object of scorn and contempt, and had ultimately witnessed His slow tortured death, as she stood by, unable to ease His agony. This woman of two thousand years ago had retained her dignity and her purpose, and had remained constant to Him who had died on the Cross. And when she remembered this, Mrs. Marris grew stronger.

She would stay at the home of Howard Harmen until she accomplished her purpose. But Mrs. Marris did not yet quite know what her purpose was.

To find it, she went to the one place where she could always be sure of an answer. She went to church.

Around five o'clock Marion Marris stepped inside a local Methodist Church. She was the only one there. She sat in a rear pew, eyes closed, hands folded in prayer. The muscles of her face and neck tightened, and every once in a while her lips moved. She remained in that position until nearly seven o'clock. She lingered a few moments and then, on the stroke of seven, she stood up quite abruptly, almost as if she had remembered an important errand somewhere else, and she left.

Marion Marris walked and walked, up and down the streets of West Haven, hour after hour. Though blisters puffed up on her feet, though her ankles were rubbed raw against her shoes, she walked on, as if on a pilgrimage, with the utter certainty and singleness of purpose of one who knows that God is with her. She sat for a while on a park bench, her head bowed, her hands folded in her lap. Then she walked again till she was beyond fatigue, as if in that exhausted state she might become pure enough to receive the sign she knew would come. The Lord would show her, the Lord would bestow upon her the light of understanding.

The dampness of the night was turning to a predawn mist. The sun would rise in a few minutes, burning away the dew and moisture, bringing another July day to Connecticut. Mrs. Marris' footsteps echoed in the emptiness of the street.

At first, she neither heard nor saw them, but rather sensed them. She felt them long before they came upon her; she sensed their frenzied, murderous force long seconds before she actually saw them. It was as if she was being drawn into a deep, whirling vortex, sucking her down and in, tearing at her, hating her, ripping her limb from limb. Feeling this, she turned around, peering into the darkness.

Then she heard the sharp barks and yelps of dogs, many dogs. But these weren't the barks of family cocker spaniels or faithful watchdogs. These were sounds of the wild, sounds of some deep primal past, where violence and madness were the rule. And then she saw them. She knew that they didn't see her and that no matter how terrified she was, she must not move. She must not let the dogs catch any movement.

Standing motionless in the dawn, Marion Marris watched hypnotized as the wild dog pack moved down the center of the street. There were about twenty of them, all sizes, though most were large rather than small, all colors, all breeds. Some wore collars, looking well-fed and cared for; others, whose homes were the streets, were dirty and ragged. Some trotted, some ran, some circled around the main body of the pack. They yelped and barked and growled at one another as they moved, snapping at each other, rubbing against each other.

Yet, in spite of the confusion, in spite of that chaos of bodies and movement, there was a unity, a single entity greater than any individual dog. That entity, as alive and as conscious and as purposeful as any single dog, was the pack itself. The pack was the higher law, and the function of the pack was murder and destruction. This pack was living rage and hatred. Mrs. Marris knew that she had stumbled into the domain of the Devil. And she knew with complete certainty that she was now with Earl.

Then the dogs turned away from the road and toward Mrs. Marris. For an instant she was sure they had seen her, and in that instant she knew terror.

They passed within ten feet of her, and they were gone.

When Mrs. Marris found her way back to the house, the first rays of the sun were creeping over the horizon, first just a glimmer of light, then within minutes the street and the houses were bathed in warm sunlight. She forced herself to take fuller, deeper breaths as she stood for a last moment on the porch.

Then she went inside and sat in a living-room chair. She let her shoes slip off and pulled her feet under her. She wrapped her sweater closer around her shoulders. She let herself doze off. In a few hours, she would be back on a bus to Boston.

Far in the distance a dog barked, perhaps in defiance of the sun.

■ There are brief periods in each lifetime when the pressure is off: halcyon days of rest between cycles, when one phase of life has come to completion and the next has not yet begun. Such days have a magical quality, as if they existed on some plane other than the world of harsh responsibilities and the fight for survival. And perhaps they do.

Such an interlude in the life of Earl Harmen began with his discharge from the Army on June 11, 1965. He had been in the Army, he had not been sent into combat, and he had gotten out safely. And now the cloud of anxiety that had been over his head for so long, the fear of being gobbled up by the military, of being wounded, of even being killed in a strange country, was gone. He was out. He was alive. They would never bother him again. Earl Harmen felt as if a hundred-pound weight had been taken off his shoulders. He was light, he could drift off on the air. He was happy.

While Earl was in the Army, his mother had moved from Boston to West Haven. His first few days of civilian life were spent sleeping late into the day in the garage apartment behind her small house. Marion Marris had decided that Earl was a man, now that he had served his country and was returning home. She knew he was not coming back as a hero, but—with a war going on and boys getting killed—her son was now safe at home with her. The apartment, which she had originally intended to rent, was a reward, the recognition of Earl's entry into manhood and his need for privacy. It had a bathroom and a separate entrance. Earl was delighted with this new arrangement.

When he first came home, it was as if he were trying to sleep off his entire Army experience, as if it were a hangover. He only came to the house for meals, joked with his mother, and then went back to sleep. This went on for about a week; then Earl finally emerged, freshly shaven, smiling, and told his mother he would like to get a job.

And so, 1965 was a good year for Earl Harmen. While the country was going through the doubts and uncertainties of growing involvement in a foreign war, while student unrest and campus rioting became a pattern of self-expression, Earl Harmen's life gradually seemed to settle into a kind of stability and purpose. He began to feel an inner concentration, a coming together of his will and his actions. Within him, as his country was experiencing a general despair and disquiet, there welled up a strange kind of power and tranquillity. He was growing into manhood at twenty-seven, and he looked forward to his new life with confidence.

He had found a job as a shoe salesman, and although the work brought him in constant contact with new people, for the first time in his life he found he enjoyed meeting them. He was no longer overcome by shyness, as he had been in the past. Instead, he found a new awareness within himself, and he could now see clearly many things that had puzzled him as a boy.

Another aspect of Earl Harmen's existence also began to manifest itself—a newfound concern for his body, a dawning awareness of himself as a creature of sensation, of skin, of muscle, and of movement. All Earl Harmen's life he had been a vaguely uncoordinated, skinny kid who avoided sports and was always picked last when forced to participate. Now, quite suddenly, he felt the need to stretch and flex his muscles, to run and jump, to test his body. At night he began taking courses in body-building and self-defense.

When Earl Harmen wasn't attending karate classes, he was usually to be found at the YMCA, lifting weights, jogging, or swimming. He never got involved in team sports, which weren't his style. He kept to himself, building his body into a powerful, well-toned unit.

When Harmen was discharged from the Army, he weighed a hundred sixty-one pounds. Three months later, in September 1965, he was up to a hundred ninety pounds. It was all muscle.

Since he was making well over a hundred dollars a week and living rent- and board-free, Harmen began to accumulate a modest sum of money. He had few expenses other than his continued membership in the Y and the karate school. He didn't smoke or drink, ate only sparingly of health foods, and never went on dates. He was a man of no discernible vices. He saved money, and his mother was proud of him. Maybe it would have been nice if, now that he was starting to find himself, he would also find a nice girl, to make everything perfect. But a mother learns not to rush things, especially when her son seems to be coming out of himself for the first time. Mrs. Marris vowed she would not be a typical interfering mother, hinting at him to settle down and get married.

With his growing bank account, Earl Harmen finally made two purchases. The first was a regulation-size pool table of the highest quality available, which cost him nearly a thousand dollars. Earl spent the day cleaning out the garage under his apartment, getting everything ready for the day when the table would be delivered. When it finally came, Harmen and his pool table quickly became very popular with dozens of neighborhood boys.

The billiard table turned out to be a happy investment for Earl. Boys who might have had nothing better to do with their time than hang around street corners and get into trouble now found themselves drifting toward the pool table. Harmen's garage became not just a hangout but a clubhouse where boys could meet, joke around, pass the time playing pool—and, best of all, stay out of trouble. For Harmen it meant that he found himself the center of an admiring circle of young boys. They valued his friendship and they valued having someone to talk to about things that were bothering them. Earl Harmen became a resident big brother to the young boys in the neighborhood. Mrs. Marris wondered if perhaps some of the boys were just taking advantage of her son, using him for gifts and a chance to use his pool table, but for the most part she too was happy with this new situation. Earl was becoming involved; she felt he genuinely liked these boys. As long as Earl was happy, Mrs. Marris was happy.

The second purchase, following shortly after the pool table, was a Chevy pick-up truck with a rear-mounted one-room van. Unlike the pool table, Harmen had to take out a loan for this acquisition.

The truck quickly became his pride and joy. He spent even more money on the inside of the van, putting in a deep shag rug, curtains, a small but comfortable bed, and dozens of pillows of all colors. There was also a small bar, with a refrigerator. And the biggest item of all was a large-screen portable color television set. The rug, the bedspread, and the curtains were all blue, Earl Harmen's favorite color. He did a complete rewiring job on the van in order to supply enough power to the television set, the lights, and the refrigerator. He added two more twelve-volt batteries, which could be easily recharged when necessary, to the trunk.

The van was an expense Earl Harmen's mother could not

fully appreciate. There were so few times that Earl had to go anywhere far from New Haven, so few times that he had to sleep on the road, so little extended traveling, that she was somewhat irritated that Earl poured so much money into his truck. She tried not to let him know that this bothered her, although it was difficult to keep things from Earl because he seemed to sense them in the air. If he had known, he probably would have just joshed her out of her irritation. Maybe this was just one of those frivolous stages that every young man must go through before he is ready to settle down. It was something Earl had to get out of his system, and Mrs. Marris would certainly not help matters any by complaining and nagging about it. She knew when to hold her tongue.

Earl Harmen's life was just about equally divided between his work, his karate classes and body-building, and the boys. Most of the boys were between the ages of twelve and sixteen. Occasionally an older boy would come over and usually monopolize the pool table until Harmen let him know that he wasn't welcome. There was no point in letting the garage become a hangout for older boys, boys who could easily find other ways to entertain themselves. It was for the younger boys that Earl was opening up his home, boys who really had nowhere to go, nothing to do, no experience to guide them.

One of the big events for the boys occurred when Earl would announce that he was taking a bunch of them in the truck for a ride, perhaps to go swimming. Only Earl's favorites were allowed on such trips, and he always made sure that they had permission from their parents. Unless a boy's parents knew where he was and where he was going, Earl would never take him anywhere. This was one of his strictest rules. Earl Harmen was not the kind of man who would needlessly worry a boy's family. It was one of the reasons the parents gradually grew to trust him, to be pleased when they heard the words "Mom, I'm going over Earl's for a while. We'll be going to the beach later on. Okay?"

Billy Rosell was thirteen years old. Though a little smaller than the average seventh-grader, Billy was an avid and talented baseball player and the youngest player on the junior high school team. And because he was blond-haired, blue-eyed, and undeniably cute in his oversized baseball uniform and well-worn fielder's glove, Billy Rosell was the true love of every girl in the seventh-grade class. He was the object of daily unsigned love letters; he received regular phone calls consisting primarily of giggles, and he often found his name in chalk on the sidewalk, linked by arrow and heart to the name of any one of a dozen girls.

Billy Rosell's reaction to all this adulation was pretty much that of any other thirteen-year-old boy. He was flattered, sometimes annoyed, and generally confused by it all. He was glad to be able to get away from the giggles and whispers of the girls by going to Earl Harmen's house, where none of that stupid stuff went on. Billy looked up to Earl as someone who was above all this kind of foolishness, a real guy who liked to work out, who took care of himself the way few adults would.

Of the many boys who now frequented the garage, Billy Rosell was clearly Earl Harmen's favorite. Billy and Earl were always having man-to-man talks, to the exclusion of the other boys. If anyone resented the increased attention Billy Rosell was getting from the revered Earl Harmen none of the boys mentioned it. Earl wouldn't stand for that kind of thing. He didn't believe in little jealousies like that.

And so, gradually, the boys who regularly frequented Earl Harmen's home, who came to consider this carefree, happy man as their only adult friend, grew to acknowledge the fact that Billy Rosell was number one. It was something they accepted. Every family has a favorite, and in this family it was Billy Rosell. There was nothing unusual in the situation. Billy was the favorite of the girls, the teachers, and now the favorite of Earl Harmen. The other boys bore no ill feelings on this score. They were content to be part of the family, part of the happy group around Earl Harmen.

Whenever the boys went to the beach, there was no question as to who would sit up front next to Earl. If Earl needed someone for running a special errand, or collecting firewood for a beach cookout, or staying late to have a midnight man-to-man chat after the rest of the boys had gone home, Billy Rosell was the one.

That Sunday night in October was an unusually chilly and windy night, and the few boys who had come to Earl's house to shoot a few racks of pool would have to leave early. Tomorrow was a schoolday, and there could be no staying out late. Three boys were still there at 8:30 P.M. One was Billy Rosell; the other two were his classmates.

"You gonna come with us, Billy?"

"Nah, I think I'll hang around for a while."

"You got homework due tomorrow, ain't you? Don't tell me you got the book report done already."

"Earl said he'd help me with it. That's why I'm gonna stay a little longer. My Mom said it was all right."

"Okay. See you tomorrow."

"See ya."

Billy Rosell was alone in the garage. While he was waiting for Earl, he took a few shots at the pool table. He had to stretch and stand on tiptoe for most of his shots, and the cue stick appeared large and unwieldy in his hands. But coordination was something that came naturally to Billy Rosell, and his shots were smooth, decisive, and accurate. He plunked in five balls in a row before he missed his first shot.

"Not bad. You're getting better."

Earl had entered the garage quietly, and Billy had no idea how long he had been there. And for some reason, Billy Rosell felt a tiny pang of fear when he heard Earl Harmen's voice in the darkness behind him. Afraid of Earl Harmen? The one grown-up in the whole world he could trust, to whom he could really talk? Billy Rosell felt his face redden in embarrassment, and he was glad the light in the garage was so dim that Earl couldn't see it.

"Practice. Years of practice," he mumbled.

"Your buddies go already?"

"Yeah. Just a minute ago."

Earl stepped out of the shadows. "So there's just the two of us, right?"

Billy took another shot, a difficult bank shot, and made it. "Just the two of us."

Earl put his arm around Billy's shoulder. "Did you say you had some homework tonight?"

"Yeah. A real pain." Billy moved away from Earl's arm and across to the other side of the table, sighting in another shot.

"I tell you what we'll do first, slugger. First we'll take a ride down to the beach. I bet the waves will be nice and high tonight, with the wind and everything. Just you and me. We'll go down to the beach, check things out, and then get that report of yours done. How about that?"

"Aw, I don't know, Earl. My Mom will be real mad if I don't get home early tonight, and I gotta get that report done. I don't think we better."

Earl skipped quickly around the table and put a playful headlock on Billy. It was a playful move, but it hurt all the same. When Earl's powerful muscles locked tight, few men could have withstood the pressure. A small-boned thirteen-year-old boy was defenseless. "Whatsa matter? Come on. Don't you want to go down to the beach? Or do you want to fight about it? Is that it? You wanna fight?"

Billy started gasping for air. Pain was burning into his neck. "Hey, cut it out. Cut it out. I can't breathe."

Earl didn't let go. He pulled his arm just a little tighter around the boy's neck. "Then we can go to the beach. Right?"

"Right. Right. Let me go, for gosh sake, will ya?"

Earl released his hold, and Billy sagged to the floor. He was near tears.

"Hey, I didn't hurt you, did I? I'm sorry. I didn't mean to hurt you."

"Christ sake, Earl. What were you trying to do?"

It was a short ride to the beach, about four miles away, and then they drove many more miles along the beach road until they came to a place where Earl said the view was best. It was a tiny parking area overlooking a rocky cliff. It was sometimes used as a lover's lane by New Haven's teenagers. That cold and windy Sunday night it was deserted. Earl pulled his van truck to a halt and switched off the lights.

"Let's take a look. I bet that surf is almost up to the road."

The night was pitch-dark, the clouds obscuring whatever moonlight or starlight there might have been. The wind howled in from the ocean and the waves crashed against the jagged rocks of the cliff. Because of the darkness, they could see nothing, but they could feel the chill, salty ocean spray in their faces.

"What do you think? Nice, isn't it?"

"Yeah. But it's kind of cold. Let's go, huh, Earl?"

"Too cold? Come here. I'll keep you warm." Again Earl Harmen's strong arm wrapped around the younger boy, drawing him closer, allowing no escape.

"Hey, come on, Earl. That hurts. You're such a damn muscle man."

"All right. I'm sorry. I didn't realize I was bruising your delicate little body."

"Let's get out of here, okay? It's kind of spooky here."

"Scaredy-cat. Afraid of the dark. Okay, fraidy-cat, we'll go. Oh, wait a minute, I almost forgot."

"What?"

"There's something I wanted to show you. Boy, a good thing I didn't forget."

"What? What is it?"

"A surprise. Come on. It's in the back of the van. Come on."

The two walked to the van truck, and Earl unlocked the rear door.

"Go ahead. It's in there. Take a look."

"I can't see in there. It's too dark."

"Go on in. You'll see."

Billy Rosell climbed in the door, and Earl Harmen followed in after him. The door closed.

The two were in complete darkness.

"Well, what is it, for cryin' out loud?"

"Here it is. Don't you see it?"

"No. I can't see it. Hey, what are you doing? Quit it, will ya?"

"Don't you like the surprise?"

"Stop it. Hey, stop it!" Then Billy Rosell screamed. But there was no one to hear.

Later Earl Harmen pulled the van truck to a halt in front of Billy Rosell's house. "Hey, stop being so sad. There's nothing to be sad about. See you tomorrow, okay?"

Billy Rosell said nothing, but opened the door of the truck and quietly got out. He sobbed softly to himself as he walked slowly up the sidewalk. Earl looked one last time and drove off for home.

It had been a very unusual night for Earl Harmen. On the way home he thought of everything that had happened, going over each detail again and again in his mind. It had been an unusual night for two reasons. First, even though Earl Harmen was into his twenty-ninth year, even though he had been away from home and had seen a little bit of the world, that night was the first time in his life he had experienced a fully realized, fully planned orgasm.

The second thing that made it an unusual night was perhaps even stranger. Earl Harmen realized that even though he deeply loved Billy Rosell, even though his heart ached for this cute-faced, blond-haired boy, the thing that he wanted more than anything in the world was to crush the life out of that boy. He loved little Billy Rosell. And he wanted to make him scream for mercy. And then see him die. He never asked himself why. Perhaps if he had, he would have said he loved little Billy Rosell so much that he wanted to love him to death.

When he got home, Earl Harmen made himself a sandwich and poured a glass of milk. He watched television before he finally went to bed.

9

■ The last of twenty-seven bodies had been dug up, this one out of the sandy beach at Woodmont on August 5, 1972. For five more days the digging continued, primarily in the general area in which most of the bodies had been found. Other, more sporadic digging was carried on in the backyards of every house Earl Harmen had lived in over the last three years. Nothing more was found. Reluctantly, body by body, the earth had given up the last of its terrible secret. After five days of fruitless digging, the people of New Haven breathed a great sigh of relief. Thank God for that, at least. Thank God there were no more children to be brought up out of the earth.

Then, in a strange way, the process had to be repeated, the grim procession of twenty-seven dead bodies had to pass by the grandstand once more before they could go peacefully to rest. At first, when they were brought out of the ground, one by one, the count mounting higher and higher, they were only scattered remains, bones, and clothing—not really boys, not really humans. But now, through the offices of the New Haven County Examiner, by means of dental records and bone structures and tattered remnants of clothes, the bones were given bodies, and the bodies were given faces and names. And so each day, another and another set of bones would be given an identity. And another family would know for certain at last.

The process of identification was slower than the digging. In many ways it was more painful.

First to be identified was Robin Allen Smith, eighteen. Soon afterward there was Henry Lattimer, seventeen. Both had been shot in the head.

A few days later positive identification was made of a pair of brothers, Bud and Joel Lepak, twelve and nine, whose family had since moved to Chicago.

John Curtis Raye was identified by dental records, hair, and stature by a friend of his family. John had been fifteen. He appeared to have been strangled.

"Many of these bodies are badly decomposed," Medical Examiner Elbert Harliss stated. "The bones are in disarray, and there's no quick way of determining which bones go together. This could take months to complete. And some of these bodies may never be identified."

Still, the work of sifting through the grisly evidence continued, and gradually more names came out. Thirteen more.

There was Frank A. Damone, seventeen, shot to death.

There was David Hollyman, thirteen, cause of death unknown.

There was Jay Sandback, fourteen, stabbed numerous times, possibly strangled.

There was Arnold Michael Tinkle, fifteen, strangled.

There was Ruben Hefferline, sixteen, shot.

There was Julius Cortez, fourteen, cause of death unknown. There was Harvey James Todde, fifteen, strangled.

And there were William Breon, fourteen; Eugene Edward Hanlen, thirteen; Scott L. Wintergreen, sixteen; Peter Robeson, sixteen; William Jackey, fourteen; and a boy known only as "Blondie." And there were ten others, ten more bodies that presented not a clue as to their identities.

Mr. and Mrs. William Lepak of Chicago had followed the Harmen case with unusual intensity. They had lived in West Haven until a year previously, at a time when Earl Harmen, Lee Criley, and Otis Hesler had been involved in kidnaping and murdering young boys. The Lepaks had not always been alone. They had had two sons, two very athletic and light-hearted boys, who for no reason anybody could understand had run away from home two years ago. There had never been a trace of them. They never wrote. Bud and Joel Lepak, then aged twelve and nine, had two years ago effectively disappeared from the face of the earth.

Mr. and Mrs. Lepak watched the Chicago newspapers closely when they became aware of the horrible case in Connecticut. They watched as news of the deaths of twenty-seven young boys gradually came to light. And then they watched intently as the names of the dead boys gradually became known. For the first time since the actual disappearance of their sons, Mr. and Mrs. Lepak did not have to strain their sanity to the limit, they did not have to force themselves to be content with little or no real facts, with blank expressions and bureaucratic indifference. There was no runaround this time. The truth came out very quickly. Yes, they were told by the Medical Examiner's office, their two sons had been among the boys murdered by Earl Harmen and Lee Criley. They had been buried in those sandy graves. Joel and Bud Lepak had been positively identified from medical records supplied to the police at the time of their disappearance. There was no doubt, no question about it. The two boys had been among the first discovered and among the first identified.

And so now they knew.

It was better that they knew. It was the uncertainty that had made them nervous wrecks, that had drained them so. At least that part was over. But then again, wouldn't it have been better to be able to hope, to feel that tomorrow or the next day the boys would come knocking on the door with a hundred stories to tell of how they had joined the circus or ridden freight trains or worked in a lumber camp or picked cotton? No. That was over now. The boys were dead. Their bones and their teeth had been positively identified.

As soon as they found out, on August 24, 1972, William Lepak and his wife packed a change of clothes into an old suitcase and drove the 860 miles from Chicago to New Haven. They drove straight through, stopping only for food, gas, and rest rooms. They didn't know exactly what they wanted to accomplish, whether or not there was any meaning in seeing the few pieces of bone and teeth that had been their sons. They only knew that they had to go back this one last time.

The first thing they did when they got back into New Haven city limits was take a motel room. It had been a long, grueling drive, they had pushed themselves too hard, and Lepak felt it would be best to nap for a few hours before they confronted the officials in the Medical Examiner's office. They showered and lay down in the cool, air-conditioned room, but sleep did not come. They had been awake many hours now, both on the brink of exhaustion, but neither could sleep. They would have to see about the boys first.

They drove to the office of the County Medical Examiner. They identified themselves to the girl at the reception desk and were immediately met by several city officials, including the Examiner, who spoke to them in hesitating, hushed tones. Mr. and Mrs. Lepak were inside the building for no more than thirty minutes. When they left, half an hour later, they had aged visibly and had to hold each other for support.

It sometimes happens in the newspaper business that a reporter, by chance, finds himself in the right place and the right time for a significant story.

On the day the Lepaks visited the office of the County Medical Examiner a young reporter was doing research on the victims in the Harmen case. He did not expect the Lepaks at that time and had not planned on doing a story on any of the victims' parents.

Perhaps because nothing had been prearranged, perhaps because the reporter was young—just a few years older than Bud would have been, really—and perhaps because at that time it was very important that the Lepaks talk to someone about their lost boys, perhaps for these reasons William Lepak readily accepted the young reporter's request to ask them a few questions.

"I realize this must be a very painful day for you, sir, and if you think it's not a good time to talk about what happened, I'd certainly respect that."

"No, I guess it's as good a time as any." Lepak had one arm around his wife's waist, as if both to protect and support her. "I think we can talk to this young man for a while, don't you, Effie?" There was a deep gentleness to his voice, a deep concern for his wife.

Mrs. Lepak, her eyes blank, her face ashen, nodded. "All right."

They decided that they would have something to eat and then go back to the motel, where they could talk undisturbed, where they would be out of the hot afternoon sun and where a tape recorder might be used without attracting too much attention.

Back in the motel room, the three sat around the small circular coffee table, gazing out the picture window to the highway and the passing cars. Mr. and Mrs. Lepak sipped coffee while the young reporter set up his tape recorder, placing the microphone carefully in the middle of the table.

"If this microphone bothers you, I can take notes instead. I don't think it'll be much of a nuisance. Most people get used to it and forget all about it."

"No trouble, son. Whatever is easiest for you."

The reporter tested out the quality of the recording, then leaned forward, still unsure as to how to begin his questioning.

"I'm going to be asking you folks a few questions. Some of

them, I'm sure, will be painful, some will bring back memories. If ever I ask you something that offends you or makes you feel uncomfortable, please tell me right away. All right?"

"We understand."

"First of all, how long had your boys been missing?"

The question was addressed to Mr. Lepak. It was apparent that he would be doing most of the talking.

"The date was exactly October 11, 1969. Almost three years ago."

"Did you go to the police?"

"Oh, yes. Sure we did. I went that first night. Right after the boys called."

"They called you?"

"Yes. It was about ten at night. We were already a little worried. They were late by that time. Then we got the call. It was Bud. He said that he needed five thousand dollars. He said he and Joel wouldn't get out of where they were unless we put up five thousand dollars."

"And what did you do?"

"At first I thought the kids were playing a joke or something —you know, sort of scare the old man. But then I kept hearing these whispers in the background, funny noises, like a lot of people moving around. I don't know why, but by then I was sure it wasn't just a joke."

"Did you make arrangements to pay the money?"

"I started to ask Bud how to get the money to him, when the phone went dead. That's the last I ever heard of my boy. That's the last thing he said to me." Mr. Lepak's eyes became moist and his voice cracked. He paused, and the reporter waited for several moments before he asked another question. The reporter noted that during that pause, when the father remembered the last words his son ever spoke to him, Mrs. Lepak did not react at all. She sat totally still, her hands folded in her lap.

"And so you went to the police?"

"Yes, we both went to the police station. They were very understanding, very helpful. They took down everything about the boys, their ages, the clothes they had on, everything. And later we handed over medical records from our doctor. But it was no use. There just wasn't much they could do. I guess they stopped looking after a while."

"Why do you suppose they stopped looking?"

"They said there were a lot of kids taking off on their parents—runaways. They said the phone call could have meant they were just trying to get money to run away with and then they suddenly changed their mind. They said it was impossible to trace every lost kid as thoroughly as they would like to. I tried to tell them that I was sure my boys weren't running away, that they were good boys who just wouldn't run off. But maybe every parent tells them the same thing. I don't know. They have a hard job. It wasn't their fault. I don't hold a grudge."

"And what did you do then?"

"Well, we did just about everything we could do. Ads in the papers, even those underground newspapers a lot of the kids read. We put their pictures all over the city, in any store that would let us. And even though I knew it wouldn't do any good, I kept driving around, looking for the boys. I didn't expect to find them, but I just drove and drove, talking to kids, looking for anybody that even looked like the boys' age. It went on for a long time like that, months maybe. You know, I think I was a little bit crazy for doing that. You don't have children, do you? Well, you know, you go a little bit crazy when they get lost like that."

"I think I can understand."

"Well, after a year or so, me and Effie just decided to leave. We left word with the neighbors where we were, just in case, but I don't think we expected anything. You get a feeling, you know what I mean? And the longer we stayed here, the crazier we were getting, looking for the boys, never getting any sleep. Every time the phone rang, we'd expect the worst. Effie has trouble with her nerves anyway, and so we just figured the best thing to do would be to go somewhere and start fresh. I'm a mason, in the union, so I can pretty much find work anywhere. So we moved to Chicago."

"And this is the first time you've been back here since, right?"

"That's right."

"How long do you think you'll stay?"

"You know, we never really thought about that. We had to come here, we knew that. But we didn't have any plans for when we got here. I don't know what we're going to do now. Now that we finally . . . finally . . . found the boys."

Mrs. Lepak spoke at last. "We'll give them a Christian burial. That's the least we can do."

"You're right, Effie. They should have that much. We'll give them a decent burial. We have to do that. We'll stay till that's over. Then we'll go back. Then we'll go home."

Mr. Lepak reached over and patted his wife's hand. It was a simple gesture, a sincere one. For a moment, Mrs. Lepak looked as if she was about to release all the emotion she had within her, but it did not come. It would come out later, finally, when the two small sets of bones were finally laid to rest in a New Haven cemetery. Then all the grief and anguish of a mother would come out. But during the interview, Mrs. Lepak still kept it all locked tight inside her. She did not weep.

Mr. Lepak, looking out the window again, broke the silence.

"You know, we found out something at the Examiner's Office. They said they figured out where the boys must have been killed. It was a house that Harmen had over on Westfield. They say he had a lot of different places. But they said the boys were probably held in a house on Westfield. The address was 2135 Westfield. And you know something? On the day the boys disappeared, I was doing some work on that same street. When I found that out, I called the company I was working for then, to check the address for that day's job. I was at 2137 Westfield that day. That *same* day . . ."

The reporter shook his head. "What a strange coincidence."

"Yes. It's just that there I was, so close to the boys, just next door. If I only could have known, if only I could have done something."

"There was no way you could have known, sir."

"But they were so close to me. Can you imagine that? They were no more than fifty feet from where I was working. I remember that place. The houses are close together. If only I had heard something. Maybe I did hear something, and didn't pay any attention. Maybe they were in there, trying to call out, trying to make some kind of noise, trying to get somebody to help."

"You shouldn't keep thinking like that, Mr. Lepak. It doesn't do you any good. There's no point to it."

The reporter was a little worried. It looked as if this quiet, strong man was beginning to lose control of himself. Mr. Lepak gripped the reporter's arm, anguish in his eyes.

"Don't you see? There might have been something I could have done. I might have saved the boys. They could be alive today."

"Stop, Mr. Lepak. No offense, sir, but the boys are dead and you just have to face it. There was nothing you could have done. You mustn't torture yourself like that."

The reporter's unexpected firmness slowed down the older man. Mr. Lepak sat back into his chair, sobbing quietly. His wife put her arm around him protectively.

The only sound in the room was the whir of the air conditioner. Several minutes passed. Finally the reporter switched off the tape recorder.

The interview was over.

The reporter spoke kindly, reassuringly. "I want to thank you both for allowing me to talk to you today. You've been very patient, and I understand what kind of strain this must be for you both. I don't suppose there's anything that will lessen the terrible loss you must feel. I just want to tell you how sorry I am."

Mr. Lepak seemed to break out of his spell. "It's a good thing we talked to you, son. Maybe you helped us more than we helped you."

The young reporter packed up his papers and the tape recorder. He was just about to step out the door when Mr. Lepak called to him. His voice was questioning, imploring.

"Can you tell me something, son? Can you explain any of this? Can you tell me what kind of man would want to hurt good boys like that? What kind of man would it take to kill so many good boys? What kind of animal would it take? They were good boys, our boys. What kind of animal would it take?"

The young reporter turned back. "I don't know, sir. I just don't know. But I can tell you no animal could ever do a thing like that. That's something that only humans could ever do to each other."

10

■ The Tenderloin, San Francisco, was a new experience for Earl Harmen. He had never really been out West, and now, here he was, smack in the middle of fabulous Action City, cruising the streets with twenty-dollar hookers, con men, soldiers on their way to or coming from Vietnam, homosexuals, topless-bottomless strip joints, hustlers, and the neon come-on of dozens of honky-tonk bars. The cool, damp October air was filled with the insistent rhythms of electric guitars and drums, doors opened and closed provocatively, showing for an instant the flashing, glistening bodies of go-go girls in cages, on swings, on bars, on stages, lowered from ceilings, carrying drinks. No cover, two drinks minimum, come on in, stranger. Earl Harmen walked alone in the autumn night. He felt like a man from another planet.

The year was 1968. Because his grandmother was ailing again, Earl's mother returned to Boston to care for the elderly woman. Earl stayed in New Haven for a month or so, unsure of the next step. Then, more on a whim than because of any planned course of action, he withdrew all his money from the bank, forty-five hundred dollars, taped it in an envelope to the underside of his dashboard, and drove his Chevy van over the mountains, across the desert, and into the magical land of California, the land of movie stars, plam trees, and sunshine.

Without knowing why, really, and without having any idea of what he would find there, Earl Harmen drifted toward the North Beach of San Francisco. He arrived in town at nine o'clock at night. He parked his van in a ridiculously expensive lot, took fifty dollars with him, and went out to see what there was to see.

As he walked down the glittery neon-lit streets, he felt as if he had walked into a foreign country, a country where none of the old rules applied, where nothing looked familiar or reassuring to him, and where he felt at the same time both excitement and anxiety. He did not understand the long line of people, men and women, stretching out in front of a topless joint, waiting to see the world's most famous go-go girl. He could not conceive of women going into that kind of place. The idea filled him with revulsion.

And on he walked. A drunk, reeling on the sidewalk, narrowly missed crashing into him. A boy, eighteen or twenty, hair dyed bright orange, with skin-tight pants, sauntered up to Earl and asked him for a dollar. Earl Harmen ignored the boy and walked faster.

As it grew late, Earl realized he hadn't eaten in many hours. He stepped into the first diner he came to, a place that was a little more expensive than he had anticipated, but once he was inside he didn't want to call further attention to himself by leaving abruptly. He sat at the counter, at one of the few empty seats.

The counterman approached with a bored, jaded expression. "What'll it be?" he asked.

"Uh, a hamburger and a glass of milk. And some pie."

"I recommend the cherry."

"All right. That's fine."

Earl watched closely as the counterman called out his order, took some new ones, and continued a steady stream of banter with the customers. It was a kind of half-friendly, half-sarcastic monologue that ultimately left Earl wondering whether he should laugh or whether the joke was on him.

An old man, possibly the owner of the diner, sat at a cash register, alternately chain-smoking and coughing into a yellowed handkerchief. He, too, was following the monologue of the counterman, but in sheer enjoyment. Periodically he called to the counterman and said, "You're all right, Eddie, you know that? They should all be like you. You got a sense of humor, you know that, Eddie? Ah, hah, hah, ah...ack...ack."

"Jesus, don't go spreading those TB germs around, will ya? This food's bad enough."

As Earl bit into his hamburger he looked around the crowded diner, trying to understand what was going on behind all the tiny pockets of activity that were developing around him. He watched an extremely short young man, under five feet, dressed in black-leather motorcycle regalia, aviator sunglasses, and a pilot's hat worn jauntily off to the side. As he walked in and surveyed the other customers, his face took on a look of contempt and disdain. Earl watched him climb up on a stool and then stare with fierce concentration at two girls chatting in a booth. When one of the girls finally looked up, the short young man snorted in scorn, wiped his mouth coarsely with the back of his fist, and looked away.

Then Harmen looked closer at the two girls. One was a heavy-set, short-haired woman dressed in ill-fitting suede and flat-heeled shoes. Her face was not made up, and her features were broad and strong. The other girl was small and dainty, with thin red lips, downcast eyes, and a sharp, delicate birdlike face. Although she was obviously well into her twenties, she was dressed like a schoolgirl, very primly, collar buttoned up tight and a ribbon in her hair. The heavier woman was stroking the smaller one's hand, saying something to her that Earl could not hear. Then the heavy woman leaned over the table, held the smaller one's face for a second against her hand, and then kissed her softly on the lips. Earl Harmen turned away in shock. He was a long way from home.

And like a parade, like the come-on to a freak show, the characters continued to drift in and out of the diner, milling about for a short time, finding someone or something, and then being replaced by others. It was a strange and disquieting experience, yet he held his ground. He continued to watch, fascinated and repelled.

A young Navy officer came in, a girl on his arm, and the two took the last empty booth. The officer had a strangely weak face, very full of himself and the impression his uniform was causing. The girl was tall and gangly, unpretty in every respect, and she responded to the officer's every move, so anxious to please him, so painfully aware that she was not. They sat for several minutes, uncomfortable together, the officer bored and looking around the diner. He finally caught the eye of a boy of about seventeen, slender in tight-fitting pants, his long lashes blinking coyly. The officer got up and spoke to the boy for a moment. He then returned to the girl, telling her that he had to go out for a short while, that she could wait for him if she wanted. The girl nodded, and the officer and the boy disappeared. The girl told the waiter they had decided not to order after all, and she too left. Earl Harmen finished his pie and his second glass of milk.

The counterman started clearing Earl's dishes, wiping the counter down with his damp rag. "Yessirree-bob, buckaroos, that sure was a good hamburger, wasn't it? People come a long way for them hamburgers, son. Y'all come see our hamburgers again real soon, heah?"

"Ah, hah, hah. You got a real sense of humor, Eddie." The old man gave Earl Harmen his change, and Earl was back on the street, drinking in the cooler, fresh salt air.

He thought he would walk to the Bay and see if he could make out Alcatraz at that time of night. He wasn't sure of just where he was going, but he sensed he was heading toward the water. Years of living by the salt water in Connecticut had made him very much aware of the smell of the ocean, and he didn't think he would have too much trouble finding the old prison island, the escapeproof prison. Something about that idea fascinated him, the idea of being locked up with absolutely no chance of escape. What goes through someone's mind when he realizes that he doesn't have the slimmest chance of getting away, when absolutely no hope is left? Does the mind snap in self-protection, unwilling to face the totally hopeless situation? Or does it remain lucid right to the end, faced with the double agony of pain and the knowledge that there will never be anything else except the pain?

But even here, on the escapeproof prison island, hadn't hope managed to win out? Didn't somebody finally escape, didn't he scale those sheer cement walls, crawl across sharp, murderous rocks to the sea, and then swim three freezing miles to the shore? Didn't somebody finally make it?

"Hi, handsome. Looking for someone?"

Earl Harmen was sure that this young blond girl could not possibly be talking to him, so he continued walking past her.

"Hey, where ya goin'?"

She *was* talking to him. She was close to him, so close he could smell the fruit gum on her breath. She was a slight girl, pretty, with heavy make-up that had the effect of making her look like a little girl who had gotten into her mother's pocketbook. She couldn't have been older than eighteen. Earl had no idea how to handle the situation.

"I said 'Hi, handsome.' Didn't you hear me?"

She spoke in a high, cloying baby-talk kind of voice Earl Harmen had never heard before.

And then, of course, he realized that this strangely painted girl was a prostitute. He had never seen a prostitute as far as he knew, not that he could be absolutely sure, and this was the first time he had ever actually been approached by one. Like everything else in this strange city, the experience both excited and frightened him.

"No. No thanks."

"Hey, whatsa matter? You look like a big strong boy. Don't you like me?"

He tried to walk away. He thought that would be the best way. But the girl followed him, hurrying to keep up with his long strides.

"Yes, I like you, but I have to go somewhere. Why are you walking with me?"

"Aw, c'mon. I can be real nice to you. Come on up to my place for a little while. Twenty bucks."

"No. I couldn't do anything like that."

"C'mon, will ya? Ya shy or something?"

"No. I said no. Now go away."

"Twenty bucks ain't much. What do you say, huh?" The girl put her hand on Earl Harmen's arm to slow him down. It was a mistake.

He whirled around, jerking his arm away from her, and slapped her hard across the face. The girl was speechless with surprise.

"Get the hell away from me, you goddam whore! Keep your goddam dirty whore hands off me." His eyes were wide with hatred, burning into the terrified girl. He pulled back to strike her again, but the girl ran off down the street. He could hear her sobs in the distance. And then she disappeared.

Earl Harmen walked on, breathing hard. The words "you goddam whore" kept repeating in his mind over and over. There was an odd, familiar ring to the words, an uncanny feeling that he had heard them before. He walked for several minutes, oblivious of his surroundings, listening to the words inside his head, trying to understand what they meant to him. So great was his concentration that he didn't see the shiny green Cadillac pull up to the curb beside him or notice the black man who got out. He wasn't really aware of the man at all until he felt the strong fingers wrap around his neck, pinching the nerves.

"This him, baby?"

The blond prostitute was sitting in the front seat, her eyes wet and blurry from crying. She nodded. The long, black fingers closed tighter and a knife appeared in the other hand.

"Hey, whitey, what you doin' swingin' on my little girl like that? Now, that ain't a nice thing to do, is it? Is it, honky?"

Earl Harmen could hardly breathe. "No," he finally choked out.

"'Course it ain't. Now just to show how sorry you are, why don't you give the little girl something so she don't feel so sad about it?"

"How much?"

"Well, let's see. Whatever you think might cover it, honky. Let's see how much you got."

Earl hesitated, and the knife flicked close to his eye. He produced the wallet and handed it to the black man.

"Well, ain't that nice. You a Eastern boy, ain't you, honky? We sure do appreciate your Eastern hospitality, don't we, baby?"

The black man opened the wallet and took out all the cash there was, about forty-five dollars, then flipped the wallet into the darkness.

"Now, just to show you me and baby-face don't hold no hard feelings for our good brothers from the East, I'm going to put away this old knife, see?" The black man folded the knife and placed it carefully in his pocket. Then the same hand whipped out again, snake-fast, the knuckles aiming into Harmen's kidney.

At no time during this encounter was Earl Harmen actually frightened. He was unsure of himself in this situation; he did not understand all the variables that had suddenly come into play, but he was not frightened. So when he saw the clenched fist about to crash into his body, he calmly took what steps he could to avoid it. It was not a very difficult punch to block, and although Harmen had been one of the least coordinated students in his self-defense classes, he had certainly managed to block much more skilled attacks from sparring partners on the mats. He stepped quickly to his right and parried the punch with his left hand. With his right hand he delivered a hard punch to the black man's neck.

Then and there, the fight was over. The black man was beaten, half unconscious from the pain of the blow. But Earl Harmen did not stop. Very slowly, very methodically, he began raining punches on the sagging man's face and into his midsection—slow, devastating, painful punches, any one of which would have been sufficient to end the fight. Except that Earl Harmen did not stop.

He became aware of the girl in the car, screaming. "You're killing him! Oh, God, you're killing him! Don't hit him any more."

As Earl Harmen momentarily stopped the flurry of punches, the black man sank to the sidewalk, moaning in a low voice. Raising himself up high, planting all his weight on one foot, Earl Harmen snapped the heel of the other foot down directly on the man's face, the center of the heel falling squarely on the nose. The black man's face seemed to swell up for just a second, and then slowly, visibly collapsed, like a deflated basketball.

The moaning stopped. The black man was still breathing, but just barely. The girl stopped screaming. The sight of the black man's shattered face made her vomit in fear.

Earl Harmen retrieved his money and then his wallet.

Because he was so unfamiliar with the streets of San Francisco, it took him more than an hour to find his truck. He took a short nap in the driver's seat, and then pulled out. He headed south, away from the city. It wasn't the kind of city he could feel comfortable in. It was full of mean people.

Palo Alto, Salinas, Monterey. Strange new names to Earl Harmen. They were somehow more mysterious, more exotic than quaint New England towns back home. Everything seemed more substantial, the majestic redwood trees, the clear skies, the people themselves. Colors seemed more intense, the grass was greener, the ocean was bluer. The ocean. That was the Pacific Ocean, the biggest ocean in the world. If one could look far enough away into the horizon, he might even be able to see China itself.

San Francisco had been an unpleasant experience. But now, cruising southward through picturesque little towns, Earl Harmen had the feeling he was going to like this state of California.

Monterey was an Army town. He had remembered hearing some GIs talking about what good duty Fort Ord was, what a good town Monterey was, not the usual dump you find spread out around an Army base.

He drove down Alvarado Street slowly, well under the speed limit, trying to get the feel of the town. There were perhaps a few more bars than one might expect in a normal town, but other than that there was little to suggest this was anything other than a pleasant, prosperous civilian town. One or two GIs could be seen strolling along, looking in store windows, but certainly not a conspicuous number. Of course. It was the end of the month. Payday wasn't for a few more days. Nobody had any money to come downtown; that's why there were so few GIs around.

Harmen was particularly impressed when he came to the wharf; the view was so pleasant that he had to pull over and enjoy it at leisure. There were fishing boats and seafood restaurants and a few shops arranged about the old, sturdy wharf. The blue-green ocean waves washed up on the beach, and directly overhead a warm sun shone down. A few young boys were fishing, mothers were wheeling babies from shop to shop, a mottled black-and-white spaniel was dodging the waves as they washed in, and everyone seemed happy and healthy. It was like a picture postcard.

But there was one more thing, perhaps the most astonishing thing from the point of view of a young man from the East. About five hundred or a thousand yards out into the bay (it was hard to tell exactly) was a tiny rocky island. On that island, around it, splashing, playing, diving, fishing, barking, was a herd of over a hundred seals. It was a sight for which Earl Harmen was unprepared. He had seen seals in zoos, but never swimming around in their natural habitat. It was a wonderful sight. He decided to get out of the car and take a closer look at this town of Monterey.

Actually, the two boys had approached him first. Earl Harmen was frankly interested in sightseeing and had nothing else in mind. They asked him if he was going south and if they could get a lift down to Big Sur with him. They were sixteen or seventeen and had that healthy wind- and sunburned look that California kids get, youngsters who spend a lot of their time on beaches when other kids in other parts of the country are in poolrooms. They looked like pleasant, happy young boys, perhaps a little too happy. They periodically broke up into strange fits of giggling that Harmen could not understand, but... Sure, he was going south. No trouble at all to let them ride along. In fact, he'd like the company.

The three sat in the front seat. It was a large cab, so there was plenty of room. As they got out of the city limits of Monterey, the two boys started whispering to each other, and finally one spoke up.

"Hey, uh, look, man. You don't mind if we smoke, do you?"

"Sure. Why not. Go right ahead."

"I mean, smoke some reefer, man. You don't have anything against it, do you?"

"Oh. You mean marijuana, huh? Well, go ahead. Just keep the windows open."

"Sure. You wanna turn on? This stuff is outta sight."

"No. I don't smoke."

"Never even tried it?"

"Nope."

"Aren't you even interested?"

"No. But you guys go on ahead. If you like it, you have a right to enjoy yourself. That's the way I see it."

"Far out, man. That's a real cool attitude."

The two boys passed the joint back and forth, involved in each other and in comparing reactions. Harmen soon found himself unable to follow their laughter or conversation and finally made no further effort at it. In spite of the fact that the windows in the cab were wide open, he still caught a whiff or two of the sweet-smelling smoke. He edged over toward the window to breathe as much of the clean air as possible. He had never been under the influence of a drug, and he didn't intend to start then.

The truck was soon winding through some lovely California country, high green hills and forests to the left, great jagged, rocky cliffs to the right, dropping off sharply into the crashing waves of the Pacific Ocean.

The boy next to Harmen, a blond, pointed off to the water. "You know, there's a nudist camp around here somewhere. Real cute chicks go there, I hear."

Harmen, glad to become a part of the conversation again, was in fact quite surprised. "Really? Right around here? Did you ever see it?"

"No, but my brother told me about it."

"I think I'd like to go down to the water and see what it's like down there. Is there a beach or anything around here?"

The blond boy shrugged his shoulders. The other boy, shorter, darker, nodded. "Um, yeah, man. A little ways up. Real groovy place. Hey, you sure you don't want to try some of this stuff? It's dynamite, man."

Earl Harmen glanced at the boy from the side of his eyes. "No. I said I don't smoke. You heard me say that, didn't you?"

"Oh, yeah, man. Forgot. Sorry."

They reached the beach just as the sun was falling below the horizon over the ocean. It was a spectacularly beautiful scene, and the beach itself, tiny, secluded, was one of the most beautiful Harmen had ever seen. The sand was white and clean for a short expanse, and then great boulders weighing hundreds of tons seemed to appear from out of nowhere, as if left there by some forgetful sea monster. In the dusk, the beautiful deserted beach had an eerie, unworldly quality. The blond boy, immediately touched by the strangeness of the scene, jumped out of the van and ran across the sand.

"C'mon, Joey. Dig this beach, will ya? Wow!"

The dark-haired boy remained in the van. He was rolling another joint. "Be with you in a minute. I feel like getting really twisted."

Harmen followed the blond boy. They walked along the beach, dodging the waves that played around their feet.

"Did ya ever see rocks like that, man? Talk about stoned. Too much."

Harmen said nothing, following silently behind, watching the boy intently.

Then, jumping around the rock, the boy disappeared from

view. For a moment, Harmen panicked. There were so many rocks, so many places to hide. Especially in the growing darkness.

"Hey, look at these little fish, will ya? Must be a zillion of them."

The boy was squatting by a tiny saltwater puddle left by the last high tide. He watched with fascination as the fish, trapped in the puddle until the next tide, swam futilely back and forth.

The blond boy was not aware of Earl Harmen standing close behind, and he did not see Harmen pick up a jagged rock.

After a while, Harmen returned to the van. The darker boy was staring into space, his eyes drugged, smiling vaguely. Earl used his belt to strangle him. He was a small boy, and certainly in no condition to put up any serious resistance.

And then, slowly, Earl Harmen drove off into the velvety California night.

The bodies were found the next day, but they were never identified.

Because his expenses were minimal, because he had no costly vices such as smoking or drinking, and because he lived most of the time in the back of his van, Earl Harmen stayed in California a little more than a year before his money ran out. He had no fixed address during that time. He just cruised the highways.

11

■ The trial of Lee Criley and Otis Hesler began to take shape, to emerge out of the mass of scattered details, rumors, and the growing list of identified victims. It was going to be spectacular. Maybe another Leopold and Loeb trial, another Manson trial. This was the crime of the century, and one might logically expect the trial of the century. There was a growing, almost tangible sense of anticipation surrounding the initial legal preparations. What kind of monsters were these two boys? What would they be like on a witness stand? What actually went on? How was it possible for so many young boys to meet their death?

Would the real story of the mysterious Earl Harmen finally be told?

Dozens of reporters were assigned to the case. There was serious talk about televising the proceedings. All the machinery was geared up for a blockbuster of a trial.

It was unusual, then, that in a trial of this magnitude, one that guaranteed instant national publicity, no big-time superlawyer stepped up to take the case. Ordinarily, this would be a case that a financially secure, skilled criminal lawyer would relish. Perhaps the circumstances of the case were so unsavory that even the more flamboyant lawyers decided that the publicity, no matter how extensive, would backfire.

The man who finally got the job was Ron Mailer, a young, up-and-coming New Haven lawyer with thinly veiled political ambitions. It would be a special public-defender assignment, no fee. The regular public defender was unable to devote the time necessary for a case of this nature, and thus the assignment went to the first lawyer unable to find a reason to refuse.

Ron Mailer got the job of defending Lee Criley on the day following Criley's arrest. He got the job simply because he was in court, defending a drunk-driving case, when Judge Lawrence Birdsell called him into his chambers, winked at him, and told him he had a new client. At the time, Mailer was so surprised he couldn't think of an excuse. Even now that he was committed to defending the alleged mass murderer, Mailer was still not sure he wanted the job.

Defending Criley would give him publicity, and having practiced for only four years, publicity would help. But as far as his political future was concerned, it was difficult to assess the kind of effect a criminal case of this nature could have. And politics was something that Ron Mailer was very definitely thinking about.

At thirty-two, he had passed the Connecticut bar and had practiced alone from the outset rather than try for a partnership with an established firm. He had a flair for independence and had enjoyed the challenge of setting himself up on his own. Maybe later on he would take on some partners. In the meantime, Ron Mailer was establishing himself as a good husband and father, a competent lawyer, and a responsible member of the community.

Since Ron Mailer would be defending Criley, another counsel had to be found to represent Otis Hesler, thus avoiding any possible conflict of interests. As is common when two defendants are charged with the same crime, a major defense of one may well be that the other is guilty.

The second counsel was Mark Edmund Lescombe, a junior partner in a small law firm. Mark Lescombe was quiet, studious, and a hard worker. He would be able to work well with Ron Mailer, letting him dictate the defense strategy while maintaining a close watch on Otis Hesler's interests. Mailer would be the genial, outgoing personality, while Lescombe would remain in the background, the leg man.

Their adversary, the district attorney for New Haven County, was Harry F. MacNamara. A subtle, complex personality, Harry MacNamara could only be fully understood in the context of his older brother, Charlie MacNamara—Senator Charles J. MacNamara—former all-state quarterback and second team all-American. Still known as Charlie by friends and family, he dominated the MacNamaras. Wise, humorous, and gentle, a man so confident of his own talents and abilities that he was able to devote his energies to a real and deep concern for his fellow man. Everyone who knew him liked and respected Charlie MacNamara because he made everyone he came in contact with feel worth while. Harry MacNamara was Charlie's little brother. This was reality for him, and he had come to terms with it early in life.

Harry MacNamara had been a good student and a good athlete, and he was now a very good lawyer. He wasn't Charlie, but he was good, and had developed a sense of his own place. At forty-two he had found a job that he could do well and that he enjoyed, and he wanted to stay there. Because he had no further ambitions, MacNamara could allow himself the luxury of seeking justice first and convictions second. He was a fair and honest man.

And so the two opposing sides prepared their respective cases.

It would be a long legal battle, one that would be closely observed by the nation. Things would proceed slowly, carefully.

The fourth figure of the courtroom drama, perhaps the strongest personality of all, was District Court Judge Lawrence Birdsell, who had a reputation for flamboyance, unpredictability, and enormous egotism.

Judge Birdsell was movie-star handsome, with strong, even features, a leonine shock of silver-white hair, and pure blue eyes. He was a widower, his wife of nineteen years having died a few years earlier. Judge Birdsell could in two hours complete a docket that would take other judges a full day. He was able to accomplish this by simply making his intentions clear to the court officers and personnel. Somehow, that was always enough.

These four would be the main figures in the legal proceedings. They were good men, men of the law, all quite aware of their special charge in conducting the trial of the Crime of the Century.

12

■ Earl Harmen returned to Connecticut in late 1969, having been gone a little more than a year. The road had been good to him. He enjoyed the wandering, the lack of responsibility, the knowledge that no one knew where he was. Earl Harmen was out there all by himself, unreachable, in the shadows, unknown. This obscurity was in some very basic way a source of strength to him. He kept to the shadows. He was seen only when he chose to be seen.

He would have preferred keeping to the open road, but the life of the wanderer was not consistent with Earl Harmen's financial reality. Earl Harmen needed things that only money could buy, and he could only secure money by keeping a steady job. That meant settling down.

It was not sentimentality that led Earl Harmen to return to New Haven. In fact, he would have preferred a place he had never been and where he knew no one in order to preserve the anonymity he had come to relish. He returned to New Haven because at the time he had run out of money his father, who now lived in New Haven, had informed him that there was a training program opening up at the telephone company. With his technical background in the Army, this might be something to look into.

And so he came back to New Haven. He could have gone anywhere.

His plan was to keep living in the van until he made enough money to start looking for a place to rent. However, Howard Harmen, who in the intervening years had also moved back to Connecticut, happy to be with his son after so many years, insisted that Earl live with him. If not indefinitely, then at least until he got his own place. This was an invitation Earl Harmen was extremely reluctant to accept. Having grown to value his privacy, he was not sure he wanted to get involved in his father's life at this stage. Since the divorce, Earl Harmen and his father had hardly seen one another, had always kept a respectful distance. It had been a delicately balanced relationship, and Earl Harmen had no intention of tipping that balance.

After living in his father's home for a few days, Earl saw that the arrangement would present no difficulty. Howard Harmen worked on a night shift, and for that reason alone, contact was minimized. And, for an older man, Mr. Harmen was surprisingly active. An avid sports fan, he was even on a bowling team. Earl was therefore free to lead his life as he wished. He saw his father occasionally at breakfast, for longer periods on weekends; that was all. They continued in that casual manner for four months, until 1970, when it finally became necessary for Earl Harmen to have his own place. By that time, he had saved more than enough money.

Earl finished the training program at the telephone company

with flying colors. His Army experience helped him, and he was also aided by the fierce concentration he was able to focus on the course. There were no distractions for him; he didn't go out at night, he had no friends. Upon completion of the course, he started to work as a service repairman. The job was easy, occasionally challenging, and paid well. His starting salary was nearly three dollars an hour, and his take-home pay, with some overtime, was well over a hundred a week, quite adequate for those days and in that place. And it was steady work.

He was making good money and living rent-free. His father would accept no help with the rent. The crisis came one night when Earl Harmen forgot to put away some magazines he had been reading. They were unusual magazines, the kind sold only at special stores, the kind that are wrapped in cellophane so that they can't be leafed through in the store, but must instead be purchased. It was Earl's habit to look through these magazines late at night, when his father was still at work. Then he would carefully lock them away and go to sleep. One night he forgot to put them away.

Howard Harmen was not the kind of man who would openly or angrily confront his son about his private reading material. But there was a change in the relationship, and tension developed between them. A few days later, Earl Harmen told his father that he had found a cheap apartment closer to work and that he had decided to take it. His father said he thought that might be more convenient.

It was at a magazine rack that Earl Harmen became reacquainted with Otis Hesler. At first he didn't recognize the short, near-sighted boy who greeted him as he was thumbing through the magazines.

"Hi'ya, Earl. Where you been?"

"Should I know you?"

"Aw, c'mon, man. Don't you remember? When you used to have that pool table over in your garage? And all the guys would hang out there? It's me, Otis. Otis Hesler."

Earl Harmen wasn't sure he remembered. Boys change a lot in their formative years. And there had been so many boys hanging around.

"Oh, sure. Otis. How've you been?"

"Great, man. Getting along. Were you gone somewhere or something? Boy, I haven't seen you around for a long time!"

"I went to California for a while. It looks like I'll be back here for good, though."

"Great, man. Hey, you don't still have that pool table, do you?"

"Had to sell it. You a pool player?"

"Yeah. Keeps me in spending money. I always like to have a few bucks on me if I can."

"You like your spending money, do you?"

"Who doesn't? Hey, what are you reading, Earl? Stroke books?" The younger boy made a grab for the magazine Earl Harmen was holding, but Harmen pulled it quickly out of reach.

"This? I don't know. I just picked it up when you came in."

Hesler smirked. "Oh, yeah. Sure, man. You wasn't reading it. Just drooling!"

Earl Harmen smiled faintly. "Some of the things they print are really terrible. You wouldn't believe some of the pictures I have."

Hesler laughed again. "What do you mean, Earl? I bet you got a whole library full of the stuff. Right?"

"I have some interesting magazines and pictures home. But maybe you're a little too young for them. I couldn't show them to just anybody."

Hesler smiled knowingly. "Only anybody who'll look, right? Besides I'm old enough. You'd be surprised the scenes I can get with."

"How old are you, Otis?"

"I was fourteen last month. I guess that's old enough. I ain't no kid, Earl."

"No, I guess you're not. But maybe your mother wouldn't like it if she knew where you were going. Would she?"

"Are you kidding? My mother don't know shit about me. Half the time I don't even go home. No sweat about that."

Harmen kept pressing the younger boy. "You don't even go home? Then a nice handsome boy like you must be staying with some girlfriend. Maybe your girlfriend would worry about you."

Hesler was getting uneasy. "I don't have any girlfriend. Look, nobody cares where I am. I'm free as the birds."

"So you think you're free as the birds. You think you're ready to try anything."

"Hey, man. I've already tried just about everything there is. Don't think you can show me anything new."

Harmen smiled. It was the smile he would always be remembered for. His eyes grew wide, flashing in intensity. He didn't laugh, because Earl Harmen never actually laughed, but the corners of his mouth turned up slowly, and he grinned down at the younger boy. "I think I could probably show you something you've never seen before."

"Yeah? Like what?"

"Why don't you come over to my place and we'll see. Unless you're afraid." He was still grinning, as if the expression was fixed in place. The effect on Otis Hesler was oddly unnerving, frightening. It was like being confronted with a grinning death's-head, its shining eyes boring into him.

Challenged, Hesler shook off the feeling. "What should I be afraid of? Let's go, man. You got a car, ain't you?"

At the time Harmen was living in an apartment building off Gilroy Street, not far from the business center of West Haven. It was a two-room apartment on the third floor. The first thing that Otis Hesler noticed was that it was immaculately clean. Nothing was out of place, not a speck of dust anywhere. Certainly not the disarray one would expect to find in a bachelor apartment. The second thing he noticed was the dozens, perhaps hundreds, of pornographic magazines stacked neatly around the place. They were on shelves, on tables, in a magazine rack, but all were placed with meticulous care, lined up with military precision. There was no need to hide all the magazines now that Earl Harmen lived on his own. And, he thought, no need to make a pigsty of his apartment either.

"Holy Christ, Earl. You really do have a collection!"

"Take a look around. You might see something you like."

"Where do you get this stuff, man? You can't get books like this in West Haven."

"You can get anything you want if you know where to look for it. Anything at all."

"Jesus. I never saw stuff like this." Otis Hesler thumbed through the pages of a magazine, hypnotized by what he saw, yet anxious to get to the next page, and the next.

Earl Harmen smiled. "I thought you might like some of the books. Why don't you just sit down and make yourself comfortable. Would you like a beer? Oh, I almost forgot. You're probably too young to drink beer."

"Ha, ha. Very funny. Yeah, I'd like a beer. Hey, I've got some grass on me. How about turning on? I bet this stuff would be fantastic if you were stoned."

"Go ahead, if you want to. There's pelnty of beer in the refrigerator. Make yourself at home. I've got to go to the bathroom. I'll be back in a minute or two."

Otis Hesler hardly looked up from the magazine. "Sure. Go ahead. Christ, where'd you get this stuff?" Harmen left the room and was gone for five, then ten minutes. Otis Hesler was anything but bored, however. He lit up and smoked a joint, then had a beer to kill the thirst he'd suddenly developed. He took a second beer, relaxed in a great soft easy chair and flipped through the magazines. He didn't mind that Earl was taking so long. He had almost forgotten about him altogether.

When Harmen did come back, he had taken a shower and shaved. He wore a light blue bathrobe, his hair was combed back, still wet from the shower, and he had doused himself liberally with cologne. The smell of the cologne contrasted oddly with the heavy odor of the marijuana.

Otis Hesler sat giggling in the chair, shaking his head disbelievingly at the photographs in the magazines.

"Why do all the kids smoke that stuff? Aren't you worried about what it'll do to you?"

"You ought to try it."

"Not me. I get my kicks other ways."

"I guess you do, man. I guess you do. Christ, I can't believe these books."

Earl Harmen came to the chair Hesler was sitting on, and perched on the arm. He put his arm around the boy's shoulder, and dropped his other arm on his thigh, rubbing it softly.

Otis Hesler looked up at Earl Harmen, half frightened.

"What do you think you're doing, man?"

Harmen increased the pressure on Hesler's shoulder and thigh. If Hesler had any thought of bolting and running, it was dispelled by the pressure he felt. He would stand no chance against a man capable of exerting that much force.

"I thought you said you could get with anything. That you were free as the birds. Let's see how free you are." Harmen's hand continued to probe the young boy's body.

Hesler knew there was no point in fighting Harmen. Something inside told him that he had better cooperate, that everything depended on whether or not he cooperated. Quickly he made a decision. It was a decision made under the influence of marijuana, beer, and his own fear, and it was the biggest decision of his life.

"Hey, relax, Earl. What's your hurry? You want a blow job? I'll give you the best blow job you ever had. Let me have five bucks, and I'll give you blow jobs all night long."

The request for money was something Earl Harmen wasn't prepared for. And because he hadn't anticipated this, he lost control of the situation. He stood up awkwardly and walked to a dresser. He opened the top drawer, reached in the back, and pulled out a five-dollar bill. And he handed the five-dollar bill to the boy seated in his chair.

And so, in that split second, reacting to some deep and ancient instinct for survival, Otis Hesler made a decision that probably saved his life.

Otis Hesler returned again and again to Earl Harmen's apartment. At first, he had the upper hand in the relationship. He would come when he felt like it, would be gone for days, sometimes weeks at a time, without letting Earl know the reason for such long absences. And every time he came to spend the night with Harmen he insisted on money, sometimes as much as twenty-five dollars. Harmen gave the younger boy as much as he could afford, and more. He bought him clothes, presents, and kept him in spending money.

And then, gradually, the relationship began to reverse itself. Otis Hesler was a street boy. Both his parents were alcoholics, and neither had ever provided any kind of security or warmth for Otis and his two brothers. To Otis Hesler, home was somewhere you slept occasionally and got away from as fast as you could. And it was in this way that Earl Harmen changed from simply an easy source of spending money to the one source of security Otis Hesler had ever known. It was in this way that Harmen regained control of the relationship, and he never again relinquished that control.

There was never any explicit agreement that Otis move in with Harmen. Just as the relationship itself had gradually developed into something entirely different from what it was in the beginning, so the living arrangement just happened. Otis Hesler stayed with Earl Harmen for two nights in a row, then three, a whole week, and then he simply never went back home.

Hesler was not a highly intelligent young man, but he had learned life on the streets and had developed a certain shrewdness, a certain subtlety of perception that most boys his age did not have. He realized very quickly that he was being used by Earl Harmen. He knew that he was now only a means to an end, and he no longer had any real personal value, but still he remained. It may have simply been that Otis Hesler had nowhere else to go, but it was as if all his willpower had been drained out of him. He no longer was the master of his actions, but instead existed only to serve Harmen in whatever plans he had.

In June 1970 things suddenly changed for Otis Hesler. He had been living with Earl Harmen for almost six months, now in the third of five apartments the two would share, when an event occurred that marked a turning point in the relationship of the teenager and the older bachelor. Perhaps if Otis Hesler had acted otherwise, if he'd gone for advice, if he had not gone along, then everything might have been different. Perhaps twenty-seven young boys might still be alive. But the fact is that Otis Hesler did not turn and walk away.

And so it was that the change took place in June of 1970, the end of Otis' sophomore year in high school. Because of upcoming graduation exercises at the school, the lower classes were let out early, giving the senior class time and space to rehearse the ceremonies.

Usually, Otis hung around the school after his last class. A slow, sullen boy in the classroom, he came alive after school, one of a number of loud, brash outcasts. He was without any outstanding talents, not an athlete, not a student, and yet in the circle of boys who were not on any team or any committee, Otis Hesler was liked and appreciated. He would often spend hours hanging around with these friends in the vicinity of the school, clowning, complaining, and killing time.

That day in June 1970, however, he did not linger at the school. He was hot and dirty and he could think of nothing better than a shower and a can of beer, and maybe a joint or two to pass the afternoon. Otis Hesler came home to Earl Harmen's place early and walked in on a scene of madness.

At first, the slight, discolored body on the chair seemed to be anything other than what it was. Otis Hesler thought it must be a doll or a ventriloquist's dummy. It hung loose and lifeless, like a dummy. But it was stripped naked. The flesh was battered and bruised, and there were small bloody areas on the arms and on the chest, areas just a little smaller than a dime. The mouth of the dummy was taped, and the hands and feet were tied together and to the chair upon which the dummy rested. Why would Earl want to tie a dummy up like that? *Jesus God, what was he doing?*

Otis Hesler stood mutely in the doorway, the midafternoon sun streaming in on him. He stood petrified, like someone who suddenly finds himself teetering on the edge of a precipice where there is absolutely nothing he could hold onto, nowhere he could turn for help.

The figure in the chair, the dummy, stirred ever so slightly, and a moan issued from behind the tape, a deep low moan from somewhere Otis Hesler had never been before.

And then realization came to him, like a cold, sick chill spreading over his body.

For some reason that was not clear to him, Otis Hesler felt his eyes fill with tears, and then sobs came in quick, short gasps from his throat. Until he began crying, he had not made a sound. He had been frozen, speechless, in the doorway. Earl Harmen had not yet noticed him. With the first choking sound from Otis Hesler's throat, Harmen whirled around to face the intruder.

His eyes were wide, flashing, and he seemed to emanate a terrible power, a murderous lust, an angry hatred, that almost pushed Hesler backward with its stark force. This was no longer a man; this was no longer the Earl Harmen that Hesler had known.

Otis Hesler had walked in on a monster, a monster in the process of devouring its prey.

"You! What are you doing here?" The voice was different, deep, demonic.

"Earl, I . . ." Otis Hesler could only stand there, choking back his sobs.

"Dammit! I said, what are you doing here? What are you doing in my house so early? Tell me. You'd better tell me, or I'll make you sorry."

"Earl. Please." It was no use. Terrified, Otis Hesler could not speak a coherent sentence.

And then Earl Harmen strode toward him, taking long, powerful steps, his face contorted with rage.

"You answer me when I talk to you, boy. Do you understand that? You answer me when I talk to you in my house."

Somehow, from some secret, undiscovered source of strength, Otis Hesler found the will and the energy to avoid the outstretched, grasping hands of Earl Harmen. He turned and ran, out the door, down all the steps at one bound. He stumbled on the sidewalk, scraping his elbows and his knees, but he kept going, running as fast as he could, running to the end of the world.

Earl Harmen did not follow the running figure. He stood in the doorway watching, his face rigid and impassive. The rays of the midafternoon sun fanned out behind his back.

Not until much later that night did Earl Harmen find Otis Hesler. Harmen had been driving slowly through West Haven for over an hour, asking Otis' friends if they had seen him, going to his hangouts, the street corners, the candy stores that Otis liked. And finally, close to midnight, he saw him, wandering aimlessly, hands deep in his pockets, walking along in the warm night.

Earl Harmen brought his van close to the curb, driving slowly beside the walking boy. He leaned to his right to call out the open window on the passenger side. He spoke in a friendly voice.

"Hey, Otis. What's the matter? Aren't you coming home?"

Otis Hesler jerked his head around. When he saw the van so close to him, he instinctively tensed, ready to run off into an alleyway, into the safety of the darkness.

"Hey, don't be so nervous. Come on. Let's go home. It's getting late."

It was a different Earl Harmen who called so gently to Otis Hesler—the old Earl Harmen, the Earl Harmen Otis Hesler had grown to know and to feel secure with. The monster, the powerful, blood-crazed animal Hesler had walked in on earlier that day was no more. The transformation was so great that for a moment Otis wondered if the scene he had witnessed wasn't a dream. Earl couldn't have been killing that boy. Earl would never have done that. But he *had* seen it. He had seen it with his own two eyes.

He still hadn't answered the voice calling to him from the van.

The van had come to a halt beside the boy and Otis heard the sound of the emergency brake being engaged, a door being opened and shut, and footsteps coming toward him in the darkness. Earl Harmen was standing in front of him, his hand outstretched, palm upward, and he was smiling.

"What's the matter? Don't worry. Everything's all right. Come on home now. Come with me."

"Earl. That kid I saw ..."

"Don't worry about that. It's all over now. There's nothing for you to worry about."

"What were you doing to him, Earl?"

"Nothing. It was just a game, that was all. Nobody got hurt."

"How come he was tied up like that, Earl? It looked like he was hurt real bad. I know he was hurt, Earl."

"He wasn't hurt, I told you. I think he was flying high on some of that marijuana you like so much. That's all it was. Marijuana."

"Where is he now?"

"How do I know where he is now? He took off, that's all I know. I don't know where he went."

"Then he was all right?"

"Sure he was all right. What did you think? You didn't think I'd hurt that boy, did you? It was just a game, we were just fooling around. If you had stayed a little bit before running off like that, you would have seen for yourself. The boy was all right. There was nothing wrong with him."

Earl kept repeating these words over and over, hypnotically, gradually reassuring Otis Hesler. It was all right. There was nothing to worry about.

Earl Harmen put his arm around Otis' shoulder and gently guided him into the van. The younger boy allowed himself to be drawn along, back into the security and comfort that had exploded in his face earlier that afternoon. He was glad to be back with Earl. After all, things were always so much better when he was with Earl.

They drove back to Earl Harmen's apartment. Harmen put his hand on the boy's knee, reassuring him.

"Otis?" The voice was kind.

"Yeah?"

"You didn't tell anybody what you saw today, did you?"

"No. Who would I tell? No, I didn't tell anybody."

"Some people might not understand things the way you understand them. That's why I have to make sure. You're sure you didn't tell anyone?"

"No. I didn't. Honest!"

"That's good. That's a good pal. Tell me something, Otis. How would you like a new car of your own to drive around in?"

For the first time that day, Otis Hesler perked up with real enthusiasm.

"My own car? Really, Earl? You'd really get me a car of my own?"

"Sure. Just a little present from one friend to another. You'd like that, wouldn't you, Otis?"

"Oh, wow. Would I, man? Hell, yes."

"Now there's just one thing, Otis. I want you to forget about what you saw today. It was nothing important, just a game I was playing. The only thing is, a lot of people might not see it the same way, so it wouldn't do to talk about it. Do you understand what I'm telling you?"

"Sure, Earl."

"So you didn't see anything going on this afternoon. You didn't see any kid on a chair, you didn't walk in on anything, because there was nothing to walk in on. Nothing happened, understand?"

"Sure, Earl. What kind of a car is it going to be?"

The two friends drove home. It was late, but they each had a can of beer before going to bed. Otis Hesler fell asleep quickly, dreaming of his new car.

A few weeks later Earl Harmen told Otis Hesler that he felt like having a party, and why didn't Otis go out and see if he could pick up some kid hitchhiking. Otis was reluctant at first, thinking back to the last "party" he had walked in on. But Earl Harmen told him that he would give him ten dollars if he could find some young boy. He told Otis that there would be nothing to worry about, that nothing bad would happen. He should just ask the boy if he wanted to have some fun, if he wanted to go to a far-out party, and if the boy said yes, then just bring him back to Earl. That was all. There was nothing wrong in that.

Besides, Otis was a little short of money, and the ten dollars would come in handy. He could use a little cash. So he agreed, and a short while later he brought a boy of about thirteen into the apartment. He left the boy with Earl and went back out to visit a girlfriend. It was an easy ten bucks.

With that act, with that decision, Otis Hesler was now not only an observer of the activities of Earl Harmen, but he was also a participant, a willing accomplice. The decision was to go along. Otis Hesler's thinking did not reach out beyond the immediate situation. He saw no larger implications—moral, legal, or otherwise—in his participation. On the other hand, he took no great pleasure in his participation. Nothing in his being drove him inevitably to the taking of human life. He allowed it to be done, he allowed himself to become involved because it was the path of least resistance. Earl expected it of him, Earl seemed to be sure of what he was doing, and finally it didn't matter that much to Otis Hesler. It didn't seem that important.

So Otis brought Earl a thirteen-year-old boy, and Earl gave him ten dollars. That was all. It was a good deal.

■ The date set for Lee Criley's trial came and went. A postponement of two weeks, from January 31 to February 14, was requested by defense counsel Ron Mailer. There were simply too many preliminary issues that still remained to be settled. Pretrial investigations were still being held; questions of evidence, of sanity, of the possibility of seeking a change of venue were still unresolved. The two weeks' continuance was granted by Judge Lawrence Birdsell, but no one involved considered it likely that a trial would actually begin at that time.

Very quickly, one legal issue began to stand out as the single most critical point in the case of the State versus Walter Lee

Criley. Indeed, the State's case stood or fell with this one issue. This was whether or not Lee Criley's confession, taken shortly after his arrest and during the days that followed, was admissible as evidence. Hesler's confession did not even come up at this time. If one confession was ruled admissible, it was certain the other would be also. All legal energy was concentrated on Lee Criley.

Without these confessions, there would be no case. The only case the State could bring against Criley without the confessions was in regard to the shooting of Earl Harmen, and that had already been ruled to be in self-defense. The most remarkable fact about this case, other than the murders themselves, was that there was not one shred of hard evidence that could tie Criley or Hesler, or even Earl Harmen, to the deaths of the twenty-seven boys.

There was every reason to believe that, without the confessions, Lee Criley and Otis Hesler would both go home and forget about a rather unpleasant episode in their lives . . . if they could.

"Of course, you're sunk even if you do get those confessions thrown out. You know that, don't you?" inquired Harry MacNamara of Ron Mailer during one of their many informal chats in the courthouse.

"Oh, really?" said the defending attorney. "I wasn't aware of that. How did you reach that particular conclusion?"

"Pretty easy. There's that slight matter of the burial sites. Even without the confession, Criley hung himself on the basis of taking the police to where those kids were buried. *That's* how I reach that particular conclusion."

"You did go to law school, didn't you, Harry?"

"Let's see. I think so."

"Did you ever come across the case of the United States versus Prescott? A very interesting case. If you look it up, I think you'll find—"

"All right." MacNamara put up his hands in surrender. "I know what I'll find."

"You'll find," Mailer went on, "that any behavior on the part of an accused, whether verbal, physical, or anything else, is to be considered subject to advice of counsel and may be used in evidence prior to obtaining counsel only when that right has been waived. You do remember that case, don't you, Harry?"

"I said all right, didn't I? What's the matter with you? I had to see if you were on your toes, didn't I?"

Ron Mailer filed a motion indicating that the confessions were obtained illegally and should be barred from any trial proceeding that might take place. There was a further postponement pending resolution of this issue.

On February 17, 1973, pretrial hearings began in the case of the State versus Lee Criley. Judge Birdsell had made certain that elaborate security measures were taken. Fourteen well-armed county sheriffs were called in and stationed strategically around the courtroom and at all entranceways. For the first time in the memory of any court officer, a special metal detector was obtained and set up. Anyone seeking admittance to the courtroom would be subject to a metal search. Judge Birdsell did not intend to have the cause of justice thwarted in his courtroom at the hands of a vengeful parent. A further technical innovation was the consideration of a closed-circuit television system. This would not be used during the pretrial hearings; but later on, during the course of the actual trial, it might be invaluable.

A pretrial hearing is different in many ways from an actual trial. Since questions of guilt and innocence are not to be considered, the rules of procedure vary markedly from a criminal trial. A wider latitude of questioning is allowed. Apparently irrelevant lines of inquiry that would never be tolerated in a trial can be followed with impunity. Though only secondary matters can be determined in a pretrial hearing, in many ways more information, more of the real "truth" of a matter, sometimes comes out.

The hearing began at 2:00 P.M., February 17, 1973. Ron Mailer stood before the judge, explaining that he intended to show that the confessions were illegally obtained. He indicated that his client would not be present in court unless he should be required to testify in his own behalf, asking if this absence met with the approval of the State. Harry MacNamara stated for the record that he had no objection.

Then Mailer called his first witness, Emma Criley, the mother of the defendant. Mrs. Criley was led in from an adjoining room by a bailiff. She was a slender woman, not fashionably slender but underweight, the kind of underweight that betrayed an extremely poor childhood. Her features, too sharp, too strained, were even. If things had been different for her, she might have been a pretty woman, but poverty had taken its toll. Her hair was grayish and thin, and her eyes, set deep, were pained and furtive. She wore a plain brown dress.

She walked into the courtroom slowly, almost too calmly. Her gait contrasted oddly with the tension that showed in her face. She had been taking tranquilizers regularly since Lee's arrest, and today she had been eating them like candy.

Mailer hurried around the table in the middle of the courtroom to lead Mrs. Criley to the witness stand. He patted her arm reassuringly and walked back to the table. A clerk approached her before she could sit down.

"Would you raise your right hand, please?"

Mrs. Criley first moved her left hand, grimaced nervously, then raised her right hand. The eyes of the clerk were boring into her, making her feel small and uncomfortable. She looked away from the stern face in front of her.

"Do you swear that the testimony you shall give is the truth, the whole truth, and nothing but the truth?"

"Yes. Yes, I do."

"Will you state your full name and address for the record, please?"

"Emma Stevenson Criley. I live at 2212 Colbert Street."

"Thank you. Please be seated." The clerk padded away silently, his feet making no sound on the carpeted floor. There was no other sound in the courtroom.

"You may examine your witness, Mr. Mailer." The voice of Judge Birdsell was firm, emotionless, and stern. It frightened Mrs. Criley.

"Thank you, Your Honor. Now, Mrs. Criley, I think everyone knows what a terrible strain you've been under these past few months. Please understand that the questions which will be put to you, no matter how unpleasant, no matter how painful, must be answered to the best of your ability. You must understand that we're only trying to get at the truth here, and the truth is the best way for you to help your son. So I'm asking you to try to be as calm and as precise as you can with your answers, and try to see that no one wants to put you through any more suffering than you've already been through. Can you understand that, Mrs. Criley?"

Mailer's voice was kind and reassuring, and his eyes were gentle. Mrs. Criley felt better almost immediately when she listened to Ron Mailer.

"Yes, I understand. I'll try to be helpful."

"Thank you, Mrs. Criley. I'm sure you will. Now, let me refresh your memory just a bit. Your son was arrested around eight in the morning of July twenty-third, 1972. Can you tell me when you found out about it?"

"Lee called me on the phone. I'm not sure if it was real late Sunday night or early Monday morning."

"Can you be any more specific about the time, Mrs. Criley?"

"Well, I was watching a late movie on the television, I guess it was around midnight."

"So it was around sixteen hours after he was arrested that your son called you?"

"I guess that's right."

"Can you recall what he said to you, Mrs. Criley?"

"He told me he shot Earl."

"Did you know Earl Harmen yourself?"

"Yessir, I did."

"And what else did Lee say?"

"Well, sir, I could hardly believe it. I guess I was so awful upset I didn't know what to say. But Lee kept saying how he felt free, that he didn't have to worry no more. He said he felt real good, and how everything was all right."

"How did he sound to you, Mrs. Criley? Was there anything unusual in the way he talked?"

"Well, for one thing, at first I didn't even think it was Lee. It didn't sound like his voice. I ought to know my own boy's voice, but when I heard him I thought it was somebody else, maybe playing a trick on me."

"How was the voice you heard different from Lee's normal voice?"

"When he talked, he seemed kind of far away. I can't really describe it. His voice was softer than it usually is."

"Was he making sense to you then?"

"I could understand what he was telling me."

"Did you try to contact your son after the phone call?"

"As soon as Lee hung up, I called up the police station to see if it was true. They told me they had Lee there, and they'd have to talk to him some more."

"Did you ask when you could see him?"

"Yes. They told me to come in the next day."

"And then what happened?"

"The cops were real mean to me, telling me how I wasn't going to see Lee for a good long time, and he had a lot of talking to do before they'd let him talk to me."

"So they didn't let you see him the day after his arrest?"

"No, sir. They did not."

"When did you finally get to talk to your son?"

"They finally let me talk to him on Tuesday. It was just for a little while. And there was a cop listening to every word we said."

"And how would you describe your son's state of mind when you talked to him? Again, was there anything unusual in the way he behaved?"

"It was terrible. He looked so tired and nervous, like he hadn't slept in days, and he was smoking one cigarette after another. It was terrible, the way they treated Lee there."

Mrs. Criley was showing signs of hysteria, but Mailer pressed on. He spoke to her soothingly, kindly; it was imperative to his case that he get her testimony on the record, especially with respect to this point.

"I'm sure it was terrible, Mrs. Criley. But you understand that he's being given the best of care right now, don't you? And you know that nothing bad is going to happen to Lee now, don't you?"

"Yes, sir."

"All right, now, Mrs. Criley. Can you tell me anything else about Lee on the day you first saw him, anything strange about the way he spoke or acted?"

"It looked like the poor boy was just going to pieces. He was crying, and talking about this, that, and the other—I couldn't understand him at all. I never seen him in such a state. It's awful for a mother to see her boy in a state like that."

"Did he know what day it was?"

"No, he didn't. He asked me how long he was in jail, and I said, 'Why, Lee, don't you know?' And then he kind of half-laughed, half-cried, saying he was going to be in jail forever and ever, and he wasn't never going to come out."

"Did you notice any nervous mannerisms in your boy?"

"Yes, sir. Every now and then, while we was talking, he'd kind of jerk his head over to one side, like he was listening to something real hard, and sometimes he'd say 'What?' or 'What did you say?' when nobody said anything. It was real scary. I never seen Lee act like that."

"Did it appear to you that Lee was hallucinating?"

"I don't know what he was doing. It was something terrible to see. I tried to give him some of the nerve pills the doctor gave him, but the guard wouldn't let me."

"What kind of nerve pills were those, Mrs. Criley?"

"Tranquilizers. Nerve pills. Lee has been taking them every now and then for a long time. He ain't crazy. It's just that sometimes he gets real nervous and needs to calm down some. That's why I wanted him to have them in jail, but they wouldn't let me."

"Now tell me, Mrs. Criley, when was the next time you talked to Lee?"

"It was that same night. He called me up on the telephone."

"Can you remember what you talked about?"

"Well, he said it was all over for him, there was nothing else for him to do. He said he signed everything they wanted him to sign, and he told them everything he could remember."

"How did he sound to you?"

"He sounded more like himself that time. He seemed tired, but he didn't sound so nervous any more."

"Did he say anything about a lawyer?"

"He said that they told him to get a lawyer, that he was going to need a good one. He told me to try to find a lawyer and a doctor for him, and to come to see him at the jail as soon as I could."

"Did he say anything else?"

"No. I think that's all."

"All right, Mrs. Criley. Thank you very much. You've been very helpful."

Mrs. Criley smiled just slightly and got to her feet.

"Just a moment, Mrs. Criley." It was Judge Birdsell. "I think Mr. MacNamara might have a few questions to ask you first. Does the State intend to cross-examine?"

Harry MacNamara stood up. "If I may, Your Honor, just a question or two. Mrs. Criley, you testified as to your son's psychological state at the time you visited him in jail, is that correct?"

"I told how he seemed to be acting to me."

"Were you aware that your son had been using drugs for an extended period of time prior to his arrest?"

Mailer stood up. "Your Honor, I object to that question. There has been no testimony regarding the defendant's possible drug use."

"Sustained."

"Mrs. Criley, did your son ever tell you that he had been deprived of the right to counsel, that he had not been allowed to see a lawyer any time he wanted?"

"No. He never said that."

"Then, to your knowledge, he could have had a lawyer with him any time he chose, isn't that right?"

"I don't know. He might have."

"That's all, Mrs. Criley. Thank you very much."

Mrs. Criley looked to the judge for instructions and he nodded, giving permission for her to leave.

She walked out of the courtroom without looking back, her head down, her shoulders sagging.

Ron Mailer told the court that he had some other witnesses he had to subpoena, and that until they could be located he would be unable to continue. The hearing was adjourned for a week.

On February 28, 1973, the second session of the pretrial hearing convened. A number of witnesses had been subpoenaed by Mailer, and the session began promptly at 10:00 A.M. On that day the courtroom was even more jammed than before, although Criley and Hesler were still not present in court. District Attorney MacNamara noted this fact. His interpretation was that the crowd was beginning to smell blood.

The first witness called was Sergeant William Rathers, the officer who had first been dispatched to the Harmen home on the day of the shooting. He had been the first policeman to talk to Lee Criley, and Mailer felt that his testimony could be significant.

Rathers testified that he had spoken to Criley at some length, that the boy seemed completely shattered and depressed, and that he was periodically tearful. The sergeant described the scene at the Harmen house when he arrived there—the body of Earl Harmen, the "torture boards," the empty pistol, and the handcuffs found near the body. He mentioned that Criley kept himself aloof from the other boy and the girl who were sitting on the porch steps. It was also determined that, at the time, Rathers had no idea that there was more to the case than that which immediately met the eye—shooting in self-defense. In the early morning hours of July 23, 1972, only two New Haven teenagers knew that vicious multiple sex-torture murders had taken place.

"Officer Rathers, please think back clearly now," said Ron Mailer. "At the time that you brought Lee Criley in, did you read him his constitutional rights?"

"Yes, sir, I believe I did."

"You believe you did. Is it possible for you to be a little more specific? I assure you, Officer Rathers, this could be extremely important."

"Well, sir, I know that every time I make an arrest, I make real sure I read those rights. That morning that I took Criley in, I think I probably read him his rights, but I can't be sure."

"Then how can you tell me that every time you make an arrest you make sure you read the rights? Why is this time different?"

"I didn't arrest Criley."

"You didn't arrest Criley?"

"No, sir. I just brought him in for questioning. If he had fought going in, I would have arrested him. But he was cooperating real good, so the arrest only came later on, when he was at headquarters."

"All right. Thank you, Officer Rathers."

It was a blunder, one that a lawyer of Mailer's experience should not have made.

The next witness was Sergeant Raymond Shaunessey, the one to whom Criley first opened up, the man who first heard the whole story. A big, burly man, Shaunessey exuded the authoritative yet compassionate presence of a good, concerned cop. Mailer was not about to get caught in the same mistake he had made with Rathers. He asked Shaunessey immediately if Criley had been formally arrested by the time he spoke to him.

"Yes, sir, he had."

"And what had he been charged with?"

"First-degree murder."

"With Earl Harmen the victim?"

"That's correct, sir."

Shaunessey had been around a long time. He had testified in perhaps hundreds of cases. His testimony was professional and, ultimately, devastating to Criley's case.

"And as a result of that arrest, were Criley's rights read to him?"

"Yes, sir."

"When?"

"To my knowledge, twice, sir. By the arresting officer, and by myself prior to the interrogation."

"Can you prove this, Sergeant?"

"I believe I can, sir."

"How?"

"The subject initialed a form which is attached to his signed copy of the confession."

In further questioning, Shaunessey stated that during his interrogation of Criley he began to feel a certain sympathy for him, in spite of the nature of the crimes Criley was confessing. Shaunessey added that in the course of a lengthy interrogation it was not uncommon for the subject to experience an almost religious feeling of atoning for his crimes, and that the instant a man made the decision to confess was always a critical one. It is in that instant—in which emotions are at a peak, in which a man's entire past is on the brink of exposure and destruction, in which he experiences solitude in its most intense form—that a rapport is often established between a skilled interrogator and the subject.

Shaunessey stated that that phenomenon did in fact take place with Lee Criley, but in such a subtle way that he, Shaunessey, felt himself being drawn into an emotional relationship. He was able to catch himself, he said, and was very careful to insure a completely professional approach to his interrogation. But he stated that during the interrogation he often felt as if he was talking to his own son, and that he had frequently spoken to his own sons in a similar way. He said that Criley was getting things off his chest, things that had troubled him deeply for a long, long time.

"We talked about a lot of things," Shaunessey said, "and it wasn't just about the killings. I felt like I got to know this boy very well. It wasn't easy, after some of the things he told me, but I felt sort of protective toward him."

"And what sort of things did he tell you that made it difficult to feel protective about him?" This question was asked by Harry MacNamara, and it sparked a day-long debate.

Ron Mailer did not want that particular question answered. He felt that any information along that line would only make his client appear in a bad light, and that it was not in the nature of the pretrial hearing to discuss matters of substance, of immediate bearing on the trial itself. Harry MacNamara argued that what they were trying to establish was Criley's state of mind in the period immediately following his arrest, and that anything he said during that time was pertinent. He was not really interested, MacNamara stated, in the factual content of what Criley told Shaunessey, at least not at this time. He was interested in establishing that Criley was in a sound state of mind and had been capable of understanding his constitutional rights and of demanding counsel at the time of his arrest if he so chose. The only way this could be determined was by learning just what Criley said during the interrogation.

It was a ticklish point, and one on which Judge Birdsell did not want to rule right away. It was getting late in the afternoon, so he called a recess until ten the next morning. By then, he told both attorneys, he would make a ruling as to whether Criley's statements would be allowed at the hearing.

The next day Judge Birdsell ruled that in order to determine Criley's state of mind during the time after his arrest it would be necessary to know what he had said. The judge indicated that there was no jury, that no one need be prejudiced by any information that might come to light, and that the factual content of this information was secondary to the manner in which it was said. He directed Sergeant Shaunessey to answer the question that had last been put to him.

When court reconvened, Harry MacNamara noted that the courtroom was again completely jammed.

"And what sort of things did he tell you that made it difficult to feel protective about him?" MacNamara asked.

Shaunessey took a deep breath and grimaced. "Well, most of this is down in the confession he signed. I don't think anything was left out. When he told me about how some of the boys were killed, he went into some detail about how...how different things had been done to them."

"And what were those things, Sergeant Shaunessey?"

"Well, he told me that they had castrated some of the boys..."

Gasps were clearly audible from the spectator's section. Shaunessey was silent.

"Sergeant Shaunessey, in what manner did the defendant Criley tell you about these things? What was his tone when he related these strange stories?"

"He was quiet, calm. But I guess he was relieved to be telling somebody all this."

"Was he making sense when he told you all this? In other words, Sergeant Shaunessey, was Lee Criley coherent?"

"He was coherent. I had no problem understanding him."

"Did he appear to be in control of himself and what he was saying?"

"His manner was very calm. I'd say he was in control."

The next witness was Detective Walt Harel. Harel had been with Criley throughout the excavation at the boat shed and for part of the excavation at the other sites. His testimony was short.

"How would you describe the defendant's attitude and behavior during the time you were with him?"

"He seemed pretty relaxed about the whole thing. It didn't seem to bother him, even when he was able to recognize some of the bodies."

"Did he seem rational to you?"

"His thinking seemed straight, if that's what you mean. I could understand him. I didn't like what I understood, but I could understand him."

"Could you clarify that, Detective Harel?"

"The kid thought it was all perfectly normal. He was even making wisecracks. He took it all in stride."

Court recessed early that day. Ron Mailer told the court that he would need a week to prepare himself for his next two witnesses. He intended, he stated, to call the defendants Otis John Hesler and Walter Lee Criley to the stand.

14

■ Day by day, Otis Hesler was progressing far beyond his depth in his relationship with Earl Harmen. He knew it, he watched it happen, and he could do nothing about it. He had never been strong-willed, but this was somehow different. He wasn't simply following Harmen, simply going along passively. Something strangely different was taking place here. Day by day, Harmen was draining Otis Hesler of will, of strength, of individuality, and ultimately of life itself.

The relationship was similar to that between a parasite and its host, or even, perhaps, between vampire and victim.

In spite of this, perhaps out of some remaining instinct for his own survival, perhaps out of a last-ditch, superhuman effort of will, or perhaps simply by chance, Otis Hesler did two things that lessened the intensity of his relationship with Earl Harmen.

The first was that he found a girlfriend. She was fifteen, a year younger than he was. She was less than attractive and considerably overweight. She responded enthusiastically to the attention and, even more, to the kind of spending money Hesler was able to produce. For Sharon Minton, Otis Hesler represented a steady boyfriend who actually had a car of his own. For Otis Hesler the stakes were much higher. He had found a possible avenue of escape from the world of Earl Harmen.

The second thing Otis Hesler did was to bring another boy to meet Harmen, one who was older than the boys he picked up hitchhiking or lured through promises of wild parties and drugs. Instinctively, Otis wanted someone to share the burden of guilt. He knew this boy from school. He knew him to be a loner and a heavy drug-user. To Otis' thinking, this boy would be perfectly suited for the kind of activities that had been going on around Earl Harmen. There were few things that Otis Hesler had predicted more accurately. This new boy was Walter Lee Criley.

At first, Lee Criley was incredulous when Otis Hesler told him what was going on. "Oh, man, wow. This is too much, man. You guys gotta be crazy, man." And yet even then, even from the first, Lee Criley's eyes shone with excitement and anticipation. Could he dare believe that such a far-out scene was taking place right under his nose? Could he believe that Otis Hesler, that weird, dumb pothead, was really into anything as flipped-out as this? It was too much.

And of course, in a very short time, he became convinced that it was all true, just like Otis Hesler had said, right down to the last detail.

If Otis Hesler thought that Lee Criley would be a substitute for him and would eventually replace him, he wasn't far off. Criley and Earl Harmen, slowly at first and then more quickly, began to react to each other. They seemed to egg each other on, to play off one another, to inspire each other. Otis Hesler had been passive. Lee Criley was active.

The parties, as they came to be called, grew more frequent

and more intense. Lee Criley fitted in well. Better than Otis Hesler could have expected. And unlike Otis Hesler, who usually disappeared soon after a party got going, Lee Criley stayed for the whole gruesome sequence of events.

If Earl Harmen had simply absorbed Otis' vital energy for his own uses, it became more of a mutual process with Criley. Energy was shared, passed back and forth, and was even amplified. It was a spiraling kind of situation, gradually growing stronger and deeper into a vortex with vast, unnatural energies whipping around and around, spinning, pulling, drawing anything weaker into its wide gaping mouth.

And that was why Otis Hesler still could not get completely out, even though he had found this substitute for himself, even though he had a girlfriend. He too was drawn into the whirling vortex he had helped to create.

Otis Hesler was in. Now Lee Criley was in. Neither would ever get out.

It was one of the hottest nights on record. Even though it was close to midnight, the temperature was still hovering in the mid-nineties. Relief in the form of morning coolness wouldn't come for many hours.

Earl Harmen sat on his porch stoop, watching a cloud of insects buzz around a streetlamp. Even the light from the streetlamp seemed to add to the heat of the night.

Harmen sipped on a can of beer. He didn't like beer, but tonight was an exception, tonight he needed a beer. He drank slowly, in oddly dainty sips; with the can still half full, the beer had turned warm. He continued sipping.

Stretched out on the lower step, his head resting on his arm, was Lee Criley, working on his sixth beer in about two hours. The crushed empty cans had been tossed in the direction of a steel trash barrel near the street. Some were closer than others, none was actually in the barrel. The two sat on the steps, allowing long periods of drowsy, uncomfortable silence to pass between them.

"How many you figure you done, Earl?"

Harmen did not answer right away. "How many what?"

Lee Criley still looked up into the stars. "You know."

"I don't know."

"I mean before me. With Otis. About how many?"

Harmen took a small sip of beer. "I told you I don't know. What difference does it make?"

"No. Really, man. What was it? Ten? Twelve? How many?"

Earl Harmen said nothing.

"And how about before Otis? How about then? Jesus mother-fucking Christ, maybe you got a hundred of 'em planted out there."

Earl Harmen took another sip of his beer, so warm now that it was almost undrinkable.

A car full of noisy teenagers cruised by. The engine, the squealing tires, and the laughter from inside the car were the only sounds on the street. Soon the red taillights disappeared around a corner, leaving only the silence and the heat.

Lee Criley crumpled his beer can, tossed it in the direction of the trash can, and missed again. Half drunkenly, he stood up. He walked to the corner of the house and urinated into the hard dirt.

"Any more beer in there, Earl?"

"I don't know. I think you swilled it all down."

"Aw, shit."

Criley slapped at his shirt pocket and pulled out a flip-top cigarette box. There were several regular cigarettes in the box and about a dozen slender, hand-rolled ones. Criley lit up one of the hand-rolled cigarettes; he sucked in the sharp, pungent smoke eargerly.

"You kids really like that stuff, don't you?"

Criley swallowed hard and said nothing. A full thirty seconds later he coughed. "Yeah," he said. "You got to try some, Earl."

"Maybe I will. Let me have just a puff."

Earl Harmen was not a drinker or a smoker. He didn't like the idea of using artificial stimulants. The smoke was more than he could handle. He blew it out quickly, coughing, his eyes watering.

"Nope. That stuff's not for me."

"You know what it does, sometimes, Earl? Sometimes it gets you horny."

"I suppose so. If you need it."

"Well, you sure as hell don't. You sure as mother-fuckin' hell don't." Criley laughed uproariously, and even Earl Harmen smiled. And then he frowned when the laughter continued long after it should logically have ceased.

Again they lapsed into silence. Earl Harmen didn't bother drinking any more of his beer. It was warm and flat by now. Criley stretched out on the steps, squinting up at the stars, smoking steadily.

"Hey, Earl!"

"What is it?"

"Let's do one tonight."

"Tonight? Are you crazy?"

"Come on. Why not? What's wrong with tonight?"

"It's too late, that's what's wrong."

"It's not late. It's only about twelve. Come on, Earl. What do you say?"

"You're crazy."

Criley was on his feet now, enthusiastic. "Come on, Earl. It ain't late. I can go out and have one back here in half an hour. Why not, man?"

"Because I don't feel like it tonight. You have to be in the right mood."

"Look, Earl. We'll never fall asleep in this heat anyway. And if we're going to be up, why not do one? You aren't working tomorrow, Earl. How about it?"

Earl Harmen was weakening. "How are you going to find one out there so late at night?"

"Don't you worry, Earl. Leave it to me. You give me the keys to the Chevy and I'll be back here before you can get things set up."

"You really feel like doing one, huh?"

"Yeah, man. Come on, give me the fuckin' keys, will ya?"

"How do I know you aren't drunk and stoned out of your mind? How do I know you won't smash up the truck?"

"Hey, Earl, I'm all right, man. Let's have the keys, man, let's have the keys." He made a move toward Earl Harmen, grabbing him between the legs, giggling. Harmen pushed him away, reached in his pocket and handed over the keys.

"Don't drive around all night. If you can't find one right away, come on back. Understand?"

Criley jumped up in glee. "Yessir, be back in ten minutes."

Lee Criley wasn't back in ten minutes as he promised. He wasn't even back an hour later. Earl Harmen felt a rage growing inside him, building to wild hatred as the minutes ticked away. When he finally heard the Chevy pull up into the driveway around two o'clock, he was ready to kill Lee Criley.

But then Lee walked in the door, smiling, leading in a skinny boy of about thirteen. And suddenly everything changed. That night they had one of their wildest and cruelest parties, but at least it seemed to satisfy Earl Harmen's lust for several weeks.

Spring is a marvelous time of the year in New England, exorcising the heaviness and chill of winter. Spring brings with it a sense of stretching out after a long sleep, with a new growth, a new buoyancy. In New Haven in 1971, spring came softly, unobtrusively, and the air was filled with a subtle but unmistakable surge of life and energy.

The young, of course, are most sensitive to such subtleties of climate. And certainly, spring is the season of the young. A time to sow wild oats, a time to raise a little hell, a time of excitement and frolic.

Otis Hesler and Lee Criley, their sensibilities only somewhat dimmed by drug use, were not immune to the new season, and they could feel its warm invigoration in their blood.

The two boys were usually not close. As a rule they regarded each other with distrust. Otis Hesler considered Criley vicious and unpredictable, capable of turning to violence at the slightest whim. Lee Criley considered Hesler babyish, soft, and stupid. They tolerated each other, avoiding contact whenever possible. Their common bond was Earl Harmen, and apart from him there was no real relationship. And so it was unusual that the two boys, cruising the streets of West Haven in Hesler's battered Chevrolet, should feel so comfortable in each other's presence. It must have been the surge of good feeling that comes with spring.

They cruised through the downtown area, slouched low in their seats, arms banging out the rhythm of a pop-music station that came blaring out of the car radio. The sunlight, a pleasant, invigorating glow, shone through the dusty windshield.

Stopped at a traffic light, Otis Hesler raced the engine. Criley glanced around him, enjoying the day, enjoying the feeling of being chauffeured through the city. To his right, a tall, attractive olive-skinned girl came out of an office building. She turned up the street, and for a moment was walking parallel to the car, only a few feet away.

"Hey, baby, where ya goin'?" Criley shouted lewdly out the car window.

The girl was startled for a moment, looked around, and then walked on, ignoring the boy in the car.

"Hey, come on. We'll give you a ride."

The girl quickened her pace and disappeared in a swarm of pedestrians.

"Fuckin' Rican."

"A Rican? How could you tell?" Otis Hesler was impressed.

"The way they bounce, the way they kind of bebop along. That one was a little taller than most, but you can tell. Rican pussy, man."

"You ever had any of that stuff?"

"Hell, yeah. Plenty of times."

"No shit! Where at, man?"

"New York. Didn't you ever get down there?"

"No. I've been meaning to, but I never did. What's it like?"

"What's it like, man? I'll tell you what it's like. It's like wall-to-wall pussy."

"Bunch of fuckin' pigs, I bet, huh?"

"Hell, no, Otis. They got some real outa-sight broads. I hear there's one place where you can get 'em looking like anybody you want. Elizabeth Taylor, Ann-Margret, anybody."

A car behind Otis Hesler blew its horn, bringing him abruptly to attention. The Chevrolet screeched away, only a little behind the flow of traffic.

"When did you go there, Lee?"

"Last year. On my sixteenth birthday. And I had me one helluva birthday party, I'll tell you."

Otis Hesler was entranced. Lee had been on an adventure that he had only daydreamed about. He gave up all semblance of cool detachment. He wanted to know what had happened. He wanted to hear everything Criley would tell him.

"Did you get much there?"

"Did I? Hell, man, those broads practically drag you off the streets by the balls. They're something else, man."

"And they're nice-looking, huh?"

"Yeah. Some of them are real knockouts. Real fuckin' beauties. They're whores all right, but don't think a whore can't be beautiful."

"I hear they have these acts and stuff they do on a stage, you know, with donkeys and dogs, and all that. Did you see anything like that?"

"Nah. I didn't go out looking for any of that kind of shit."

They cruised near the waterfront, feeling a warm onshore breeze from Long Island Sound and noticing the oceangoing vessels tied up in the port of New Haven.

"You know, Lee, I always wanted to get on some big ship like that and see the world."

"Me, too, man. The Merchant Marine. That's what to hook up with. I got an uncle who does that. Goes all over the goddam world. Makes pretty good money. Sounds like a good way to make a living."

"Yeah. I figure I'll join the Navy."

"Are you nuts, man? Swabbin' the goddam decks? Yessir, no sir, all fuckin' day? You can have that shit."

"How old do you have to be to get in the Merchant Marine?"

"I don't know. Eighteen. Twenty-one. I don't know."

"You only have to be seventeen for the Navy. I already did some checking on it."

"I'd keep checking if I was you. You'll never see me in any goddam uniform."

The two boys had never spoken to each other at any length before, certainly never of personal matters or plans. It was a new experience. It was as if they were friends at last, not just companions.

"You know where I'd like to go? I'd like to get on one of those big boats and go all the way to China. See Hong Kong and Shanghai and all those places."

Criley nodded. "Yeah. I saw a movie about a guy who did that."

"The one where a guy shoots his friend so the Chinks can't torture him? I saw it too."

"I guess the Merchant Marine goes out to China. They'd have to. That's what you ought to get into. Not the fuckin' Navy."

"Don't you ever want to take off somewhere like that, Lee?"

"Me? Sure."

"Where? Where would you want to go?"

"I guess I'd like to go out to California. Earl said he was out there for a while. Maybe me and him will head out there sometime."

A subdued "Oh" was the only response. The mention of that name, the other name, changed the focus of things, as if a lens had suddenly been adjusted and things were back to normal. Almost imperceptibly, both boys shifted in their seats, Hesler feeling renewed tension in his shoulders and arms, Criley sensing a familiar excitement, a rush of anticipation.

Earl Harmen and everything he had come to mean to the two boys was again the dominant factor, both in their minds and in their actions. There would be only rare instances in each of these boys' lives when that would not be the case. Earl Harmen did not have to be physically present to exert his dominant, tangible influence over the two.

It was shortly later that they spotted the hitchhiker. A boy of fifteen or sixteen with a shock of light-blond hair.

Wordlessly Otis Hesler pulled the car to a halt about fifty feet in front of the boy. The boy ran up to the car, panting, and Lee

Criley opened the rear door for him. The boy rushed into the back seat, slamming the door behind him. He was in.

"Hey, you guys, thanks a lot! I've been out there about an hour already."

"Where you headin'?"

"Not real far. Just about twenty miles up the road here. You goin' that far?"

"We could. We could. By the way, my name's Lee, and this here is Otis." Lee Criley reached his hand to the boy.

"Pleased to meet you. My name's Cal Fenten."

Lee smiled. "I think I'll just call you Blondie. Anybody ever call you that?"

"Yeah. Lots of people do."

"Want a cigarette, Blondie?"

"No, thanks. I don't smoke."

"You don't smoke? I bet he smokes this kind of cigarette, huh, Otis?"

Otis Hesler nodded. He smiled tightly but said nothing, concentrating on the traffic.

They drove on a few miles, Lee and the blond boy talking and joking. Then quite suddenly, Otis Hesler turned right and off the main road.

"Hey, hold it, you guys. You better let me out here. I gotta keep on going straight."

"Hey, don't worry, Blondie. We'll take you right to where you wanna go. I just have to pick up something at a friend's house. Just take a minute."

They took another right, and then Otis Hesler pulled the Chevy up in front of a small ramshackle house.

"This is it, Blondie," Lee said. "I won't be a minute. Oh, hey, listen. There's something in there you might be real interested in. Why don't you come on in?"

The boy hesitated, suddenly uncomfortable. "I don't know, Lee. I think I'll wait here."

Lee Criley opened the back door, beckoning the boy out.

"C'mon, will ya? Nobody's goin' to hurt you. Just for a minute. I'll show you something you never seen before, I swear."

Reluctantly the boy stepped out. "Okay, but just for a minute."

"Sure. You coming in, Otis?"

"Yeah. Yeah. Go ahead, man. I'll be there in a minute. Something I want to check on the car first."

Otis Hesler watched Lee Criley and the blond boy walk up the sidewalk, through the door and into the house. The screen door slammed noisily shut behind them.

He sat in the car, chewing on a fingernail. He did not go inside.

Hesler spent the rest of that night with Sharon Minton. He ate dinner at her house, and then the two went to a drive-in movie where *Blood of Dracula* was playing.

The next day he went to school, then spent the night with his girlfriend again. For some reason, one thing led to another, and before he realized it, four full days had elapsed since he had dropped Lee off at Earl's house.

When he got there, both Lee and Earl were asleep. The surprising thing was that the hitchhiker, the boy they called Blondie, was still alive. He had been tortured and abused for four days, but he was still alive. Hesler knew he couldn't last much longer.

15

■ The corridors and steps of the New Haven County Courthouse were crowded long before the hearings were scheduled to begin. This was to be a big day, the day the two teenaged killers would at last come out of the obscurity of confinement and make their appearance in court. The New Haven townspeople would no longer need to depend on newspapers and television commentators for details of the killers, how they acted and what they looked like.

Because of the huge crowd pushing into the courtroom, security was heavy and the metal detector was being used on every individual seeking admission. The two guards operating the detector explained patiently that all metal objects should be taken out of pockets before attempting to pass along, and that these objects would be returned immediately. A man in his forties, dressed in work clothes, took a keychain and a metal eyeglass case out of his pockets, put them on a small table, and submitted to the metal detector. The small needle dial still fluctuated crazily.

"You sure you ain't got any metal on you, bud?"

The man looked about nervously. "No, I told you I didn't."

"Why don't you step out of line for a minute? We're going to have to search you if you want to get in there."

"I told you I don't have nothin'. Can't you believe me? I don't have nothin'."

Both guards approached him. "Better come this way, fella."

The man lurched out of line, picked up his belongings from the table, and broke free of the guards.

"Is that fair? Is that fair that these bastards are walking around and my boy is dead? Is that fair?" The man was now weeping bitterly.

The guards made an attempt to stop the distraught man but he disappeared into the crowd. He did not return and was never identified.

The rest of the line moved uneventfully into the courtroom.

At precisely 10 A.M. Judge Birdsell opened the door behind his bench and a bailiff called the court to order. The two prisoners were brought in. One was the defendant in the immediate case, Walter Lee Criley. The other was a defense witness for Criley, Otis John Hesler.

Because of the care taken to keep them separate while incarcerated, it was the first time the two boys had seen each other since they had been arraigned. The two boys avoided eye contact.

Criley was dressed in blue prison denims and a white shirt, open at the collar. His hair was combed neatly, his features were composed. He appeared relaxed, sure of himself and self-contained. Only once did he look into the audience, his eyes seeking his mother. When he found her, he winked, then retreated back within himself. He sat next to his lawyer, facing the bench.

Otis Hesler sat between two guards. He was dressed in a blue suit, the kind that is issued in jail on request. The suit was big on him, even though Otis Hesler had gained weight while in jail. His wide-open eyes, terrified, moved ceaselessly around the courtroom. His hands fidgeted in his lap, scraping dried skin from around his badly bitten fingernails. He looked at Lee Criley a couple of times, but Criley did not notice.

The formalities of opening the court were gone through quickly. And then Attorney Ron Mailer called his witness to the stand: Otis John Hesler.

Hesler looked around at the two guards, who pointed to the witness stand, directing him to move toward it. He stumbled slightly as he rose and walked forward. And as he was walking to the stand, his lawyer, Mark Lescombe, approached, put his arm on his shoulder, and whispered something into Otis Hesler's ear. Hesler nodded and walked on.

Hesler was sworn in, and Ron Mailer stood to ask the first question.

"Mr. Hesler, how long have you known the defendant, Lee Criley?"

Hesler coughed, looking down at his feet. "I refuse to answer on the grounds that it may tend to incriminate me."

"Did you know a man named Earl Howard Harmen?"

"I refuse to answer on the grounds that it may tend to incriminate me."

"When did you first become aware that Lee Criley had been arrested?"

"I refuse to answer on the—"

Mailer threw up his hands. "All right, Mr. Hesler, all right. Your Honor?"

Judge Birdsell addressed the boy sitting in the witness stand.

"Mr. Hesler, is it your intention to refuse to answer all further questions on the grounds that they may tend to incriminate you?"

"Yes."

"What?"

"Yes, Your Honor."

"Are you doing this under the advice of counsel?"

"Yes, Your Honor."

"Very well. That's certainly within your rights. You may step down."

As Hesler stepped down, he looked one last time at Lee Criley. This time Criley was looking back. It was the first time their eyes had met in more than six months. The eyes of the two boys shifted, found each other, locked onto each other, and shifted again. That was all. Only a second, yet it was enough. For Otis Hesler, the second was an eternity.

Otis Hesler had been frightened and nervous, but still relatively composed. When he saw Criley, Hesler was shattered. He would not take the stand again, either against Lee Criley or in his own defense. For the remainder of the trials, he would be no more than a still, mute figure, expressionless, impassive. With that one glance from Lee, Otis Hesler's spirit shriveled and died.

Then Lee Criley took the stand.

He almost sauntered to the witness stand, waiting patiently while a court clerk put him under oath. Then he sat down, calm, motionless, with no indication of the intense strain he was under. He folded his hands in his lap, the nicotine stains visible on his fingers. The courtroom was still. For the first time that day, the spectators were silent, aware and conscious of the air conditioner whirring away.

Ron Mailer shuffled some papers in front of him and moved to the witness stand.

"Lee, I'm going to ask you some questions about certain events that occurred on the night of July twenty-second, 1972, and the early morning of July twenty-third. Can you remember where you were on those dates?"

"Yes, sir. I was at Earl Harmen's house." Criley's voice was thin, high-pitched.

"Who else was there at that time, besides yourself?"

"There was me, Veronica Metcale, and Don Simonds. And Earl."

"And what was the purpose of those people being there at that time?"

"We were having a party."

"Were there any drugs consumed?"

"We smoked some dope for a while. And there were some pills."

"When you say dope, what do you mean?"

"Marijuana. Grass."

"Was there any other kind of intoxicating substance used?"

"Yeah. We sniffed some acrylic paints, too."

"Would you describe how that is done?"

"Well, you know, you squeeze some paint out of the tube and into a plastic bag. Then you cover up your mouth and nose with the bag and just breathe it for a while."

"And that will cause you to become intoxicated?"

"Sure will."

"All right, now, let me just review what you told me. You said that you smoked some marijuana, took some pills, and then you sniffed paint out of a plastic bag. Were you in an intoxicated condition after all this?"

Lee Criley smiled, revealing yellow-stained teeth. "Intoxicated? Man, I was stoned out of my mind."

"Do you have any trouble remembering the events of that night?"

"Some of it's not too clear. I think I remember most of it, though."

"Suppose you tell me what you remember," said Mailer.

Criley described the flow of events of that evening. What he said was consistent with information that had appeared in the newspapers on the day after his arrest. He told how he had passed out and then awakened to find himself handcuffed to a plywood board. He explained how he had talked Harmen into setting him free, and how Harmen then began to molest Veronica Metcale and Don Simonds, who were also cuffed to boards. He explained that he feared for the lives of Veronica and Simonds, as well as for his own. He grabbed Harmen's pistol, he said, and shot him several times, he didn't remember how many. He said he believed that if he didn't shoot Harmen, Harmen would have killed all three of them.

"Now, then, can you tell me how you came to be arrested?"

"No, sir, I can't."

"What do you mean, you can't?"

"It's just that I don't know how I got arrested. They told me I called the police myself, so I guess that's how it happened. But I can't remember doing that."

"Can you tell me the first thing you do remember after the killing?"

"I remember sitting in a room with some cops. One of them was telling me how all I had to do was sign some papers for him and everything would be taken care of."

"Did you sign those papers?"

"I don't know. I think so."

"Do you know what was in those papers?"

"No, sir. I don't."

Throughout his examination of the witness, Mailer remained physically close to him. It was as if he wanted to keep Criley's mind as close as possible to the subject of the questions, and if he allowed too much space between the two of them Criley's mind would have opportunity to wander, perhaps into areas best left alone.

"Can you tell me a little about how you felt during that time, the first time you can remember being in the police station?"

"Well, sir, I felt awful tired. I don't know how long I had been without sleep, and I was coming down off the booze and the paint. My body felt like it weighed a ton. And I had a headache."

"Anything else?"

"I was hungry."

"Didn't the police give you anything to eat?"

"They said I could go to sleep and have everything I wanted to eat as soon as I signed the papers."

"Now, how about mentally? How did you feel mentally?"

"I felt real nervous. Sometimes I take these tranquilizers for my nerves, and I wished I had them. It seemed like my mind was going all over the place. Sometimes it would go real slow, and I couldn't remember what I was talking about. Then sometimes it was like I was seeing everybody real far away, like they weren't talking to me, but to somebody who looked just like me. It was scary."

Mailer continued to question Criley about his use of tranquilizers, how he had first sought medical help for his nerves, how he had trouble sleeping, and how sometimes he heard voices talking to him, telling him to do things. He stated that often he wasn't sure during the police interrogation whether the questions were coming from real policemen or from inside his own head.

"Now, Mr. Criley, just a few more questions. Can you tell me if at any time during the questioning by the police you were physically struck?"

"No. Nobody hit me."

"Did anyone threaten to hit you?"

"No. I don't think so."

"And while you were being questioned, did any officer inform you of your rights under the Constitution, your right to keep silent, your right to a lawyer? Did anyone tell you that you didn't have to answer any questions at all?"

"No. Nobody said anything about that. They said I could see a lawyer after I finished talking to them, after I signed the papers."

"So all the statements you made, all the papers you signed, all that was done without informing you of your rights under the United States Constitution, is that correct?"

"Yes, sir. That's correct."

"Thank you very much, Mr. Criley. Your witness, Mr. MacNamara."

Ron Mailer had done a good job. He had clearly and concisely established most of the points he would need if he hoped to have the confessions thrown out. He had shown that Lee Criley was under the influence of a number of intoxicants, that he had suffered blackouts both before and after the arrest, and that he was in a general state of mental and physical turmoil. Mailer returned to his seat, expressionless but inwardly pleased with the testimony so far.

Harry MacNamara didn't look up, but shuffled through the papers in front of him for at least a minute. The most noticeable effect was on Criley himself. He shifted uncomfortably in his chair, frowning, chewing at a fingernail.

Finally, Harry MacNamara rose. "Your Honor, if it please the Court, there are a few things the defendant has brought out here that I would like to research a little further. For that reason, then, I am requesting a recess until two o'clock this afternoon."

There was nothing further that Harry MacNamara had to research. There had been no surprises for him that morning. His tactic was simply to break the flow of Criley's testimony, to give him a few more hours in which he had to keep the same facts straight in his mind. It was the tactic a basketball coach might use when the opposing team seems to be in control of the game. He called a time-out.

When court reconvened at two o'clock, Lee Criley was where he was supposed to be, ready and waiting to take the stand. Harry MacNamara was late. First five minutes, then ten. At twelve minutes after two he walked into the courtroom, begging the court's and his learned colleagues' indulgence. Criley was visibly irritated at the casual, elegant manner in which the prosecutor carried himself.

Harry MacNamara was an experienced professional. He knew that his manner was irking this young boy from a poor family in West Haven. There was something in the expensive, casual cut of MacNamara's clothes, his soft-spoken self-confidence, his razor-cut hair style that suggested all the comfort and security that Lee Criley could never aspire to. They suggested money, country clubs, shiny cars, beautiful girls, the finest that life had to offer, things that a boy from a broken home in West Haven could only dream about. Harry MacNamara was quite aware of the effect he was causing. He intended to break the carefully studied pattern of responses and find out, if he could, what was going on in Lee Criley's mind.

MacNamara remained seated, his face down, not looking at Criley. When he spoke, his voice was just barely audible.

Criley cocked his head to one side. "What did you say?"

Suddenly, like a cat springing out of a crouch, MacNamara whipped out of his seat and said loudly, "I asked you if you remember any police officer reading you your constitutional rights."

"No. No. I never heard my rights."

"Are you absolutely sure?"

"I don't remember hearing my rights read to me."

"If I could prove to you that you did hear them, do you think you'd remember then, Mr. Criley?"

Ron Mailer stood up. "Your Honor, I must object to that question."

MacNamara didn't wait for the judge's response. He withdrew the question and proceeded to his next one.

"Would you recognize your own signature, Mr. Criley?"

This question bothered Criley. "Yes. I think I would."

"I am going to hand you a paper with your signature on it, and you tell me if it's yours. All right? Do you think you can do that?"

"Yes. I can recognize my signature."

"Fine. Now, Mr. Criley, take a look at these." He was just about to hand some documents to Criley, when he stopped. "I'm sorry, Mr. Criley. There will be some other writing on this paper. You'll be able to read that, won't you? You *are* able to read and write, aren't you?"

Criley breathed a sigh of exasperation. "If I've a mind to."

"Do you have a mind to today, Mr. Criley?"

"We won't know till we try, will we, Mr. MacNamara?"

Judge Birdsell looked down sternly at the defendant. "Mr. Criley, I must warn you to answer the questions with a simple yes or no, and to refrain from sarcasm here. This is a court of law, no matter what it may seem to you."

Criley reddened but did not answer.

"Can you tell me what is on those papers, Mr. Criley?"

"It's the rights."

"And is that your signature on the bottom?"

"Yeah."

"I can't hear you, Mr. Criley. Could you please speak up just a bit."

"Yes. I said yes, it's my signature. But I don't remember signing nothing like this."

"Do you remember the officers reading these rights to you?"

"No."

"Do you remember them saying anything to you about signing this paper?"

"They were saying a lot of things to me. I can't remember everything. I wasn't paying any attention to half the things they were saying."

"You were being arrested for the murder of a man you had known over a period of years, and you weren't paying attention to what the police were saying to you? Isn't that a little hard to believe?"

Criley shook his head in irritation. "Mr. MacNamara, I just killed a man. I wasn't thinking straight. I didn't pay attention to everything the police said to me."

"I would think that someone in your position would want to pay the strictest attention to everything that was going on, especially something as important as rights under the Constitution."

"Well, then, I tell you what you do, Mr. MacNamara. You go out, and you kill a man, shoot him dead, and then come back and tell me how *you* feel. Suppose you do that."

There was a shocked gasp from the spectators, followed by laughter. Judge Birdsell rapped his gavel. "Mr. Criley, one more smart remark like that and you'll be found in contempt of this court. Do you understand me?"

Criley looked down at his hands. He pulled his lips tight across his teeth. He wanted a cigarette badly. "Yessir, Your Honor."

MacNamara continued to cross-examine Criley about the events on the night of Harmen's death, going over and over each detail of testimony, seeming to be listening indifferently to Criley's responses, simply questioning, questioning and questioning again. It was a cross-examination technique MacNamara had often used, a technique that usually made the witness irritated, confused, and off-guard. MacNamara remained cool and poised, never raising his voice, relentlessly asking one question after another. Criley squirmed in his chair, discomfort and anger in his eyes.

"Can you tell me what time you got to Harmen's house on the night he was killed?"

"I don't know."

"Was it before midnight or after midnight?"

"I don't know. Before midnight, I guess."

"How did you know it was before midnight?"

"I'm just guessing. I'm not sure."

"Was it a long time before midnight? An hour, two hours? Can you be more specific?"

"No. I can't be more specific."

"And yet you are able to tell me it was before midnight. Isn't that a little strange?"

"Maybe it is strange. I don't know. I don't believe in keeping up with time. It's against my religion. That's why I don't wear a watch."

And still MacNamara pressed on, with Criley growing more defiant with each nagging, probing question.

"You say you cut the clothes off Veronica Metcale before killing Harmen. Where did the knife come from?"

"It was Earl Harmen's knife."

"How did you get it?"

"I told you. It was laying on the table."

"How big a knife was it?"

"Things were happening pretty fast that night. I didn't get a chance to analyze it."

The afternoon wore on. Ron Mailer realized it had been a mistake to allow his client to testify. At least it was at the pretrial hearing that he had made this mistake, he told himself, and not at a formal trial. At least a jury wasn't going to see Criley on a witness stand. If he could just get through this one day without

Criley's incriminating himself, Mailer would never let him open his mouth in court again.

And there was something else, another association that clicked on in Ron Mailer's mind as he watched the cross-examination. Something from his own boyhood, something he hadn't thought of in years, was floating up out of the murky depths of his unconscious. There was something about Criley that gave Mailer a feeling of *déjà vu*. But Mailer knew that he had to concentrate on the activities going on before him; there was no time to indulge in the kind of reflection he was drifting into. He made a short note to himself, and directed his full attention back to the court.

"Mr. Criley, you stated that you had put some handcuffs on the Simonds boy, is that correct?"

Criley was tired. He needed a cigarette badly. "Are you telling me what I said or asking me what I said?"

Judge Birdsell banged with his gavel. "The witness will answer the question."

"Yes, yes, that's correct."

"Did you have a key to the handcuffs?"

"Yes. That is, Earl had it somewhere."

"And how did you place the handcuffs on?"

"I put them on, that's all."

"How was that?"

"You've seen handcuffs, haven't you? I put them on just like any pair of handcuffs go on."

It was getting close to five o'clock. Criley had testified all afternoon. Although no new ground had been broken and no glaring contradictions had been turned up, MacNamara was satisfied with the testimony he had elicited.

"Just a few more questions, Mr. Criley. How long have you been using drugs?"

"If you mean aspirin and coffee, just about all my life. If you mean like pot and pills, like that, I guess about four or five years."

"You're seventeen now. That would mean you began using drugs at age twelve or thirteen, is that correct?"

Criley smiled. "Very good. That's right."

"And had you been using drugs up to the time of your arrest?"

"Yes."

"How often were you using drugs during the time just before you were arrested?"

"Just as often as I could get my hands on them"

That was the last question of the day. All that remained at this point was the final summation from Mailer and MacNamara, each arguing as to the admissibility of the confession taken by Sergeant Shaunessey as evidence. This would take a few more hours and would have to go forward to another day. Court was recessed. Criley was taken away quickly, and equally quickly the courtroom cleared.

Ron Mailer had excused himself from going out for a drink with some of the court personnel. It was unlike him to be antisocial, but he felt that he needed just a little time to himself that afternoon. He drove to a quiet, out-of-the-way bar he knew and relaxed in the cool, air-conditioned darkness. He ordered a double Scotch and soda, drank it down quickly, then ordered a second. Ron Mailer was not a drinking man, and the second drink took him a little longer to consume. That was all right. He needed a little time to sort some things out.

There was something about Criley that rang a bell in Ron Mailer's mind, a flash of recognition, a glimmer of understanding. Maybe it was something he had said, a gesture, a look in the eye, even, but Mailer was sure he had the key to understanding his client. It was just on the tip of his tongue, an idea, a memory, if he could only summon it from the depths of his unconscious. He knew it would be nothing that could help him with his case, just a personal clue to comprehending this incomprehensible person and the incomprehensible things he had done.

Mailer finished the drink, and he could feel the effect. Better slow down; he wasn't used to putting them down that fast. He ordered one more, a single shot, and munched on some peanuts placed in front of him.

His mind wandered back to when he was a Boy Scout, the camping trips, the hikes, the good times. The idyllic world of innocence, of energy to burn, of unfettered joy in being alive. He had been on his way to collecting quite a few merit badges, he remembered. How many he wasn't sure, but quite a few. He had been very much interested in nature, in animals, collecting all sorts of pets, studying them and their habits. Mailer had spent several boyhood summers in south Texas, near the Mexican border, and most of his nature study had been in the desert—the great, hot, dusty desert, where only the hardiest can make it.

And then the jigsaw in his mind fell into place, and he remembered how he had come to associate Lee Criley with a childhood experience. It had taken place in the desert. Young Ron had been hunting lizards, alone, when he was maybe thirteen or fourteen years old. And he remembered the rattlesnake he had surprised, and how he had pinned the snake's head to the ground with his forked stick. It was a big snake, and he remembered how the fat, muscular body had squirmed and writhed in rage. He had looked down at the snake's head, and the slitted reptilian eyes looked right back at him, hating him, beckoning him, the sharp fangs curving out at him from the silent, deadly, gaping mouth. Ron Mailer had the snake pinned, but that was all. He couldn't reach a rock big enough to kill it, he couldn't maneuver it into his lizard bag, and if he let go, he was sure the snake would attack him. He must have held the snake for a quarter of an hour, terrified of what would happen if he let it go.

Finally, out of sheer desperation, thirteen-year-old Ron Mailer pushed the stick as far into the ground as it would go, and then he ran. He ran faster than he had ever run in his life, sure that if he slowed up just a bit the snake would have him, would sink its fangs into his leg, filling him with murderous venom. After that, Ron Mailer never went back into the desert.

And that was what Lee Criley brought back to him. Lee Criley was the snake all over again. Pure poison.

Ron Mailer paid for his drinks, left a good tip, and went home.

16

■ Bud Lepak was twelve years old. In less than four months he would be thirteen, a teenager, and he was looking forward to the age and the change of status he was sure would go with it. At twelve years old, you're a kid, nobody cares what you think, but once you get into the teens, you're part of the world. People listen to you. Bud Lepak had high hopes for his teen years.

It was a hot summer afternoon, and he and his brother Joel were off to see what they could catch at the lake. Fishing was good at the lake but, unfortunately, it was illegal. Bud had found a little spot where he could fish in reasonable security as long as he didn't make too much noise. Today he was taking his brother along with him. It wasn't altogether by choice; Mrs. Lepak had made it clear that Bud wasn't going anywhere that day unless he took Joel with him. Joel was nine, but even Bud had to admit he was a likable, alert kid. You didn't have to repeat something a million times before Joel understood it. He could be trusted to keep the fishing place a secret and to keep his mouth shut while they were there. Maybe it wasn't such a bad idea having the kid along. If you stopped to think about it, he was more dependable than a lot of the older kids.

Joel Lepak was on top of the world. His greatest joy in life was to be with his brother Bud. Bud knew everything; Bud could do everything; and somehow, when Bud was around, exciting, magical things happened. Joel was unashamedly thrilled with the idea of spending the afternoon with his big brother, doing something his brother liked to do. He made up his mind he would be no trouble. He wouldn't make Bud sorry he had taken him along.

The two brothers walked in the midafternoon sun, balancing their fishing poles, Bud carrying a pail and a small can of worms in his left hand.

"How do you think they're running today, Bud?"

"I don't know. Pretty good, I hear."

"Can you catch enough to eat?"

"Hope so."

"Boy, we better not catch too many, and drop 'em *all* on Mom. Remember how mad she was that time you and Hank cleaned all them fish on the back porch?"

"This time we'll clean the fish right at the lake. That way, we won't make any mess."

"You got a knife, Bud?"

Bud pulled out a jackknife with a four-inch blade from his pocket. It was sharp, with a serrated edge for scaling.

"Wow! Let me see, Bud."

The older boy put the knife back in his pocket. "Mom'd kill me if I let you touch this thing."

They were out of the residential section now, about a half mile from the lake. The two boys kept to the right-hand side of the road, facing away from oncoming traffic, in order to stay in the shade as much as possible. It was going to be a real hot one.

Joel was the first to notice the car cruising slowly behind them. It was a white Chevy, dirty, and beat-up. He could see that it was driven by a smiling T-shirted boy. There was no way of telling how long the car had been following them like that.

"Hey, Bud. Somebody's calling you."

Bud turned around and squinted into the windshield. The glass was dirty and the morning sun reflected directly off it. He couldn't quite see the driver, only a slender, suntanned arm waving to him from the open window on the driver's side.

"Hey, Bud. Where ya goin'?"

It was a familiar voice, but Bud couldn't place it. He didn't know many boys who drove cars.

"Who is it?"

"It's me, Lee. Who'd you think it was, your girlfriend or somethin'?"

"Hi. Hi, Lee." Bud remembered Lee Criley from a year or so back. He used to live in the neighborhood but he hadn't been around for a while. He never hung around with Lee much, although a lot of his friends did. He could have, he supposed, even though Lee was several years older. But Bud was more interested in playing baseball or fishing, things Lee and his cronies considered kid stuff.

"Where are you guys going?"

"Down to the lake."

"Better watch out nobody catches you. It's against the law to fish there, you know."

"We'll be careful."

"Yeah, you better. Hey, what do you think of this car? Pretty hot stuff, huh?"

"Yeah, it's nice, Lee. Is it yours?" Bud wasn't sure how long he should continue this conversation. He and Lee had never had a conversation this long before, and he didn't know why Lee would want to start one now. However, Lee was older and bigger, and Bud didn't want to risk offending him. "Is it yours?"

"Sort of. A friend of mine lets me use it whenever I want. Want a lift?"

"No thanks. We just got a little way to go."

"Who's that? Your little brother? Hey, shorty, you want a ride, don't you? You don't want to do all that walking on those little legs of yours, do you?"

Joel flushed, embarrassed. He didn't know what to say; he looked to his brother for help.

"He don't mind walking, Lee. Thanks, but we'll be all right."

"Hey, no trouble, fella. I'm going down that way anyway." He leaned over and opened the door on the passenger side. "C'mon, get in. What are you scared of? Nobody's going to bite you. You'll get there before the fish do. What do you say?"

Bud Lepak shrugged and moved to the car. He motioned for his brother to follow him.

"That's right, hop in. Just throw that fishing stuff in the back seat."

The door slammed and the car roared off into the flow of traffic.

Lee seemed very excited. Bud couldn't be sure, but he thought Lee might have been using drugs or something. It was hard to tell with Lee, because even when Bud knew him a year ago, he often acted strangely.

"This your brother, Buddy? Didn't you say that?"

"Yeah."

"What do you know? Last time I seen him he must have been wearing diapers, you know that? And now here he is, a real cute kid. Ain't that right? You're a real cute kid, aren't you?" Lee grinned at Joel. The boy blushed and said nothing. There was something new in Lee's voice now, something that Bud Lepak had never heard. There was a shrill note to it, an edge that threatened to go out of control. Bud knew he shouldn't have gotten into that car.

They had just come to the cutoff where a dirt road led to the lake, but instead of pulling over Lee kept going straight on the main road, increasing his speed.

"Hey, Lee, where you going? Let us off, will ya?"

"Don't worry, crybaby. There's something I want to get at a friend's house. It won't take a minute. Then I'll take you right back to your fish, okay?"

"But why? Why can't we get out here?"

"If I let you out here, you'll still have to walk a long way, won't you? Don't sweat it, will ya? We'll be back in a minute."

Bud considered jumping out of the car, but he couldn't leave his brother behind. His mother would kill him if that happened, and for some reason he was more worried for his brother than he was for himself. There was something about the way Lee was looking at Joel.

Lee took a left off the main road and went down Letney for just two blocks. He took a hard right on Westfield and pulled up near the curb. They were in front of a small three-room bungalow, run-down but with a big air conditioner buzzing in a front window. Just beyond the bungalow was a huge excavation site and the beginning of the foundation of a large building. A sign indicated that a new twelve-story apartment building was being erected on that spot. The air was filled with the sound of jackhammers, generators, and trucks. Hard-hatted laborers, their backs glistening in the sun, moved about the excavation pit. Bud Lepak breathed an almost audible sigh of relief.

Joel called out, "Hey, Bud, look where we are."

"Yeah, Joel, I see."

"What are you guys talking about? Where do you think you are?"

For a reason that even he did not understand, Bud tried to keep his brother from speaking out. But it was too late. The words came rushing out of his younger brother's mouth, a mixture of relief and enthusiasm. "It's our dad. This is where our dad works. He takes us here to show us the work he's doing here."

Lee Criley was visibly shaken by this information. He stopped short. "Your dad? Is he here now?"

"Sure. Look, Bud. There he is. Dad! Hey, Dad!" The shouts of the younger boy were lost in the noise of the construction going on around them. The man at whom they were directed, busy supervising the loading of some cinder blocks, did not respond to the shout. William Lepak did not hear his son call out.

"Ah, what do you want to bother him for? Look, as long your old man's right here, why don't you come in for a minute?"

Lee Criley bounded out of the car and opened the door for the two boys. A look of invitation and confidence was back on his face.

"I don't know, Lee. We're in a hurry."

"It won't be a minute. Your father's right here. What's to worry about?"

Bud shrugged his shoulders and got out of the car, his younger brother following. Just before they went into the bungalow Lee Criley had brought them to, Bud Lepak glanced once more at his father. Mr. Lepak's back was turned. He did not see the screen door, and then the heavy wooden door, slam shut behind his two sons.

Lee Criley led the two boys into a sparsely furnished living room. There was a ragged fold-out sofa, a coffee table with an empty beer can on it, and a small black-and-white television set. On the floor was a telephone. The two windows were shut tight and the shades were pulled. Although it was early afternoon, the room was almost completely dark.

"You guys sit here for a minute, will ya? I'll be right back. Just hang loose."

Lee walked through another door to what appeared to be a bedroom. It was so dark in the little bungalow that it was impossible to tell just where Lee was going. The door closed and the two boys were alone.

"I don't like it here, Bud."

"We'll be going soon. You heard what he said."

"I don't think Ma would like it if she knew we were here in this place."

"Can't you be quiet, for gosh sake? We'll be out of here and fishing before you know it. If you'll just shut up."

"I want to get out of here now."

His brother's fear was beginning to be infectious, but Bud

Lepak refused to panic. After all, he was going on thirteen, and a thirteen-year-old didn't run away from things that scared him.

"Sit down and be quiet like I told you, Joel. I mean it."

The younger boy sat quietly. As time passed, their eyes became accustomed to the darkness. The room was coming into sharper focus.

They waited. Still Lee Criley didn't return.

Another minute passed. Still nothing. "Do you think he just left us here, Bud? Do you think he just took off and didn't tell us?"

Bud felt more and more uneasy. "Nah, he wouldn't do that. But just to make you happy, let's go out and talk to Dad. Then we can come back and get a ride to the lake. How's that?"

The two boys got up and were moving toward the door when the room exploded behind them. The bedroom door crashed open, and suddenly the room was full of activity and shouting and grunting. For a split second Bud caught sight of Lee wrestling Joel to the floor. But that was all. There was nothing else in the flurry of noise and confusion that he could make out.

Bud felt a great weight pressing in on him, then a sharp pain in the back of his head. Something covered his face, something cold and wet, something that burned his nostrils and lungs. And then he was aware of nothing.

There was no way for Bud Lepak to tell how long he had been unconscious. When he awoke, the first thing he felt was the pain in his arms, especially his wrists. All his weight was suspended from his wrists, and something, a chain or a rope, was digging into the flesh. Both arms and both legs were spread out wide, immobile, and he was facing up against an upright board. His eyes darted about; he twisted his head as far as he could against the surface of the board. He couldn't yell out because his mouth was taped shut. And he knew that he was naked.

It was a game, that's what it was. It was some kind of game that Lee had thought up, like ring-a-lievio or capture the flag. Bud had never played any game where anybody was tied up the way he was, but Lee was one of the bigger kids, and maybe that was the way they played. He was stiff and cramped, and his wrists were hurting terribly, but he knew it had to be a game. He'd better just go along with it and not make Lee think he wasn't old enough to play a game like this. That might make Lee do something even worse.

He wondered about Joel. Joel was certainly going to be all scared and maybe even start crying or something. Joel was really too small to play anything like this. He wouldn't understand at all. But Lee would see that. He would see that Bud was older and stronger and might be able to play a game like this, but Joel just couldn't hack it. Lee would see that and he'd let Joel go. Of course, that's what must have happened. Joel was probably outside with his father, or maybe he even went all the way home. It would be just like that kid to walk all the way home. Then his mother and father would ask where Bud was, and Joel would stall for a while, but sooner or later he'd tell them. And that meant he wouldn't be staying tied up to this board much longer. Either Lee would have to let him go and call it quits on this game or his father would come busting in and take him home.

Knowing that he'd have to be set free in a little while, Bud Lepak felt better. He understood the situation, and he could handle it as well as anyone his age, or even older. Still, there was something wrong here. There was no sound in the room. Had he been left alone here? Had Lee taken him somewhere else when he had lost consciousness?

Fear overcame him in a great rush. He wished with all his heart that his father would come in and untie him and take him home. He felt tears roll down his face. He wanted to go home. Any minute now, any second, and his father would be there. Right *now*!

There was only silence. He would count to three, and in three seconds his father would be there to take him home. One, two, three! No sound.

All right, then. His father was just walking toward the door now. In ten seconds he would be inside. He would count slowly and give his father plenty of time. One, two, three, four, five, six, seven, eight, nine . . . nine and a half, nine and three quarters, ten!

Silence.

All right, then, he would give his father one more chance. This time he would be sure to give him enough time. This time he knew his father would be there; he prayed with all his might that his father would be there. He wouldn't rush things, he would count very slowly, very carefully, and this time he would count to twenty-five. He would count slowly all the way up to twenty-five, and then, for sure, his father would be there. No need to rush. Take it easy, and then begin to count slowly.

He took deep, slow breaths, as deep as he could, breathing through his nose since his mouth was taped. He reached twenty-five. And his father did not appear.

Once more. One last time. Oh, please, please, Dad. I want to go home now. Please come. If I count hard enough, then you'll come. You're on the way now. You're coming up the steps. Just ten more seconds. Oh, please, please come this time.

One, two, three, four, five . . .

He thought he heard something. Was he here? Had his father finally come?

He twisted his head around, scraping his nose and cheeks against the board.

When he turned his head around, Bud Lepak saw the face of a monster, of a grinning, wide-eyed madman, the face only inches away from his own. The eyes were flashing in excitement, and Bud went dizzy with terror.

A scream of fear welled up from some primal source in the boy's being, from his very entrails, through the throat, and then resounded back on itself, held inside by the tape over his mouth. What came out was only a long, low guttural moan.

The monstrous face was saying something, the lips were moving and sounds were coming out, perhaps laughter, he couldn't be sure. Then he felt fingers on the side of his neck, probing, pinching, at last settling on strings of nerves, pulling them, tearing them. Pain shot through Bud Lepak's twelve-year-old body. Vomit exploded in his mouth, backed up, and dribbled out his nostrils.

A great, fleshy body was all over him, squeezing him, rubbing him. Hands and lips and teeth scurried over his body like spiders, enveloping him, covering him. Then there was something pulling him open, tearing him in two, and it pushed into him, invading, destroying, ripping him inside. It roared into him, huge and merciless, filling him with agony. And then, as the teeth clenched down on his shoulder, biting into the flesh, before he passed out again, he was filled with a burning pain that went deeper and deeper into him.

Minutes or perhaps hours later, he could feel hands on him again. They were untying him, setting him free. They would let him go home now. It was over.

His arms and legs were numb, and so when the locks were taken from his wrists and ankles, Bud fell in a lump to the floor. A strong, steel-like grip caught him under the arm, squeezing the tendons under the arm, and lifted his body as if it were weightless.

"Time to wake up, handsome. Time to wake up."

"Can I go home now? Please?" He was crying softly.

The man picked Bud off the floor and carried him like a baby in his arms.

"The little boy wants to go home? Isn't that cute. See how the little boy wants to go home. Isn't he the sweetest little boy you ever saw, Lee? Isn't he?"

"He sure is."

The man carried Bud to the sofa and sat down, cradling him in his arms. The slight, nude body was small and defenseless in the man's arms. Except for the sobs that would not stop, the boy made no sound. The man's blazing eyes continued to seek Bud's eyes, holding them hypnotically.

"What a sweet little baby boy. Why don't you give nice old Uncle Earl a great big kiss? Why don't you do that, hear?"

The man bent down and pressed his mouth against the boy's.

He pressed his face down hard, at the same time bringing the boy's body up closer with his powerful arms. Bruised and torn from the treatment it had sustained, the inside of the boy's mouth was puffy with pain. The man's tongue forced its way inside the mouth, twisting and searching like a snake.

The man pulled away. His eyes blazed wildly. His face was smeared with blood from Bud's mouth.

"Did I hear you correctly? Did you say that you wanted to go home? Is that what you said before?"

Bud nodded, his face contorted with fear.

"Well, now, why didn't you say so? I didn't know you wanted to go home. You should have said something earlier. Now, just to show you what nice guys we are here, we're going to let you call your mommy and daddy. See how nice we are? Wouldn't you like to do that?"

Bud was overcome with relief. At last it would be over. At last he could call his parents and it would be all over.

"You really mean it?"

"Of course I mean it. I wouldn't fool you, would I? I don't look like the kind of guy who'd fool somebody, do I?"

Bud shook his head. His body continued to shake from the sobbing.

"All right, then. Don't worry. Uncle Earl and Uncle Lee are going to take care of everything." The man picked up the telephone, still holding Bud on his lap. "There, now. You can remember your telephone number, can't you? A big smart boy like you. What's your number?"

"Three-four-seven-two-eight-nine-one."

The man dialed the number, repeating each digit under his breath. He held the phone to his ear and waited for perhaps fifteen seconds. The click on the other end of the wire told Bud that someone had picked it up. The man held his hand over the receiver, whispering to Bud.

"Now, you tell your mommy you're all right, hear me? Tell her how good we're treating you."

And he handed Bud the phone.

At first he was unable to speak. His voice stopped in his

throat, and he just held the phone close to his ear. A female voice at the other end echoed in his ear.

"Hello? Hello? Who is this? Hello?"

It was his mother. It was really her after all. They weren't fooling him. He would be going home. Bud Lepak could no longer control his tears. The sobs turned to great cries from the bottom of his heart.

"Momma, it's me. It's me, Bud, Momma. Momma, I want to come home."

"Bud, where are you? Where have you been? Are you all right, Bud? Bud, what's the matter?"

The man covered the receiver again. "Tell her you're all right. Tell her nothing's the matter."

Bud continued to cry. "I'm all right, Mom. Nothing's the matter. I'm all right."

"Bud, where are you? Are you with Joel? Bud, for God's sake, what's wrong with you?"

The man covered the receiver once more. "Tell her we need some money. Tell her she won't ever see you again unless she comes up with five thousand dollars. Tell her she better have five thousand dollars or else."

"They want money, Momma. They say they want five thousand dollars."

"Who wants five thousand dollars? Buddy, tell me, are you all right? Is anybody hurting you?"

"Oh, Momma, Momma. They hurt me, Momma. They hurt me so bad. Please come and get me, Momma."

"Give me that fuckin' phone, you little cocksucker!" The man grabbed the phone and slammed it back on the receiver. "You talk too much, you know that, you goddam little cocksucker?"

He picked Bud up by the shoulders and threw him onto the floor, his head hitting the wooden board from which he had just been released. The man's eyes raged as he stood over him, and he kicked Bud in the legs and buttocks. "You goddam little cocksucker, you better learn to do what I tell you in here. You think your momma's gonna come and get you? Well, just forget it, sonny-boy. You aren't going to see your momma ever again. This is the last stop for you. Do you understand me? You're never going to see your little old momma again."

A long low moan issued from Bud's throat. It was soft, almost musical, and it had a strange effect on the man standing over him.

"Hey, come on, don't feel so sad. Come on, now." The man bent down, kneeling over Bud's body, caressing him gently.

"Hey, don't cry. It isn't all that bad. Don't you be sad." And the caresses built up in intensity. The hands roamed all over the small body, tenderly at first, then harder, touching him all over. And again, the body of the man enveloped the boy. He lay still, yielding, suffering the terrible obscene pain silently as the man penetrated him once more. He lost consciousness again.

Bud awoke cuffed to the board once more, but this time his back was to the board and he was facing the empty room. He was alone. The tape on his mouth prevented him from calling out.

It was very hot in the room. The air conditioner had been turned off. Bud figured it must be nighttime, but there was no way of telling. He was hot and thirsty, and his body ached. He slipped in and out of a nightmare, never sure exactly which was nightmare and which was reality.

He saw his mother come into the room, a look of calm concern on her face, carrying a glass of water. He tried to call to her, to tell her to stay with him, but he could make no sound, and she disappeared again. He saw the lake where he had been taking Joel fishing, and he sat in the cool shade of the tree as he and his brother pulled fish after fish out of the clear, fresh water. His father walked by, dressed in his heavy work clothes and construction boots. He waved as he went by.

The minutes and hours passed by. At first his body was drenched with sweat from the heat of the room. And then the sweat simply stopped coming. He was still hot, still aching for water, but the sweat stopped rolling off him. And then he drifted into blackness. There were no more visions.

He came to when the tape was being ripped away from his mouth. The skin around his mouth was torn, and some ripped away with the tape. Except for the blood that started to flow again, his mouth was completely dry. His tongue felt swollen and sandy.

Lee was standing in front of him. What was Lee doing here? What was he going to do to him?

"Hey, Buddy. You look dried out. How about some water?"

Lee walked out and came back in a moment, carrying with him a glass of tap water. He held it to Bud's lips, tilting the glass gently so that he could drink. The water was lukewarm and the glass was dirty, but to Bud it was life. He felt strength come back to him as he gulped down the water, and his head began to clear. With his regained lucidity the pain in his body became more intense.

"Not so fast. Don't drink it all at once."

"Can you let us go pretty soon, Lee? Me and my brother have to be going home. My folks will kill us."

"Well, no, I don't think so."

"Please, Lee. If you let us go, we'll never tell anybody. Honest. I promise."

"Can't do it."

In spite of his words, there was something reassuring about the way Lee was talking to him now. At least he wasn't the crazy man who had hurt him last night, or whenever it was. For a while Bud wondered if he might have imagined everything that had happened. But there he was, handcuffed to the board. His body was stiff and aching, and the torn tissues reminded him only too painfully that he had not imagined anything. Yet here was Lee, talking to him almost normally. Maybe he and his brother would be going home soon.

"Lee, where's my brother? Can I see him?"

Lee had sat down on the sofa and was lighting a cigarette. He was calm and relaxed. He kept his eyes lazily on Bud, smiling at the corners of his mouth.

"Joel? I don't guess you'll be able to see him any more."

"Why, Lee? Did you let him go home already? Is he all right?"

Lee laughed. "Hell, no, we didn't let him go. We killed his little ass."

Bud couldn't believe what he heard. "You didn't do that! C'mon, Lee, where is he? You let him go home, right?"

"Nope. I strangled him. It wasn't easy either, you know that? A lot of people think it's easy to strangle people, even a little kid like your brother. Well, believe me, it isn't. Took me a goddam long time."

Just at that point, the older man came in. He was dressed only in tight, faded dungarees. His chest was bare. Bud gazed up at the muscular arms and chest, not daring to look as far up as the eyes. He was sick with terror.

"What the hell's the matter with him?"

"I don't know, Earl. I told him I strangled his brother and he started puking."

The man walked to Bud and lifted his face up by the hair. He looked closely into his eyes, and then let the head fall limply down.

"No reason to keep this one any more, is there?"

"No, Earl. You want me to finish him off?"

"Yeah."

Tears started to roll down Bud Lepak's cheeks. He looked pleadingly at Lee.

"Don't kill me, Lee. Please don't kill me. I won't tell anybody, ever. Please, Lee, don't kill me."

The muscular man looked at Bud in disgust and left the room. When Bud looked back at Lee he saw a small pistol in his hand. The pistol was pointed directly at Bud's head.

"Lee, please. I promise."

"Bye-bye, Buddy Boy."

The gun exploded and a small round hole appeared in the center of Bud Lepak's forehead. His head dropped forward, and he was still.

Lee placed the gun on the table and lit another cigarette. He walked to the air conditioner and turned it up to its coldest setting.

He shouted above the noise of the air conditioner, "Hey, Earl. Earl, you in there?"

Harmen replied from the other room, "What do you want?"

"When you wanna clean up this mess? It's gonna get pretty hot today. We can't leave 'em here too long."

Harmen came into the room. He looked for an instant at the inert body of the boy, still cuffed to the board, then came to the window.

"Wait till tonight. We'll take them out to the boat shed after dark. See if you can find Hesler and he can help bury them."

"Okay."

Then, suddenly, eerily, the head of the boy raised up. His eyes gazed far off at some point beyond the confines of the room.

Lee Criley snapped around. "Jesus Christ! Will you look at that? That kid ain't dead. I shot him in the head and he ain't dead. I'll be a son of a bitch!"

Earl Harmen grabbed the gun from the table and held it to the boy's temple. He fired and the boy's head dropped to his chest.

He did not move again.

17

■ Lee Criley was doing what is referred to in prison terminology as laying up, doing time behind bars after arrest and before sentencing. It is a limbo period and in many jails, because of the increased edginess and tension men feel during this period, the pretrial prisoners are kept in different facilities from the sentenced prisoners. For a number of reasons, Lee Criley was not subject to the same anxieties as other prisoners who were similarly laying up.

First, Criley was kept segregated from the entire jail population, both the pretrial and the sentenced prisoners. As a result, he was not subject to the constant jailhouse chatter about lawyers, court dates, and statutes. There were, in fact, extended periods when he didn't think about his legal situation at all. Second, Criley did not expect to see the light of day as a free man ever again. It was difficult to tell just when he had come to this conclusion. Perhaps he knew it when his lawyer quashed his elation over the ruling that he had killed Earl Harmen in self-defense. Perhaps, on a deeper level, he had sensed the inevitability of his destiny long ago. At any rate, Lee Criley had resigned himself to being a caged bird. He did not expect things to change when he finally stood before the judge for sentencing.

The only visitors Lee Criley received were his mother and his attorney. The visits from his attorney were infrequent and uneventful. There would be no further legal proceedings until the question of the admissibility of the confessions had been decided, so in the interim there were no pressing matters to discuss. The visits from his mother were more frequent, twice weekly, but were painful for both of them. They would sit facing each other through a glass partition, Lee tense and uncomfortable, his mother constantly on the verge of tears. Then they would try to make small talk. The visits were always abysmal failures. Both wished they could stop the pretense; and neither could.

Then, one day, Lee made a request of his mother that made her gasp for joy. It was the one thing she had allowed herself to hope and pray for, the one thing her son could do to make his mother happy.

Lee Criley asked if Reverend Denning could come to see him and talk about Jesus.

It was a great day in the life of Emma Criley. At last, at last, her boy seemed as if he might be seeking salvation. She left New Haven County Jail on that day breathless and excited and went directly to the First Church of Christ, where she had a brief talk with the Reverend Wilton Denning, telling him of her son's request. The minister was only too glad to be of help, he said. He assured Mrs. Criley that he would make arrangements to see Lee as soon as possible.

Mrs. Criley went home that night, and for the first time in

more than six months she felt a sense of tranquility and relief. She prayed, as always, before she went to sleep, and thanked God for finally coming to Lee. For the first time in all those months, Emma Criley fell asleep immediately, without tossing and turning for hours.

As a member of the clergy, it was easy for Wilton Denning to arrange a visit with Lee. He did not have to wait for the regular visiting hours, but was allowed to come and go pretty much as he pleased. The first two or three visits with Lee were short and tentative. Denning did not want to pressure this young man who had called for help from the Lord, and at the same time he did want to make available to him any kind of help he would accept. After the first few visits, however, the two spent more and more time together. They sat and read over passages in the Bible, they conversed in low, intimate tones. From time to time, the two could be seen kneeling, praying together.

It became apparent that, at some basic level, Lee Criley and the Reverend Wilton Denning had quickly become very important to each other. Denning was soon devoting more of his time to counseling Lee Criley than he was to his parish responsibilities. As for Lee, while there were certainly no real demands on his time, he spent every free moment either with the minister or reading his Bible. The relationship between them continued, quietly and steadily. And Lee Criley continued to pray and read the Bible in his lonely cell.

On March 21, 1973, the headlines of the southern Connecticut papers announced the newest and certainly most significant development in the mass murder case. One headline told all: CONFESSIONS RULED ADMISSIBLE.

After weeks of preliminary hearings, motions, conferences in chambers, Judge Birdsell had finally announced his ruling that the confessions made by Lee Criley and Otis Hesler concerning their activities in the case could and would be used as evidence in any upcoming trial. He had decided that both defendants had been warned of their legal rights to keep silent and to counsel, that no duress had been used to extract the confessions, and that both defendants were in posession of their faculties at the time they made the statements. It was a ruling that sealed their fate.

Lee Criley's attorney, Ron Mailer, noted Lee's peculiar lack of emotion when he was told about it. If Lee understood what it meant, as he claimed he did, he gave no indication. It may have been that Criley had simply lost interest in the complicated issues surrounding his trial. It was, Ron Mailer thought, as if someone had told Lee that it appeared he just might have to pay that traffic ticket after all.

Then another legal question began to be seriously dealt with by the lawyers: the death penalty.

In the state of Connecticut, the death penalty could be invoked only in a few special cases, such as when a police officer was killed, when murder was committed by someone hired to commit it for pecuniary gain, or in the course of a kidnaping. Harry MacNamara told Ron Mailer that, in spite of the kidnaping aspect, he would not seek the death penalty if the defendant were to plead guilty to the six charges of murder. In exchange for guilty pleas, he would ask only for a life sentence.

Ron Mailer did not accept. He concluded that it would be impossible for the State to establish the kind of situation needed for the death penalty—for kidnaping was, in law, very narrowly defined. After a brief conference with his client, Mailer stated that pleas of not guilty would be entered in response to all charges, and that a trial by jury would be requested. Mark Lescombe, Otis Hesler's attorney, submitted motions for an indefinite continuance on the grounds that Criley's trial would be prejudicial to his client's interests.

Through it all Lee Criley sat in his lonely cell, visiting occasionally with the Reverend Denning, poring over his Bible, and sometimes, head bowed, eyes closed, just moving his lips silently.

18

■ Something was naggingly wrong about the Fourth of July weekend in 1972. It wasn't anything specific, nothing you could put your finger on; it was more like a continuing series of events that just weren't going right for Earl Harmen. Harmen was usually careful and meticulous; he appreciated things that went along correctly, smoothly, with the grain. And yet, in spite of preplanning, in spite of his attention to detail, he could sense that things were working against him, and it was an irritating, uncomfortable sensation that he didn't like.

Of all the holidays, he had always liked the Fourth of July the best, primarily because of the fireworks. He had never actually used any himself, but he liked to watch the displays that were put up by the fire departments of the various cities he had been in. And because, as a boy, he'd never had the fun of a family outing on the Fourth, he liked the idea of a jovial, happy-go-lucky cookout with hot dogs and hamburgers and potato salad and beer. On the Fourth of July it was good to sip a can of cold beer and watch the sky light up in bright colorful explosions.

His Aston Street home was just right for a cookout. There was a long, grassy backyard, separated from the few neighbors by a small grove of trees. There was a picnic table and even a stone fireplace. Not a metal charcoal grill, but a real outdoor fireplace. And so Harmen invited Otis Hesler and Lee Criley for an evening cookout and then a drive to see the fireworks. He even mentioned to Lee that it might be a good idea to see if he could find somebody else to bring along, somebody who might perhaps be talked into spending the night.

The first thing that backfired was that Earl found out he would have to work on the morning of the fifth. He had requested this day off weeks previously, but his supervisor had simply forgotten to make a note of it, and Earl was scheduled to work. There was no way out.

This meant that the cookout would have to break up early, that he wouldn't be able to watch the fireworks, and that any extra fun for the evening would have to be interrupted. It was the way things happened when you depended on somebody else. There was only one way to be sure, and that was to do it yourself. He had been stupid enough to depend on somebody else, and he would have to suffer for it. Son of a bitch, he'd like to kill that stupid supervisor of his.

The anger remained, bubbling up every now and then throughout the rest of the day. It wasn't an anger that expressed itself; it was simply there, in Earl Harmen's eyes, in the tension in his arms, in his stomach.

He had already spent the money for the food and beer, so there was no sense in calling it off. He could never eat all that food by himself. Like it or not, the cookout would go on.

The weather on the third of July only served to increase

Earl's growing moodiness and anger. All week long the weather had been pleasant and comfortable, almost springlike; on the third the sky hung low and bleak, and from time to time there was a drizzle, increasing the oppressiveness in the air and in Harmen's mood.

Otis' girlfriend was taking up more and more of his time, and occasionally it looked as if he might break free of his involvement with Earl and Lee. But he knew that it was important to Earl that he be at this cookout, and despite Sharon's protestations he decided to go. Perhaps, if Otis had known the kind of hostility he would encounter, if he had known how close Earl was to total loss of control, perhaps he would not have come.

He arrived at the house at 3030 Aston at seven o'clock. He knocked on the front door, waited a moment, and walked in. The three rooms were empty, and Otis Hesler walked on through to the backyard. Harmen was stooping over the barbecue pit, about fifty feet away from the back door. He stood alone under the New England clouds.

"Hi, Earl. What do you say?"

Harmen looked up. He focused on Otis, then glanced around behind him. He turned back to the charcoal fire without a word. Otis walked toward him, his hands deep in his pockets.

"What's happening, man?"

Harmen whipped around, looming over the startled youth. "'What's happening, man? What's happening, man?' Jesus fucking Christ, is that all you goddam kids can ever say? 'What's happening, man?' I'm trying to light this fucking fire, can't you see that, you cocksucking bastard? That's what's happening, man."

The flood of words was a shock to Otis. Earl Harmen never talked this way, never. Profanity was something he had always avoided. But what was much more frightening to Otis was the look on Harmen's face. He had seen that look before, many times, but he had never seen it directed at him. It was a look of murderous ferocity. Otis Hesler's blood ran cold.

He had no idea how to respond. He stood paralyzed, blinking like a jackrabbit caught suddenly in the lights of an oncoming car. He wasn't ready for this at all.

Earl Harmen turned away just as suddenly, his anger changing to contempt. He poked at the burning bits of charcoal.

"Ah, forget it. Go get yourself a beer. There's a bunch in that cooler over there."

Otis did as he was told. He popped open the beer and then stood quietly to one side, giving Harmen plenty of room. He didn't know whether to try to start a conversation again, whether he should help with the fire or just leave the man alone. What he did was simply to stand there, eyes down, always aware of where Harmen was.

The two were silent for almost five minutes before Harmen spoke.

"You see Lee today?"

"Uh, no, Earl, I didn't. I guess he ought to be here pretty soon, though. You know how Lee is sometimes."

"He said he was going to bring someone along with him."

"Yeah? Fine, Earl. Real fine."

"I'd just like to know where the hell he is right now, that's all."

"He'll be by, Earl. Lee always is."

"So you tell me. Here. How about trying a hamburger?"

"Great. Thanks. I could eat a horse. No kidding. Thanks a lot."

"I can cook it a little more for you if you want."

"No. This is perfect. Just the way I like it."

"Look, I guess I was a little snappy with you back there. Don't pay it any attention, hear?"

Otis laughed, but the nervousness was still in his voice. "No sweat, Earl. You got a right to get touchy if you want to, just like anybody else. I don't mind."

"I just wonder where the hell Lee is, that's all."

They sat across from each other at the picnic table. Otis ate voraciously in spite of his uneasiness. As usual, Harmen ate little, munching on one hamburger and sipping the same beer for almost half an hour. It was obvious to both of them that there was really nothing to say to each other. In spite of all they had experienced together, there was now nothing for the two to talk about while they waited for their mutual friend. It was a thought that irritated Earl Harmen and frightened Otis Hesler.

The screen door behind Otis screeched open and slammed shut. Without turning around, just from observing the change in Earl's expression, he knew that Lee had arrived. And he knew that Lee had brought someone with him.

"Where the hell you been, Lee? What took you so long? Come on over and sit, for God's sake. Have something to eat. And who's your handsome buddy?"

Lee came over, staggering just a bit. He was already high on something. Otis guessed it was amphetamines, but he couldn't be sure.

With him, just a pace or two behind, shy and blushing, was a red-haired, freckle-faced boy of thirteen or fourteen. He wore the uniform of the local boys: sneakers, blue jeans, and T-shirt. Lee Criley pushed the boy forward, clumsily, toward Earl Harmen.

"This here is Smiley, ain't that right, Smiley? At least that's what I call him 'cause he's always smiling. Smiley's the smilingest dude in the state of Connecticut, ain't you, Smiley? I said, ain't you, Smiley?"

The boy looked at his feet in embarrassment. "I guess so, Lee."

"Smiley here says he'd like to come to our party and have himself a little fun. Right, Smiley? Says how he'd like to see what a real wild, grown-up party is like. Smiley's my main man. Ain't that right, Smiley?"

Earl sat up, his mood obviously elevated. "Hey, don't be so rough on him, Lee. How are you, Smiley? My name's Earl. Glad to have you. Come over here and sit by me, and have some of these hamburgers. You're too young for beer, aren't you? Don't worry about that. Otis, get Smiley here a short beer, will you? Smiley and I are going to be real good friends, I can tell that."

The four of them sat and the boys gorged themselves on the

food Earl Harmen had provided. Harmen focused all his attention on the boy, while Otis was relieved that Harmen was no longer interested in him, that the incredible anger that had momentarily surfaced was no longer in evidence. Lee was in a world of his own, laughing and giggling at nothing, chattering constantly, and generally ignoring the others.

The gloominess Earl Harmen had experienced earlier had almost dissipated. It was turning out to be a good party after all. The weather was bad, things would have to be rushed somewhat so that he could get to work in a few hours, but the boy Lee had brought made up for everything. A pleasant, happy, handsome boy, the kind of boy that seemed so hard to find in this depressing area. It was turning out to be a damn good party.

The boy was not used to drinking beer, and not only did he feel tipsy right away but he began running to the bathroom. Earl Harmen was thoroughly amused by the staggering boy's attempts to hold it as long as he could before he was forced to race for the back door of the cottage. Otis and Lee paid little attention.

During one of the boy's trips to the bathroom a gray Pontiac station wagon pulled up in front of the house. At first no one noticed it, but a door slammed and an attractive woman in her early thirties walked up to the edge of the backyard. As Otis Hesler was the closest to her, she spoke to him.

"Excuse me, but is this where Mr. Harmen lives?"

The woman had a soft, lovely voice. Otis was immediately captivated by it, and by the woman's striking good looks.

"Yes, ma'am, it is."

"Someone told me he saw my son coming into this place with another boy. Ordinarily I wouldn't bother him, but we're going to his grandmother's tonight, and he should be coming with us. I wonder if he's here."

Harmen watched the conversation. His face was frozen, expressionless. Lee Criley saw Harmen's face and instantly recognized the danger signal. He quietly moved away to a corner of the backyard.

Otis Hesler was not aware of the expression on Harmen's face. If he had been, he might not have responded to the woman as he did. Instead, however, he was spellbound by her laughing blue eyes, her red hair, and the faint cloud of perfume that surrounded her.

"Well, what's his name, ma'am?"

"His name is Ronald. Ronald Ashten. Is he here?"

"There's a boy here, ma'am, but I don't know his name. About thirteen or fourteen years old? About that age?"

"Yes, yes, that's right. I knew he'd be here. Where is he now?"

"Oh, he just went to the bathroom for a minute. He'll be right out."

At that instant the screen door swung open, and the boy's face flashed recognition, disappointment, and then embarrassment.

"Ronald, you'll have to say goodbye to your friends. We're going to Granny's tonight."

"Aw, Ma, do I have to? I'm having a good time here."

"Yes, you have to." She turned to Otis. "Thank you very much, young man. I'm sure Ronald will be able to come back again sometime. Come on now, Ronald."

The boy shrugged his shoulders and followed his mother to the car.

Before he turned around, before his eyes made contact with the eyes of Earl Harmen, Otis Hesler realized he had made a terrible, possibly fatal, mistake. A knot of fear formed in his stomach. His throat went dry. Oh, Jesus, God, why had he done it? Why had he let that kid just walk away like that? Why hadn't he lied to the mother? Oh, Jesus, God, what would Earl do to him? His mouth went slack, his lips turned blubbery, and tears rolled down his pale cheeks. Mechanically, like a robot who has no choice about his own actions, Otis Hesler turned to face Earl Harmen. From his corner in the backyard, Lee Criley, now alert to what was going on, watched quietly, intently.

Harmen's voice was subdued and low but it quivered in the steady, concentrated timbre of a man bent on nothing less than murder.

"Are you trying to fuck me up?"

"No, Earl. Honest, I . . ."

"You're trying to fuck me up, aren't you?"

Otis Hesler was crying. Harmen advanced toward him, eyes wide, the muscles on his neck tense and pulsating.

"Earl, please. I wasn't thinking. I'm sorry, Earl, there was nothing I could've done."

Closer and closer he came. Otis stood paralyzed, frozen in terror of this man he had known for so long. He knew that now . . . now it was his turn. And that there was no escape.

"I'm going to kill your ass, you bastard."

He was almost up to him, and his hands, those strong, powerful, murderer's hands, were reaching out for his throat.

Somehow, from some hidden recesses of his being, from some vestigial instinct for survival, the will to break loose, to run away and to live, rose up in Otis Hesler.

He ran as he had only once before—the day he had first discovered Earl Harmen's fearful secret. The tears streamed down his face. His heart pounded. He ran away from Harmen's outstretched hands, across the yard, over the fence, and down the tree-lined streets. He ran as long and as fast as his legs could carry him, and he swore to Almighty God that if he ever made it, if he ever really got away, he would never go near Earl Harmen again.

Harmen watched Otis Hesler escape from his grasp. He watched him run off, and he bellowed out his rage to the sky. He bellowed from the bottom of his stomach. He cried out his hatred and his murderous anger. He roared into the hot, muggy air like an enraged prehistoric monster watching his prey flutter away beyond his grasp. And with that great bellow, something changed permanently in Earl Harmen.

He stood there, a low, long moan coming from somewhere deep inside. His powerful fingers clenched and unclenched, and his blue eyes clouded over, unseeing, and in a strange, utterly different way, uncaring. Then, still moaning, he staggered into the house.

Lee Criley, who five minutes ago had been drinking heavily and had been under the influence of drugs, was now sober. His brain snapped into focus with the sharpness and clarity of a flash of sunshine. He saw Earl Harmen go out of control, and he knew that he would have to go to him right away. He knew that he would have to understand and respond to everything that was happening in Earl's mind, and that, if he didn't, the relationship that had become so important for him would be lost. In that instant, Criley realized that he was not an independent person. He was alive only to the extent to which he participated in the life of Earl Harmen.

It was a shocking realization, overwhelming in its intensity. Lee Criley sobered up, straightened up, and went to his friend Earl Harmen.

Criley found him in the living room, still moaning softly to himself. He was pacing rapidly, almost running around the room in large, counterclockwise circles. His eyes were focused on something Lee could not see.

"Hey, Earl. Take it easy, will ya? Sit down, will ya?"

If Earl Harmen heard what was said to him, he gave no indication. He kept pacing, moaning. Every once in a while he would kick out at a piece of furniture, but he never broke his heavy, long-legged stride.

"Hey, Earl. What's the matter? So a punk got away. What the fuck, man? Take it easy, will ya, for God's sake?"

Earl Harmen ignored Lee's entreaties. Instead, he seemed to retreat deeper and deeper into his own rage and hatred.

Lee had never really been afraid of Earl Harmen until this day. And yet he knew he would have to approach him, he would have to break through this sudden new barrier if he was still to be a part of Earl Harmen's life. He never stopped to ask himself why he had to be a part of Harmen's life. He only knew that he just had to.

Criley moved in front of Harmen's powerfully built frame, his own slender, unmuscled body even smaller by comparison, and he put his scrawny hand on the bigger man's shoulder. Earl Harmen stopped short. Then he focused on Lee Criley. Automatically, he raised his arms, his fingers moving slowly for Criley's throat.

"Earl, it's *me*! Don't you see that? What the fuck are you doing? You wouldn't hurt *me*, would you, Earl? Come on, old buddy, you wouldn't hurt *me*, would you?"

Earl Harmen stopped, blinking. A dim light of recognition flickered behind his eyes.

"What are you getting all pissed off for, man? We got lots of things we're gonna do together, ain't that right? We're gonna go places, get out of this crummy town, right, Earl? Remember how we got it all planned? So why are you gonna spoil it all and hurt me? You wouldn't do that, Earl. I know you wouldn't do that. What do you say?"

Harmen dropped his hands to his sides. "You're right. I'll be okay in a minute."

"Sure you will. Forget that asshole Hesler. We don't need an asshole like that. Just you and me, Earl. We'll stick together, just the two of us."

"Okay. But why don't you go home now? The party's over."

"Yeah, sure, Earl. Just so everything's still okay between you and me, you know what I mean? You wouldn't forget all that travelin' we were planning, would you? That's still on for you and me, isn't it?"

Earl Harmen was preoccupied, only marginally aware of the younger boy pumping him for answers. All he wanted was to be alone, to think some things out. "Traveling? Yes. That's still on."

"Great. That's what I wanted to know."

"All right then. How about going home now? I have to get to work pretty soon."

"Okay, Earl. Don't let that asshole get you down. I'll come by tomorrow. Maybe we can get something goin' by then. I'll see what I can find. How's that?"

At last Lee Criley left Harmen alone, secure in the knowledge that he had cleverly, even bravely, restored their relationship.

Earl Harmen sat in the growing darkness immobile, his arms resting limply on the arms of the chair. More than an hour passed before he got up and walked to the bathroom.

It was full dark in the little bungalow by then, and he stumbled once or twice, banging his shins painfully against the furniture. At last he reached the light switch outside the bathroom. He stepped inside and stood at the sink, looking at his reflection in the mirror before him. For a long time he stood there, gazing into the reflection of his own eyes, almost as if he were seeking something there, almost as if he were drawing some subtle vitality from his own image.

Then, slowly, the edges of his mouth turned up and a smile formed.

It was not a smile of happiness that came to the face of Earl Harmen. It was a smile of complete malevolence, of sheer mockery. The rest of the world lived by certain set values. Earl Harmen knew better.

Not until the middle of July did Lee Criley see Otis Hesler again. After the first few days of Otis' disappearance, Lee forgot all about him. He even forgot the incident of the Fourth of July. He thought Otis might have left town with his girlfriend, or maybe even taken a job somewhere. It was not Lee Criley's nature to worry about things like that, and he hardly thought about Otis at all.

Lee was a late sleeper, and it was about two in the afternoon of July twentieth that he left home. Before he could adjust his eyes to the sunlight, Otis appeared from out of nowhere, calling out to him.

"Hey, Lee, I gotta talk to you."

"So talk, man. Where the fuck you been, anyway?"

"I been around. You seen Earl lately?"

"Sure. Why not?"

Otis Hesler was nervous. His hands shook as he lit a cigarette. "Listen, did he say anything? I mean, about what happened? Did he say anything about me?"

Lee nodded his head a few times, smiling. "So that's why you been keeping your ass out of sight, huh? Still worried about Earl."

"Did he say anything to you? That's all I want to know."

"Yeah, well, he talked about it for a little while. He was pretty damn pissed off there, man. I don't know, man."

"You think he's still mad? You think he'd come after me?"

Lee laughed. "Shit, man. What the hell's the matter with you? You scared of Earl?"

"Damn right I'm scared of him. I sure don't want him pissed off at me. That guy was gonna kill me, Lee."

"Are you kiddin'? He was just fooling around, for Christ sake."

Otis inhaled deeply on his cigarette. His hands were still shaking. He spoke softly. "He wasn't fooling around. I saw him. I saw it too many times with the others. He wasn't fooling around. He would have killed me if he could've caught me."

"You know what your problem is, Otis boy? You're just plain pussy-whipped, that's all you are. Let's go over and see Earl now. He won't hurt you."

Otis shook his head. "No more for me, man. I'm through. I'm not going over there any more."

"So do what you want, it's okay with me. See you around, half-wit."

Lee turned to walk away, and Otis called after him. "He's crazy, Lee. I'm warning you. You shouldn't go there any more either."

"Aw, get fucked, will ya?"

Lee turned the corner and headed in the direction of Harmen's house.

Otis Hesler would never see Earl Harmen alive again. And the next time he was to see Lee Criley, they would be together at the New Haven County Courthouse.

■ "Let the dead boys have their day in court."

So requested State's Attorney Harold MacNamara in his summation of his case against Walter Lee Criley. There had not been a lengthy trial, as had been expected—or, if truth be told, as

had been hoped for by the morbidly curious public. Lee Criley
had decided to stop fighting. He entered pleas of guilty to all of
the charges pending against him. The charges were six counts of
murder.

There was little that defense counsel Ron Mailer could offer
in explanation of his client's crimes, and it was to his credit as an
attorney that he did not alienate the court by painting an
unrealistic picture of Lee Criley as a misunderstood, sympathetic
figure. He simply, humbly, asked the court, when considering
sentence, to be as fair and as merciful as God and conscience
would allow.

Harry MacNamara was brief, dignified, and eloquent in his
summation for the prosecution. "Let the dead boys have their
day in court," he pleaded. "Let us never forget the victims whose
fate brought them into contact with the young man who sits
before you today and whose lives were so cruelly, so mon-
strously cut short ... the State asks, instead, that Your Honor in-
voke our law to the fullest in passing sentence on this young man.
The State asks for maximum consecutive sentences. The State
asks, Your Honor, that twenty-seven dead boys have their day in
court."

Judge Birdsell listened without expression to the final
arguments of both attorneys and then recessed court until July
23, 1973, at which time he would pronounce sentence upon the
defendant, Walter Lee Criley.

■ He couldn't see the slimy snake under the porch, sliding, inching along in the darkness where no one went. And he didn't see the fangs close down into the body of the tiny bird or the venom seep into the terrified, fluttering body. He didn't see the slow ebbing of life that took place in the darkness under the porch. It had been witnessed by the silent black beetles, by a black widow spinning her web, and by other creatures that made their homes in the darkness under the porch.

Earl Harmen didn't see any of this, but he knew with certainty that it had happened. After all, there were things that killed and things that died.

"Want me to bring anybody around tonight?"

The bird had fallen from its nest, tried to fly too early, its mother off foraging, tearing mucoid worms from the cool earth with her beak. Turn about was fair play. The snake was hungry, too. The tiny bird had fallen through the branches, its wings beating ineffectively against gravity and the doom that awaited it below. It couldn't fly but it managed to hop underneath the porch. Harmen knew this without seeing. He knew what happened in the cruel world of nature.

"Earl, you want me to find somebody for tonight or don't you?"

The voice was high, insinuating, aggravating. It hurt him to listen to it. He wanted to shut it out, to stop it some way. If he could only understand what it wanted of him. Maybe if he said nothing it would go away, leaving him alone with his knowledge of the dark place where crawling things lived in silent awareness of one another.

"For Christ sake, Earl. Should I get somebody or not? I asked you a million times."

"Yes, yes. Get somebody. Get somebody." And suddenly, so easily, there was the sound of footsteps and the voice was gone.

Alone. He *was* alone, wasn't he? The house was quiet, almost as quiet as it was down there where the crawling things lived. What was that? Was it a shadow? Was there someone else in the house with him? He went to a window, and across the street a light flashed on and off and on again, and then another did the same, and then they all flashed and twinkled erratically in the darkness. Tiny, unblinking eyes, following his movement. He couldn't see them, but he knew.

He was sure now that there was something else alive in the house. Not human, perhaps, but alive, breathing, and watching him. He ran from room to room, turning on all the lights, looking in closets, under the bed, tearing drawers from his bureau. There was nothing he could see, but he knew it was there.

"Who's there? Who's watching me?"

Movement, shadows, but nothing definite, nothing substantial. Whatever, whoever, it was laughed at him. It was a thing, not a person at all, and it followed him from room to room, sometimes breathing on him, sometimes brushing against the back of his neck.

It was there to kill him. There could be no other reason.

He went into the bathroom and filled the sink with cold water. He held his face in the sink, under the running water, rubbing the water into his hair and around his neck. Yes, it was colder, cooler, and the thing retreated, leaving him exhausted. But he was still alive.

And then his bowels churned and rumbled and a pressure built up within him. The urge was insistent. If he had not been right there in the bathroom, he would not have had time. Lucky. Funny. He lowered his pants and sat down, and foul vapors filled the air. Not healthy, the smell of death and putrefaction, the smell of rotting things and of hell. There was a spasmodic movement of his stomach muscles, and his insides twisted. And then a great emission of soft, loose excrement splashed into the bowl, cascading like the sudden rush of a broken dam. The stuff was warm as it passed through his body, and as he emptied himself, he felt a new kind of relief and tranquility. He was empty, and clean, and tired, and he thought back to some half-remembered dream that maybe he'd had as a child, or maybe it was in his mother's arms, the baby's eyes looking up at her in warmth and security. All the fears and anger had passed through him now, and he was innocent and peaceful. The snarling viciousness, the murderous rages and the killing, so much killing, was gone now. It was all over, purged. Tears of joy and gratitude welled up in Earl Harmen's eyes. Thank you, God, thank you, Jesus, oh, thank you.

It was only a moment later, when he stood and looked down, that his shrill scream of terror and despair filled the room.

A living thing writhed and undulated in the foul water. It was a living thing that had been nourished inside him and had been born of him.

He tried to run, but he stumbled, hitting his head against the door. The blood, hot and sticky, streamed down his cheek, bubbling in his nostrils. He crawled and scurried across the floor, whimpering, sobbing, blinded by his own blood. The thing would kill him. He knew that.

He did not remember their coming in. He didn't think he had actually lost consciousness. There didn't seem to be any blank, black spaces. It was just as if, suddenly, someone had turned on a light, a bright, blinding light, and he was sitting in the living room with three other people. It puzzled and frightened him, but he held his body rigid, motionless, careful lest he betray himself to these others. He could see them clearly, sharply defined, yet far away, as through a reversed telescope. He could hear and understand every word they said, yet their voices seemed to come from miles away. He didn't know who they were.

He sat, removed and yet aware of the minutest detail, observing these people in his house. No one addressed him, and he was silent for a long time as the conversation of the three progressed.

"I thought you said this was going to be a party. I thought there'd be a lot of kids here." A girl was speaking, a strange, pouty-mouthed girl he was sure he had never seen before.

A thin, long-haired boy answered her. There was something more familiar about this boy. "You don't need a lot of people to make a party. The dope's good, isn't it?"

The slender boy handed the girl a sweet-smelling cigarette. She inhaled deeply and murmured "Yeah," stretching her body sensually, like a cat. Smiling to herself, she handed the cigarette to the third person, another young man, whose eyes were half-closed, but he waved it away.

"How about your friend, Lee? Don't he want none?" The girl looked coyly at Harmen and he stared back, expressionless. She shrugged her shoulders and looked away.

"Hell, no, Earl don't smoke any of that shit. He likes for everybody to have a good time, but Earl never gets high. He don't need it. Right, Earl?"

"Yes," Earl Harmen said. The sound of his own voice seemed foreign and hollow.

He remembered now. He remembered who Lee was. Odd he

should have forgotten something like that. But the other two. He had never seen them before. And the girl. Who was she? A girl! What was a girl doing here?

He continued to watch them smoke another cigarette. They didn't seem to mind his silence, almost ignoring his presence altogether. That was fine. They would let him alone and he would let them alone. For now.

He watched them smoke a third and a fourth cigarette, and then Lee reached in his pants pocket and extracted a small plastic prescription bottle. It was half full of pink capsules. He rattled the pills gently, smiling. "Anybody interested in a tour of outer space?"

The other boy, who had been silent for as long as Harmen had been aware of him, sat up. "Whatcha got?"

"Nothin', really. Just some jellybeans. You're too old for jellybeans, aren't you?"

They divided the pills up among the three of them and washed them down from a single can of beer.

"How long does this shit take, man?"

"I don't know. You got a bus to catch? Hey, I got something that'll help you catch that bus!"

Lee took some tubes of acrylic paint and some plastic bags out of a closet. He showed the boy and the girl how to use the bags, placing them over their noses and mouths to get the full effect of the paint. He managed to get in quite a few sniffs for himself in the process.

Harmen watched them talk and giggle among themselves. Gradually the level of activity in the room, never more than minimal, sank even lower. The boy snuggled up next to the girl, his arm around her shoulder, his hand brushing absently against her small breast. She seemed to be unaware of the boy. She traced the shape of a figure eight on the chair with her finger, over and over, her face slack and dreaming. Lee had lain down on the floor, staring up at the ceiling. They were motionless in those positions for ten minutes, twenty minutes, and then almost an hour. The only movement in the room was the shallow, almost imperceptible rising and falling of breathing.

Earl Harmen watched them like a malevolent flesh-eating bird. His eyes flicked back and forth, from one to the other. When an hour had passed, he rose up from his chair. He was himself again. He was ready.

He moved quickly, efficiently, because he had gone through the process so many times before. He knew what he was doing, and he knew he was doing it well. The pride of the skilled, experienced technician. He moved with a purpose.

First he brought out the three plywood boards from the bedroom closet. He placed them side by side in the living room, leaning them securely against the wall. He left no more than a foot between each one, and the three boards covered one entire wall. In each board, toward the corners, were four holes roughly the size of a baseball.

Back to the bedroom. High in the back of the closet were the handcuffs. There were only four pairs, each pair with the key tied to it. He would need more. Well, that was no problem. No problem at all. That was why he had the rope there, wasn't it? Where had that rope gone? Yes, there it was, right where he had left it. He laughed. Didn't they think he knew what he was doing? But of course they were practically unconscious.

He took Lee first. He fastened a set of handcuffs to each wrist, then hoisted the slender, limp body up to the first board. Placing Lee's back against the board, he slipped the other half of each pair of handcuffs through the top two holes on the board and snapped them shut.

Lee Criley's eyelids fluttered open a fraction of an inch. "Where are we goin', Earl?"

"That's all right. That's all right."

Lee offered no resistance, and Harmen fastened his feet to the board with rope threaded through the bottom holes. Lee Criley was now completely immobilized. No chance of escape. It was a perfect job of tying, really it was.

He hoisted up the other boy. He was heavier, more difficult to swing around than the slender body of Lee Criley. But Earl Harmen was strong, he knew he was strong, and with only a bit more effort, this boy, too, was tied up the same way as Lee, handcuffs on top, rope on the bottom. The boy remained unconscious through the entire procedure.

The only difference was that this older boy was tied with his face to the board.

Finally, the girl. A slut, a tramp, with painted mouth and yellow hair. He was not gentle with her light body, and the back of her head slapped against the board as he leaned her up. He used rope both for her hands and her feet. For an instant she opened her eyes and looked straight at him. She moaned, rolled her eyes back, and dropped back into whatever world she had come from, humming to herself.

That was all there was to it.

Except for the dog.

He didn't remember the dog coming in. Funny he hadn't noticed it before. It must have been a spaniel of some kind, a mutt really, with black-and-white spots, and it lay asleep in the middle of the floor.

"Hey, fella, how ya doing?" He knelt down to pet the dog, quietly, gently, so as not to wake it. He put his hand on the dog's head, but his hand passed into thin air.

The dog opened one eye and gazed directly up at him. It was not a dog's eye, but a human eye, the eye of a boy. It was an eye that had gone through fear, pain, all the pain it could stand, and then despair. And, finally, death. All that was left now in that eye was hatred, and it was focused directly up at Harmen.

He backed away, but the dog stood up, growling deep and low in its throat. At last Harmen was backed up to the wall, and still the dog kept coming, eyes now glued on his eyes, the long, sharp teeth bared. Saliva dribbled from the dog's mouth, the head thrust forward in challenge. Then, like a coiled spring, the dog leapt through the air, flying into Harmen's face. He could no longer see the dog, but he could feel its teeth tearing into his neck, his face, his eyes. He could feel the flesh being torn away from his skull, and the needlelike teeth digging, probing into his body. The dog's breath was steaming hot, and the saliva left a sticky slime wherever it drooled on his skin. He tried to protect his face with his arms, frantically pushing the dog away from his neck. The dog kept snapping at him, at his arms, biting into his shoulders and chest, tearing his shirt and then his trousers.

Somehow he got the dog away from him, back onto the floor, and the two stood facing each other, panting, Harmen exhausted and terrified, the dog growling his hatred. Then, without any preparatory flexing of muscles, without any warning, the dog sprang again, this time sinking his teeth deep into Harmen's genitals.

"Earl what's the matter with you? What did you get me all tied up for?"

The pain screamed through his body like a river of fire. He pushed and kicked at the dog, vainly trying to escape the pain.

"Earl, come on, untie me, will you, for Christ sake?"

Somehow Harmen managed to pick up a wooden chair, and brought it down with all his might on the dog. The chair passed into thin air. The dog was gone. The pain was gone. All that remained was the exhaustion and clamminess.

"Earl, let me the hell off this board, goddam it. Will you, huh?"

He felt his face, neck, and shoulders, and then, more delicately, ventured a hand to his genitals. There was no blood, no torn flesh. He had not been bitten to pieces.

He wondered how he could have imagined all that. Could it have been a dream? Maybe he was being affected by all the marijuana those goddam kids were smoking. There was so much smoke in the room. He was sure that was what it was. Goddam these crazy kids, anyway. He'd make sure they paid for this. And there they all were, tied up so carefully. Just waiting until he was ready. And the man who had only moments earlier screamed in terror now smiled to himself in anticipation.

"Hey, Earl, untie me, will ya? What are you doing?"

The question struck him as hysterically funny. His mouth dropped open in surprise and delight, and the laughter filled the room. "What am I doing? I'm killing you, you goddam fool, that's what I'm doing. First I'm going to fuck you, and then I'm going to kill you all. Does that answer your question?"

And then, again, the speed of events in the room increased, as if a merry-go-round had suddenly changed gear. There was a pickup of tempo, and it was impossible to focus on any single thing. For a while, Harmen wasn't sure if he was moving or if somehow the room itself was spinning on some invisible axis. His legs were wobbly, his balance was going, and he didn't know if he was stumbling into the furniture or if the furniture was actually crashing around the room, striking his shins and thighs.

"It's me, Lee, Earl. You wouldn't kill me, would you, Earl? You don't want to kill *me*?"

The room was still. It was he who was pacing about, his own legs that were carrying him back and forth, round and round in strangely purposeful patterns and circles. It was as if he were being whirled about as fast as he could run in counterclockwise circles, as if he were being pulled by some agent other than himself.

"Let me out of here, Earl. Let me out and I'll help you with the others."

He heard a low, droning, humming sound in the room, and then discovered that it was coming from his own throat. It was a song he had to sing, unearthly and strangely vibrant. There was no melody, only a periodic variation in pitch, almost like the dark, wandering tones of a monastic chant.

His circuits of the room continued. Something he had to do, as if he were being pulled around the room. And then, like a marionette controlled by strings, Harmen felt his arms and hands lifted away from his sides. His outstretched hands traced sharply angled geometrical figures in the air. At first he was able to feel the shape of stars and triangles and quadrangles, then the figures became too complicated to keep track of. He gave in to the forces that were causing this strange, frightening dance. There was nothing else he could do.

"I'll kill 'em for you, Earl. I know what to do with them. I promise, I'll kill 'em for you."

"Shut up, you bastard. Shut up!"

There was a gun in his hand now, and it was waving like the

head of a poisonous snake, poised in front of Lee Criley's face. "Shut up, goddam you, or I'll blow your goddam head off. I mean it. You know I mean it."

"Earl, listen to me. Don't you know me? It's me, Lee. Don't you remember? Come on, Earl, quit foolin' around. Unlock these cuffs, and I'll take care of those creeps."

Harmen put the weapon down on the sofa, retrieved the key from his pants pocket, and set Lee Criley free.

He was surprised by what he had done. He thought he had intended to kill Criley along with the others. He thought that was what he had planned. But maybe that wasn't what he wanted at all. He wasn't sure any more. It was hard to keep his attention on any one thing.

He began blurring, an instant here and an instant there, as if he were in a film, and at random intervals a number of frames were blank. He lost all continuity to his actions, to his thoughts. He no longer knew what was going on in that room.

He found himself with no clothes on, and he felt his body against the body of another. He felt a stirring of excitement, and then, everything went blank.

He saw Lee Criley leaning over the body of a girl, holding a knife against her skin, and then it all went blank again.

When he came back he was no longer in the room, but was somewhere far away, someplace many miles and many years away. He was a little boy again, going on five years old and getting ready to start school pretty soon. It was early in the morning, before his mother woke up. The air was still chilly as the dawn sun rose rapidly through the trees. He had put on his shorts, shirt, and sneakers all by himself, and he walked outside near the back porch. And then he saw himself hopping down the steps the way he used to do and going to the garbage can. It was an old garbage can, dug into the ground two or three feet deep; to open it, you had to step on a small metal lever. He was just a little boy, and looking down, down, to the bottom of the hole made him dizzy, afraid of losing his balance. Yet he was fascinated by what was at the bottom of the hole. The metal that lined the wall of the hole was rusty and rotted, and the smell of decaying and rotten food assaulted his nostrils. Yet he kept peering through the darkness, trying to make out something at the bottom of the hole.

Whatever it was, way down there, was white, and it glowed in the darkness. It was a large patch of white, and around it were two or three other smaller patches. He looked closer, down on his knees now so that he could see more clearly.

There was movement within the white patches, waves, undulations, and the shape of the patches gradually shifted. He looked more closely. And then he saw that each patch was composed of thousands of tiny squirming, devouring worms, white worms that burrowed and dug, that pushed their sharp-ended forms back into the slimy mass from which they had emerged. They were maggots, though he didn't know the name for them. But he did sense that they were the kind of life spawned by filth and rottenness and decay, living creatures born of death and disease.

Harmen saw all this as he stood in his living room. It was not an hallucination so much as a very clear, sharp, perfectly remembered image. The image was as sharply etched in his mind's eye as if he had just seen the garbage hole a split-second previously rather than more than twenty-five years ago.

Then a realization insinuated itself into the awakening consciousness of Earl Harmen. It came to him unobtrusively. It was as if the greatest of truths do not require any stirring of emotions to proclaim themselves. Such truths simply are.

Harmen knew with a cold, deadly certainty that he was not really looking into the bottom of a maggot-infested garbage pail. He was looking into the mind of God.

Then, abruptly, he was facing Lee Criley again. There was a dark object in Lee Criley's hand. A pistol, and it was pointed at him.

And slowly, as if in a dream, Harmen ran straight toward the gun, laughing. A voice he vaguely recognized as his own said, "Yes, yes! Kill me, kill me!"

He saw a flash at the muzzle. And he thought he saw the bullet spinning and tumbling toward his chest.

EPILOGUE

■ July 23, 1973, was exactly one year to the day after the West Haven Police Department received a call from a distraught young boy who said he had just killed a man. After precisely one year of questioning, confessions, and legal proceedings, the case of the State of Connecticut versus Walter Lee Criley would be closed.

The atmosphere was peaceful in the New Haven County Courthouse on July 23, 1973. Lee Criley sat with his attorney, Ron Mailer, waiting for the judge to enter the courtroom. Criley had gained weight during his year in jail. He was almost chubby, would almost have been healthy-looking if his complexion hadn't turned sallow after twelve months without sun. He sat rigidly, nodding only slightly when his lawyer relayed messages to him from his mother.

Emma Criley sat immediately behind her son and to his right, just behind the wooden partition separating the defendant from the audience. Next to her sat the Reverend Wilton Denning. Mrs. Criley sobbed steadily, blowing her nose frequently into a white handkerchief. After patting her shoulder once or twice in his most consoling manner, the Reverend Denning relaxed into himself, folding his hands over a tiny Bible he held in his lap.

At ten-thirty, Judge Lawrence Birdsell opened the court, called the first and only case on his docket, and asked the defendant if he was ready to be sentenced. The defendant stated that he was.

On each of the six counts of murder, Lee Criley was sentenced to a minimum of ninety-nine years, each sentence to be served consecutively. The total effective sentence was five hundred ninety-four years, less the year already served. There would never be the possibility of parole for Lee Criley, as there would for Otis Hesler, who two months later would be sentenced to life imprisonment.

Throughout the sentencing, Lee Criley stood still and erect, his hands clenched behind his back, his fingertips and knuckles showing white. For an instant, it seemed as if there might have passed across his lips the trace of a smile.

1